Don't Say a Word

ALSO BY JENNIFER JAYNES

Strangers Series

Never Smile at Strangers
Ugly Young Thing

Don't Say a Word

JENNIFER JAYNES

THOMAS & MERCER

Published by Thomas & Mercer, Seattle

www.apub.com

Amazon, the Amazon logo, and Thomas & Mercer are trademarks of Amazon.com, Inc., or its affiliates.

ISBN-13: 9781503933422
ISBN-10: 1503933423

Cover design by David Drummond

Printed in the United States of America

To Sage Gallegos
Thank you for being such a wonderful friend and
auntie . . . and believing in magic with me.

PROLOGUE

TWELVE-YEAR-OLD ZOE SHUDDERED as a fly buzzed past her ear.

Her eyes filling with tears, she pinched her nose closed. She'd never smelled decaying human flesh before. It was a heavy, sickening, awful smell. Kind of like the reek of the dead cat last spring that she and her sister had walked past every morning to get to their bus stop.

The stench overpowered the odors of paint, sawdust, and freshly installed carpeting—the new house smells that had, just a couple of days ago, promised her family a fresh start.

Before *everything* changed.

She stood in her bedroom doorway, frightened to step out into the hall, but she was so hungry her stomach ached. She knew there was a big stash of gummy worms in the first drawer of her mother's bedside table, but there was no way she was going to step foot in her parents' bedroom, because she was terrified of what she would find in there.

She'd have to pick through what was left in the kitchen.

Don't think about it, just do it, she told herself.

She darted down the hallway at lightning speed, the wood floor cold beneath her bare feet, the sounds of each footfall echoing through the large, mostly empty house. She sprinted down the steps to the first floor.

The house was eerily quiet. Her mother wasn't lazing on the couch. No soap operas blared on the new flat-screen television in the living room. No television judges barked admonishments. No drugs were strewn haphazardly across the coffee table.

In the kitchen, Zoe yanked the refrigerator door open and stared inside. Aside from a few condiments, some empty food wrappers, and crumbs, it was empty. Her stomach churned as she opened the door to the snack cabinet. She found two small boxes of raisins for her twin sister, Carrie, and stuffed them in the back pockets of her jeans. Then, dodging corrugated moving boxes and stepping over empty potato chip bags and an assortment of other food wrappers, she went to the pantry. Behind a giant carton of baking soda, she discovered one last can of raviolis.

Her mouth watering, she tore the pull-top open, dipped her fingers in the can, and plucked one out. She shoved the sweet pasta into her mouth, barely taking the time to chew before letting it slip down her throat.

The phone rang in the distance.

A bolt of terror shot through her, and she almost dropped the aluminum can.

The phone had been ringing a lot, but she had been too scared to answer it. Because if she did, it would finally make everything real. And she didn't want it to be real. She had to believe that if she waited a little longer, everything would go back to normal. She'd wake up to find that all of this had just been a dream.

After six rings, the house became still again, and she felt her shoulders relax. She resumed stuffing the pasta into her mouth.

What the heck happened? she wondered for the millionth time, trying to remember.

Think! Think!

She knew only that one, or possibly both, of her parents were now gone. The events two nights earlier were like the images she'd seen in toy kaleidoscopes. They didn't all fit together or make sense. Since it had all happened, her brain refused to work right. Every time she tried to remember, her thoughts fell away, like dominoes that were standing, but then suddenly weren't.

Her father had been on a haul that night, and her mother's greasy boyfriend, Gary, had been at the house. Zoe heard her mother talking to Gary about something. Something scary. It'd had something to do with the Texas Lotto money her father had won a few months back at a gas station across town. He'd won $1.2 million—and the jackpot had paid for the huge new house she was now standing in.

Suddenly, an image flashed through Zoe's mind that made the hairs rise on the back of her neck. The ravioli can fell from her hand and landed with a big *plop!* on the floor. Wide-eyed, she watched it roll across the ceramic tile until it hit the pantry wall.

More memories, painfully vivid ones, rushed forward. Memories of things she might've seen.

Zoe took a step back. She shook her head. *No, no, no, no, NO!*

Clamping her hands against her ears, she squeezed, trying to crowd out the awful images. Attempting to remember had been a mistake. She no longer wanted to know.

Humming loudly to block out any new images, she went to the phone and dialed her father's cell phone again. And again, he didn't answer. Tears streamed from her eyes, burning her raw cheeks.

She sprinted back up the stairs. But when she reached the hallway that led to the bedrooms, she froze. Her parents' door was partially open, and she could see the corner of her parents' bed . . . and maybe, just maybe, a hint of her mother's head, her blonde hair splayed out across the floor.

Had their door been open before?

No, she decided. It had definitely been shut.

Okay, maybe not definitely, but she was pretty sure it had. So . . . was it possible that she . . . they . . . *everyone* . . . was really okay? That this had just been a really vivid nightmare? That maybe her mother had only been lying on the floor drunk all this time?

Please, please, yes!

"Mother?" she called, her throat raw from crying. Hopeful, she crept toward the door. But when she got close, the overpowering stench of death twisted her belly. A fly buzzed out of the room and landed in the middle of Zoe's forehead.

Swatting weakly at it, she burst into tears and backed away.

In the safety of her bedroom, Zoe locked the door and went to the closet. Her twin sister, Carrie, was lying where she had left her, partially covered in clothes, her eyes clenched shut, her cheek pressed against the scratchy new carpet.

She had been lying there so long, Zoe couldn't tell if she was still sleeping or simply ignoring her. Since that night, Carrie had barely moved. She hadn't even gotten up to use the restroom.

With trembling hands, Zoe dug the raisins out of her pockets. "Want raisins?"

Her sister didn't budge.

"You haven't eaten anything."

The girl was silent.

Zoe nudged her with her foot.

"Stop," Carrie croaked.

"But you have to eat."

"No, I don't."

Zoe set the raisins next to her sister and went to the bedroom window. Peering out at the cloud-darkened sky, she watched a streetlight flicker in front of her house. She sat down on the window seat and cried fresh tears, not knowing what to do.

A few minutes later, she heard the rumble of a car's engine, then tires *whooshing* over wet asphalt. She waited for the vehicle to pass her house and continue on.

But it didn't.

Suddenly headlights cast a blue-white glow on the front of the house . . . and across Zoe's face. Panic zigzagging through her stomach, Zoe jumped up and ran to the closet. She squeezed in next to Carrie and hurriedly slid the door closed.

CHAPTER 1

"FEAR MAKES THE wolf bigger than he is," twenty-two-year-old Allie whispered to herself as she lay in her dimly lit bedroom. The expression was a German proverb Bitty Callahan, the woman who adopted Allie six years ago, had taught her. It was something she always tried to remember when her mind began to spin with negative thoughts.

Although Allie was much stronger than she'd ever been—more confident, more sure of herself, kinder, and more gentle—in the privacy of her mind, she still struggled with fear. Even though many of the heinous things that had made life so frightening when she was growing up no longer existed, she now had new fears.

As she listened to the autumn wind rattle the window next to her, she thought about how drastically her life had changed. She used to live in perpetual fear of losing her older brother. Now she feared losing her mental health and becoming incapable of being the type of mother her four-year-old son, Sammy, deserved. Sammy was her reason for living. He was her everything.

But having him in her life also frightened her—which led her to be overprotective.

She tried not to think negative thoughts because, supposedly, thoughts you dwelled on long enough could become true. Not that she really believed that (or maybe she did), but she had constantly worried about her brother leaving, and one night when she was fifteen, he did. He blew his head off in their living room while they were in the middle of an argument.

Over the last several years, Allie had read anything and everything to learn how to be and *stay* "mentally healthy," to think more positively, to become a better person and a better mother—anything that would help her distance herself from what her biological mother had been, and what Allie had started to become. But no matter how far she traveled—physically or mentally—her mother's grim words still stung her ears.

You're going to be just like me, Allie Cat. Just wait and see.

Of all the dreadful things her mother had told her, this was the one that frightened her most—and Allie worked hard to make sure her mother's prophecy would never come true. Her mother had been a mentally ill small-town prostitute who had killed several people. After she died, Allie's older brother had taken care of her the best he could. He paid the bills, bought the food. But then he became ill, too, and when he committed suicide, Allie found herself suddenly orphaned and on the streets.

Then she'd met Bitty. The kind older woman took her in as a foster child and eventually adopted her. Bitty introduced her to a clean and relatively safe world that was so different from the dirty, unkind world Allie had always known. She taught her how to be a decent person, and every day, Allie strove to become more like her—and the exact opposite of her biological mother.

She'd really lucked out to be placed with Bitty. The woman had helped her turn her life around. But Allie had never been lucky before, and a part of her was always waiting for something to happen, for the other shoe to drop.

For something that might ruin it all.

The heat in the house kicked on, snapping Allie back to the present. The scent of vanilla wafted from the air vent above her. Bitty was in the kitchen doing some late-night baking. She was constantly experimenting with new recipes, making healthful versions of old favorites.

Allie shook the dark thoughts of her past from her mind and set her Kindle on the nightstand. Sheets of rain crashed loudly against the window, and the lamp next to her flickered. She was reaching to turn it off when the landline rang.

Allie froze. It was already half past eleven.

Late-night phone calls rarely brought good news.

The phone rang twice, then stopped. Allie wondered if Bitty had answered it. Curious, she climbed out of bed and shrugged on her robe. But as she neared the kitchen, a chill crept up her spine. She stopped in her tracks, feeling strongly as though something terrible was about to happen. For a second, she considered crawling back in bed with her son. Instead, she yanked her robe closer to her body and started walking again.

The wind outside rattled the windowpanes as she entered the kitchen. Bitty stood in front of the refrigerator, a dish towel slung over her shoulder, her back to Allie. She was in her robe, and her shock of white hair was piled, messily, on top of her head. "Did the phone wake you?" she asked without turning.

"No. I was awake," Allie said.

The bad feeling Allie'd had moments before knotted in her gut. *Relax,* she told herself. *There's nothing to be worried about. Just stop already.*

"Who called?" she asked.

"That was the agency. Twin sisters will be arriving within the hour."

Cold fingers of disappointment tugged at Allie's heart.

More foster children.

Allie sat down at the bar, and her dog, Piglet, jumped into her lap and curled into a tight ball. Most of Allie's carefully constructed, consistent, peaceful world now existed inside the house with her beloved Bitty, her perfect little boy, and their loyal dog. But when foster children were around, the house didn't feel half as comfortable. Their presence disrupted her sense of normalcy.

But although Allie felt uneasy each time a new kid arrived, she could never tell Bitty. Allie admired the fact that Bitty fostered kids. It was one of hundreds of things she admired about the old woman. After all, how could she not? Bitty had literally saved her life when she'd taken her in. Bitty had given her a second chance at happiness—a chance most kids with pasts like hers never got.

"Where are they coming from?" she asked.

"About two miles away. Sherman's Landing."

Sherman's Landing. Where the rich people lived.

They'd never taken in rich foster kids before. This would be a first. Most came from trailer parks and the little unkempt tract homes scattered around East Texas. They also usually took in one kid at a time. Not two.

The teakettle hummed softly on the stove. "Want a cup of tea?" Bitty asked, pulling a tray full of cookies from the oven.

"Yeah . . . sure."

Bitty grabbed two mugs from the cupboard. She dropped a tea bag into each and filled them with steaming water; then she slid a mug and a cookie in front of Allie and sat down.

She smiled, the thin skin around her eyes crinkling. Allie noticed the lines in the old woman's face looked deeper than usual—and she felt a pang of sadness at the realization that she was getting older. That maybe one day in the not-so-distant future she'd no longer be a part of her and Sammy's life.

"You feeling all right?" Allie asked.

Bitty raised her eyebrows and sighed. "Oh, I'm fine. I'm not sure if those twin girls will be, though," she said. "They were found a few hours ago, hiding in a bedroom closet. Both of their parents were found dead in the master suite, and from the looks of it, they'd been dead for some time."

CHAPTER 2

TEN MINUTES LATER, Bitty ushered the twin girls and an exhausted-looking caseworker into the living room.

Rain lashing the windows behind her, Allie sat in the recliner and studied the girls as they took seats on one of the couches. Both girls were pale and frail looking, very possibly malnourished. They also had the same long, wavy hair, except one was blonde and the other a dark brunette.

"This here is Zoe Parish," the caseworker said, motioning to the dark-haired girl and setting a weathered-looking box of files on the coffee table.

Bitty knelt down in front of Zoe.

"Hi, Zoe. I'm Miss Bitty."

Zoe glared at Bitty. "We want to go home."

"She had a difficult time leaving her house," the caseworker said. "I'm afraid she's angry and a bit confused."

Her eyes still on Zoe, Bitty nodded. "I completely understand," she said, gently. "I don't blame you. I probably wouldn't have wanted to leave my home either."

Zoe wore a jacket far too large for her, and beneath it, Allie could see a yellow T-shirt stained with some sort of red sauce. As Bitty spoke to Zoe, the girl stared down at her hand and nervously chipped off glittery pink nail polish with a thumbnail.

The caseworker continued. "And this is Carrie Parish," she said, motioning to the blonde girl, who seemed significantly smaller than the brunette. Her skin was paper-white, her eyes sunken, and she was clutching a tattered stuffed bear. "She hasn't said a word since they were found."

"Hi, Carrie," Bitty said, softly.

Carrie pulled the stuffed bear closer to her chest.

Bitty had said the twins were twelve years old, but they looked— and seemed to behave—younger. If she had to guess, she'd say they seemed only about ten. She'd seen other children regress after experiencing trauma and wondered if that was also the case with these girls.

"Like I told your sister, I'm Miss Bitty. I'll be taking care of you tonight, okay?"

The girl remained silent.

Bitty turned to Allie. "This young lady is my daughter, Allie," she said, motioning to her.

Daughter.

Allie's heart swelled at the word because Bitty was the only real mother she'd ever had—and it had taken her sixteen years to find her. She still pinched herself sometimes, stunned that out of all the children Bitty had fostered over the years, she was the one the woman had chosen to adopt.

It still made no sense to her . . . why *she* had been the lucky one.

"Hi," Allie said, smiling one of her confident smiles. One she'd practiced thousands of times over the years. Confidence had never been something that had come easy to her. She'd had to work hard on it.

The brunette girl, Zoe, studied her with big, watchful eyes.

"Would you girls like something to eat or drink?" Bitty asked. "I made cookies."

Her eyes still on Allie, Zoe shook her head. Carrie remained silent.

"I have chocolate chip," Bitty said.

Neither girl responded.

"I'm afraid we found them in dire conditions," the caseworker said. "Covered in urine, vomit. We tried to clean them up a little at the hospital, but they didn't—"

Bitty cut her off with a raised hand. She didn't like people talking about the children in front of them as though they couldn't hear. She believed that children should receive the same respect any adult would expect. "Allie, please show the girls to the bathroom and run a bath," she said.

"Yeah, sure."

"Help them if they need it, then show them to their bedroom while we finish talking, okay, honey?"

"Okay." Allie stood up and crossed the room. "C'mon, follow me," she said, motioning to the girls.

Eyes cast downward, the twins dutifully followed.

Both girls stood quietly in the bathroom doorway as Allie prepared a warm bath. Now much closer to them, she could smell the stink of urine and vomit the caseworker had been talking about.

Allie stood on the toilet seat and gathered supplies from the upper shelves of the overhead cabinet, then climbed down. She placed everything neatly on the counter. "These are for you. There's also shampoo and conditioner next to the tub," she said, gesturing to both bottles. "Can I get you guys anything else?"

Zoe was staring at her again. Up close, Allie could see how bloodshot and frightened the girl's big green eyes were.

"No, thank you."

"Carrie?"

Carrie stood silently, hugging her bear and watching the bathtub fill with water.

"Did they call Grandmother?" Zoe asked, her voice quivering.

"Who?"

"Grandmother. Is she . . . is she coming for us?"

"I don't know," Allie said. "Bitty didn't say anything about her, but I'll ask."

"We won't go with her," Zoe said, shaking her head. "There's no way," she said, sounding both obstinate and terrified.

Allie nodded, then squeezed past the girls. She stepped out of the bathroom to give them some privacy. "I'll be out here. Just let me know if you need anything, okay?"

"Okay."

Allie left the door open a crack. She listened to the girls undress and step into the water. Then she moved closer to the living room, where Bitty and the caseworker were sitting, talking on the couch.

"I'm afraid they haven't had the best home environment," the caseworker was saying. "About three years ago, their younger brother was hit by a truck and killed. The girls were there when it happened. Witnessed the entire thing."

Allie winced. She went to the bathroom door to listen in on the girls again. Hearing water sloshing around, she went to the closet where Bitty kept extra clothes for the kids. She chose two cotton nightgowns and pairs of underwear that looked like they would fit the twins.

A few minutes later, she led the freshly scrubbed girls to the bedroom where the foster kids slept. It was decorated in warm browns and soft blues, and outfitted with bunk beds along the far wall and a twin bed on the opposite wall. Functional and comfortable.

"This is your bedroom. You can sleep wherever you like," Allie said.

Zoe bristled. "This isn't *our* bedroom," she said, her green eyes icy. "This isn't even our house. We're only here until our dad gets back from his run and picks us up."

A strangled sound came from deep within her sister's throat. She buried her pale face into her teddy bear and sobbed.

———

"Their father's dead, right?" Allie asked after she and Bitty had left the girls' bedroom, leaving the two curled up together on the lower bunk, a plate of chocolate chip cookies and some almond milk on the nightstand next to the bunk beds.

"Yes, I'm afraid so."

"Zoe told me he's just out of town. That they're expecting him to pick them up."

The woman exhaled loudly. "The caseworker said she hasn't fully accepted that her parents have died."

"So what do I say if she says it again? About her father."

"I'd gently remind her about the conversations she's already had with her caseworker and the psychiatrist at the hospital," Bitty said. "Tomorrow morning, I'm taking them to the Child Advocacy Center. The police want to find out what they know about the murders . . . and they'll also start seeing a counselor there on an ongoing basis. Hopefully, the sessions will help."

"Did the caseworker mention a grandmother?" Allie asked. "Zoe's worried that she's going to pick them up. She seemed scared that they'll have to stay with her."

"I was told the maternal grandmother was contacted, but she refused to accept the girls."

Allie frowned. "God. That's awful."

"Yes, it is. It happens far too often, I'm afraid. People can be selfish . . . and cold."

Yes, they can, Allie thought.

Over more tea, Bitty filled Allie in on everything the caseworker had shared. About their three-year-old brother being hit by a truck, about the $1.2 million the family had just won in the lottery, and their recent move from a trailer on the edge of town to Sherman's Landing.

"Guess the good life didn't end up so good," Bitty said. She stood and carried the plates to the sink.

"Yeah, I guess not."

Zoe's fear-filled eyes flashed into Allie's mind. She remembered how miserable Carrie had looked . . . like she'd simply wanted to fold into herself and die. Although all of the foster kids looked pretty miserable when they first arrived, Allie found that she felt worse for these girls because their family had been ripped apart by murder.

Just as hers had.

She also had a good idea of what the road ahead of them would look like . . . and it wouldn't be pretty. People never healed from the horror of murder.

Not completely.

Her eyelids suddenly heavy, Allie said good night. Back in her bedroom, she kissed Sammy's soft cheek. She pulled away and stared at his little face, letting pure joy wash over her.

She still couldn't believe he was hers. That he had actually come out of her body. Before Sammy, she hadn't understood the meaning of joy. Now she felt it several times every day.

Sammy was her world.

He and Bitty were her everything.

Trying to block further thoughts of the girls from her mind, she crawled back into bed and closed her eyes. Almost instantly she drifted off, into the comforting arms of sleep . . . where she rested soundly until the first of the horrible screams rang out.

CHAPTER 3

ALLIE LEAPT FROM the bed and ran toward the screams. They were coming from the girls' bedroom.

She flipped on the overhead light to find the blonde twin, Carrie, standing in the middle of the room, her eyes wide, her arms rigid at her sides. She was screaming at the top of her lungs.

Zoe was standing a few feet from her sister, holding her ears. "Stop, Carrie! Stop! You're freaking me out," she pleaded. "Stop, Carrie! You're scaring me!"

Carrie's voice was so loud and shrill, Allie's brain vibrated in her skull. Allie hesitated, staring at the screaming girl. She didn't know what to do.

She knew someone more normal would reach out to Carrie and embrace her in a hug. But Allie couldn't. As she looked at the girl, she noticed several angry red lines on the insides of both arms, just below her elbows.

They looked like cutting scars.

Bitty flew into the room. She immediately went to Carrie and wrapped her arms around her. Carrie, her face nearly purple, continued to scream, tears spilling down her cheeks. "Shhh, honey. It's all right," Bitty soothed.

Bitty freed a hand, grabbed a blanket from the twin bed, and pulled it tightly around Carrie's shoulders.

Feeling useless, Allie wrung her hands and turned to the doorway, expecting to see a frightened Sammy, but the doorway was empty. She glanced at Zoe, who was still holding her ears. There was raw terror in her eyes. She hummed and rocked back and forth on her tiptoes. Allie watched her, her own pulse racing.

Finally the screaming stopped. Carrie began to pant, as though desperately trying to pull air into her lungs.

"It's going to be okay," the old woman continued to soothe. Bitty's eyes found Zoe. "Has she had these fits before?"

Zoe shook her head. "No. What's . . . what's wrong with her?" She stepped tentatively toward her sister now that she was no longer screaming, and gently touched her back. "It's okay, Carrie. Dad'll be here soon to get us, okay?"

Carrie opened her mouth and started screaming again.

Zoe's hands shot to her ears. She backed away from her sister and sobbed.

Perplexed at the excitement, Piglet jerked her chin to the ceiling and howled.

Zoe blinked at Allie, those watchful eyes of hers seeming to want . . . need . . . something. They reminded her of the look Sammy got on his face when he was upset and wanted to be held. *Did she want a hug, maybe?* Allie wondered. Allie was pretty sure it was what any normal, caring human being would do in the situation. But she couldn't.

She always helped Bitty with the foster children, but she never got involved. Not emotionally anyway. She ran errands, prepared food— did the menial stuff—but she never got to know them on a personal level. And she certainly didn't hug them. She was too afraid of making her world any bigger. The girls' presence alone was already a disruption.

She knew her hesitancy was selfish . . . and she felt bad about it, but she also feared coming undone.

And she couldn't let that happen.

Realizing Piglet was still howling, Allie gathered the dog in her arms. She stood nervously for a moment, randomly noticing that the cookies and milk on the bedside table were gone, then she went to Bitty. "What can I do?"

The old woman's voice was calm. "A glass of water, please."

Relieved to finally have something to do, Allie set Piglet down and hurried to the kitchen for a glass of water.

Before returning to the girls' bedroom, she stopped to check on Sammy. She was relieved to find him lying exactly where he was before the screams, still sound asleep. Sammy had always been an incredibly deep sleeper. Even as a baby. In the beginning, the fact that he slept so much—and could sleep through practically anything—had concerned her, but his pediatrician said he was simply a good sleeper . . . and told Allie not to worry so much . . . that it was a problem most new mothers would love to have. But she still worried sometimes. She couldn't count the times over the years when she'd checked just to make sure he was still breathing.

Ears still ringing from the high-pitched screams, Allie took a deep breath and carried the glass of water to the girls' room.

CHAPTER 4

BITTY CALLED THEM night terrors, and they were definitely terrifying—for the person having them as well as everyone else within earshot. As Allie climbed her way out of a deep sleep the next morning, she could still hear Carrie's gut-wrenching screams.

When she finally managed to pry her eyes open, Sammy was looming over her. Seeing that she was awake, he grinned. With his blue eyes, fine sandy hair, and dimples on both cheeks, she thought he was the most beautiful sight ever.

Allie smiled back at him. She'd fallen in love with Sammy during her first ultrasound. That was the day she realized her life wasn't about her anymore. Her life was all about him now, and she knew it always would be. He was going to give her life meaning, and she was going to give him the best childhood she possibly could. She only wished Sammy had a more involved father. Since he'd been born, Johnny had only visited a couple of days a month.

"Who here?" Sammy asked.

"Who *is* here," Allie corrected. Sammy was a little behind his peers in verbal skills and was working with a speech therapist twice a month.

She answered his question: "Two little girls. They got here late last night."

Sammy straddled her stomach and plopped his little bottom down. "What their names?"

"Carrie and Zoe. Why? Did you hear them this morning?"

"Yes, they was in the hallway."

"Want to go and meet them . . . and say good morning to Grammy?"

Sammy's face lit up. "Yes!"

———

The girls sat at the dining room table, still in the nightgowns Allie had picked out the night before.

Both had swollen eyes and looked miserable. When Allie and Sammy walked into the room, Zoe looked up, her eyes reproachful. But when she caught sight of Sammy, they softened a little. Allie remembered what the caseworker had said about their little brother, and the gruesome way he'd been killed. She wondered if maybe Sammy reminded Zoe of him.

"You guys get some rest?" Allie asked.

"Yes, ma'am," Zoe said, quietly, her swollen eyes still glued to Sammy.

Clutching Allie's thigh, Sammy quietly stared back at her.

"Sammy, this is Zoe and Carrie. They're going to be staying here awhile."

Zoe's eyes narrowed. "That's not true. Our dad is going to pick us up as soon as he gets back from his run," she said, angrily. "Didn't you hear me say that last night? Because I'm pretty sure I said it twice."

Allie's eyes stung. *No, I'm afraid he's not. You're never going to see him again. At least not alive.*

"Why, good morning, sleepyheads," Bitty said, walking into the room and seeing Allie and Sammy. She set plates of food in front of the girls.

"Grammy!" Sammy shouted, and released Allie's leg. He wrapped his arms around the old woman as she arranged the plates. Bitty picked Sammy up and he kissed her on the cheek.

Allie noticed dark circles beneath the woman's eyes from staying up so late the night before. And the night before that. As Allie'd guessed, the lack of sleep was beginning to wear her out.

"Are you hungry?" Bitty asked.

"Yes!"

Bitty set Sammy down and smiled warmly at Zoe. "Can I get you anything else, dear?"

Zoe shook her head.

"Okay, just let me know."

Bitty went to Carrie's side and knelt down. "Go ahead and eat, honey. You need your strength."

The blonde girl dodged Bitty's eyes, but dutifully picked up her fork and moved a little of her eggs around.

"There you go," Bitty said, patting her on the shoulder.

Bitty gestured to Allie. "Go ahead and sit down. I'll bring out your plates."

"Need any help?" Allie asked.

"Everything's pretty much done. But maybe you can sit with the girls for a few minutes so I can get dressed? I'm taking them to the Child Advocacy Center in an hour."

"I'll drive you," Allie offered. She'd bring her Kindle and the iPad for Sammy to play games on, and they'd wait for Bitty and the girls in the truck, then drive them home.

"Oh. Well, thank you. That would be great," Bitty said. Allie could tell the woman was relieved she'd offered. Bitty just didn't like to show it. Although she was always helping others, she wasn't comfortable accepting help herself. Allie suspected part of the reason was she didn't want to acknowledge that she was getting older—and that the lack of sleep took much more of a toll on her body than it once had.

The phone rang. Allie reached for it and answered. "Hello?"

There was silence on the other end.

"Hello?" she said a little louder.

She could hear someone breathing. Then, after a few seconds, the call disconnected.

A shiver moved through her.

When she looked up, Bitty was watching her expectantly. "Who was it?"

"I don't know," she said. "They didn't say anything."

Allie rubbed the goose pimples that had risen on her arms and tried to tell herself that it had been nothing. A bad connection or a wrong number. But given her past, alarms were sounding in her head.

She glanced at Zoe, who had stopped eating her eggs, midbite. "It might've been my dad trying to call," she said, her tone hopeful. "Sometimes when he's on the road he hits dead areas and he can't hear us."

A chair screeched against the tiled floor, making Allie jump.

Carrie stood and burst from the room.

CHAPTER 5

COLD RAIN SLAPPED the gutters of the one-story brown brick building that housed Johnson County's behavioral services department. While Allie and Sammy sat in the warm truck, Bitty walked the girls in.

Allie lowered the windows an inch to let some of the cold, crisp air rush in. There was something about the chilly, rain-cleansed air that she'd always found soothing. Breathing in the tangy scent of wood smoke, she peered in the rearview mirror and saw Sammy also watching the girls. He'd had a million questions about both of them as he'd dressed that morning. She wondered what he was thinking now.

"You warm enough back there?"

Sammy nodded. "Why we not go with them?"

"Why *didn't* we go with them," she corrected. "Because it's going to be boring in there. Someone's just going to ask them a bunch of questions, then they'll be done. They shouldn't be long."

Sammy returned his focus back to the game on his iPad.

Her thoughts shifted to the breather on the phone earlier that morning. The call was still creeping her out. If someone had simply gotten the number wrong, why didn't he or she say something? Why just sit there like a freak, breathing on the phone?

She found the big Stop sign in her mind and waved it in front of her eyes.

Stop! she told herself. *Relax. It was* just *a wrong number.*

It was a technique Bitty had taught her years ago that helped her suppress negative or obsessive thoughts. It worked really well . . . most of the time.

Prone to depression and anxiety attacks, Allie had learned that if she controlled negative thoughts, ate well, took a low-dose antidepressant and a handful of supplements, the bad feelings usually went away very quickly. On the other hand, if she didn't do all the above religiously, they often spiraled out of control.

She powered on her tablet and was in the middle of reading a nutrition article she'd bookmarked when someone tapped on the driver's side window.

She almost flew out of her seat.

Her eyes darting to the window, she realized it was just Bitty. Exhaling loudly, Allie lowered the window and cursed her exaggerated startle reflex. It was going to end up giving her a heart attack.

"Sorry, honey. I didn't mean to scare you," Bitty said. "But Zoe said she won't talk to the therapist unless you're in the room with her."

Allie frowned. "What? Me?" That didn't make sense. Bitty was the one good at connecting with people . . . comforting the children. Not her. So why did Zoe want Allie there? They didn't even know one another.

Besides, Allie's rule was to never get involved with the foster children. "But that's crazy. Why would she ask for me?"

"I don't know." The woman watched her. "If you don't feel comfortable, you don't have to do it."

Allie *definitely* wasn't comfortable.

"I can go back in and say it's not an option," Bitty continued. "And they'll just have to find some other way."

But Allie had never said no to Bitty, and she wouldn't now. She pulled herself together and unbuckled her seat belt.

The building's lobby smelled of lemon disinfectant and stale coffee. When they entered the waiting room, they found Carrie slumped over in her chair, sound asleep.

Allie set Sammy down and pointed to a small play area. "Looks like there are some fun toys to play with," she said. But Sammy wasn't interested. Instead, he climbed on the empty seat next to Carrie and studied her while she slept.

"Okay, well, sit here for a few minutes while I go in. Grammy will stay out here with you, okay?"

"Okay, Mommy," he said, powering on his iPad and staring at Carrie some more.

"Make sure if you leave that chair, you tell Grammy first, okay?"

Sammy nodded.

Footsteps sounded on the tiled floor, and a large black man wearing a police uniform rounded the corner with a police hat and a leather-bound notebook in his hands.

"Allie, this is Sergeant Lyle Davis," Bitty said. "He's one of the investigating officers on the girls' parents' case. Lyle, this is my daughter, Allie."

Allie shook the man's hand, trying as she always did in public to appear cool and confident. Fortunately these days, it was an act she was able to pull off well enough to impress even herself.

"Nice to meet you, ma'am," Sergeant Davis said. He had a kind smile and brown, watery eyes. But what Allie was most aware of was the gun that rested in a holster on his hip. She hated guns after seeing what her brother had done to himself with one. It was the main reason Bitty didn't keep any in the house.

"It's nice to meet you, too," Allie said.

She heard more footsteps from around the corner. A moment later, another man appeared holding a Styrofoam cup. When Allie saw him, her stomach did a somersault and her hand instinctively went to her cheek. It was one of several ways she used to hide the many parts of her face that she'd loathed.

All her life, she'd suffered from BDD (or body dysmorphic disorder), a condition that distorted the way she saw herself. With her long dark hair and big gray eyes, people had always said she was beautiful . . . stunning even . . . but when she looked in the mirror, she found the girl who peered back at her to be far from attractive. She'd healed significantly the past six years, but she still had a ways to go.

Realizing she'd been trying to hide, she immediately dropped her hand to her side. *Stop that, dammit. You don't do that anymore.*

"Allie, this is Detective Lambert," Bitty said.

Swallowing hard, Allie looked at the man who was staring back at her. He appeared to be in his early to mid-thirties and was wearing plain clothes: a crisply pressed blue button-down, a brown leather jacket, and a pair of black jeans. He had dark, tousled hair and blue eyes. He stood taller than Sammy's father, Johnny, who was six foot, so she put him at about six foot two. He was easily one of the most gorgeous men she'd ever seen.

Suddenly she realized Bitty was still talking.

". . . worked with many of the same kids over the years and have gotten to know one another quite well. Detective, this is my daughter, Allie."

Detective Lambert's eyes continued to hold hers as he reached to shake her hand. She fought the urge to look away because, as usual, she questioned her appearance. This morning, aside from a little mascara and some lip ointment, her face was essentially bare. She was also wearing her long dark hair in a ridiculously messy knot on the top of her head. But eye contact had become very important to her over the years, especially since she'd become Sammy's mother. She wouldn't show fear or weakness, let on that she had body issues, or be submissive to anyone . . . if she could help it.

Not anymore.

She wanted Sammy to have a mother he could be proud of. A *strong* mother.

She shook the detective's warm hand and forced her eyes to remain steady on his, wondering what he was seeing. The person she saw in the mirror or what Bitty and other people seemed to see.

He smiled, showing perfect teeth. Her heart fluttered, which made her angry at herself . . . for her lack of control.

"I don't think I've ever seen eyes quite that shade of gray before," he said. "They're . . . well, they're striking."

"Thank you."

"It's great to finally meet you, Allie," he continued. "Your mother's a very good woman. But I expect you already know that."

"I do."

The light bar above her head buzzed. Suddenly conscious of the bright fluorescent lights that made everything a little uglier, herself included, she cleared her throat and turned her eyes to the sound of footsteps approaching.

A young woman with red hair rounded the corner. Her eyes immediately found Allie and she smiled. "Hi, are you Allie?"

"Yes."

She held out her hand. "I'm Renee. I'm the lead forensic therapist here. I'll be the one talking with Zoe this morning."

Allie shook the woman's hand. "Nice to meet you. What do I need to do?"

"Just sit in the room and be there for her. That's all."

"Okay."

"Great. Follow me."

CHAPTER 6

ALLIE FOLLOWED THE therapist into the small treatment room and found Zoe sitting on a vinyl couch, the sleeves of her borrowed shirt stretched out over her hands as though she were trying to protect herself.

Allie took a seat in a chair next to the couch and peered at the girl. Zoe's eyes flitted to Allie, then to a desk in the far corner of the room, the dark circles beneath her eyes and worry lines on her twelve-year-old forehead exaggerated by the overhead lighting.

The therapist took a seat in a recliner across from her. Allie studied the woman, who looked only a few years older than Allie. She wore casual clothing, a University of Texas pullover and yoga pants. Her red hair was up in a high ponytail, her legs casually crossed in her chair. Allie wondered if the casual clothes and posture had a purpose—to make frightened kids more comfortable. To help put them at ease.

The woman's voice was soft and rich. "Like I explained before, Zoe, we're recording our session so the investigating officers can hear your answers," she said. "They're listening to what you say today in hopes that it will help them identify the person who hurt your parents."

Zoe stared at her. "But my father's not . . ." Her voice trailed off. She looked down at her hands and started picking at her pink fingernail polish. When she looked up, her eyes were glistening. "Why . . . why is everyone saying my father's dead?"

"Because he is, Zoe," Renee said, gently. "You have been told that, right?"

Zoe folded her arms across her body and looked down.

"No one wants to make you uncomfortable . . . or to feel any pain. But there are a few questions we need to ask now. Okay?"

"But I don't *want* to remember."

The therapist leaned forward a little. "I understand, but it's important that you try. There's a bad man out there, and the police need to catch him before he hurts anyone else."

Zoe stared into space.

"Do you know who killed your parents?" Renee asked.

Zoe's face reddened. "Please. Quit saying my father *died!*"

"I'm sorry, Zoe, but he did die," the woman corrected, gently. "Both your mother and father died Tuesday night. You do understand that, right?"

Zoe blinked.

"I know that your caseworker, Miss Judy, spoke with you and Carrie when—"

Zoe's face suddenly crumpled. She buried her face in her hands and sobbed.

Allie shifted in her seat. She felt like she was eavesdropping.

Renee stood and grabbed a box of tissues. She set them on the table in front of the girl.

When Zoe surfaced again a few minutes later, Renee asked the question again. "Do you know what happened that night? Who hurt your parents?"

Zoe reached for the tissue and shook her head. "You should ask Gary. Not me. Because I have no idea."

"Who's Gary?"

"My mother's boyfriend."

Renee furrowed her brow. "Were your parents separated?"

"No. My mother was cheating on my dad with Gary."

"Oh." Renee nodded. "Did your father know about Gary?"

"I don't know. I don't think so."

"Do you know Gary's last name?"

Zoe shook her head.

"Why do you think we should talk to Gary, Zoe?"

"Because he was there," she said, softly.

"At your house . . . on Tuesday night?"

"Yes."

"Do you think it could've been Gary who hurt your mother and father?"

Zoe wrung her hands. "I guess. Maybe."

"Can you tell me exactly what happened that night?"

"I don't know what happened!" Zoe said, her tone whiny. "We were in our bedroom."

The therapist nodded, then tried a different tactic. "Who was in the house the night your parents got hurt?"

"Just me, Carrie, my mother, and Gary."

"Good, Zoe. Thank you." Renee scribbled in her notebook. "So Gary was there. And your mother, you, and Carrie? Only the four of you?"

"Yes."

"No one else?"

Zoe shook her head.

"So you're saying your father wasn't there?"

"No. He was working."

"Are you sure?"

"Yes."

"Would you say Gary's a violent person?"

Zoe seemed to think about the question. After a while, she shrugged.

"Did you ever hear him yell?"

Zoe nodded.

"Did he and your mother ever argue?"

"Yes."

"Did he ever hit your mother?"

Zoe thought about it. "No, I don't think so. But I saw him push her before. Just once or twice."

Renee nodded. "Was anyone acting upset that night?"

Zoe got a faraway look in her eyes. "Yeah."

"Who?"

"My mother."

"Your mother was upset?"

"Yeah."

"What was she upset about, Zoe?"

"I don't know. She's always upset."

"Who was she upset with?"

"Gary."

Renee jotted something down. "Do you know why your mother was upset with Gary?"

Zoe squeezed her hands beneath her buttocks and rocked. She shook her head.

"Do you think you can tell me everything you remember? *Anything* would be helpful. It doesn't matter how small or unimportant you think it is."

A baby cried from somewhere else in the building. Zoe's eyes flicked to the door, the direction of the sound, then she stared at the floor. She took a deep breath. "Our mother told us to stay in my bedroom because Gary was visiting, so Carrie and I watched a movie. While we were watching the movie, I heard my mother yell at Gary a couple of times. I remember because I had to keep turning the volume louder so we could hear the movie."

"Okay, good. Very good, Zoe. Do you know what your mother and Gary were arguing about?"

"No."

"Okay, so they were arguing. What happened after that?"

"It was kinda late, so we went to sleep."

"And after you went to sleep?"

Zoe's eyes welled up with tears. "I . . . I heard something."

"What did you hear?"

The tears were now streaming out of Zoe's eyes. "I'm not sure, but it was loud," she said, her words thick with emotion. "Then a little while later, the front door slammed. I looked out the window and saw Gary leaving. His tires made noise on the road when he left. It woke Carrie up.

"After he left, it was really quiet. My mother always, *always* keeps the TV on loud when she's alone, but she didn't have it on. It scared me because it was really weird . . . it being so quiet in our house."

The room was silent.

"What happened next?"

"Carrie and I knew something bad had happened . . . so we hid in my closet beneath a bunch of clothes. We were scared."

Renee nodded, the expression on her face gentle. "You were in the house two days after it happened. Did you or Carrie talk to anyone during that time? Try to get help?"

"I kept trying to call my dad's cell phone, but he didn't answer."

"I see," Renee said, softly. "Did you hear anyone come or go after Gary left in his truck that night?"

"I don't think so." Zoe suddenly looked up at Renee. Her eyes no longer had that vacant look. They were very focused. "They were shot, weren't they?"

"Yes, Zoe. I'm afraid they were."

Zoe blinked, and her ears pinkened. "Where was my dad when he was shot?"

"I believe they said they found him in the master suite. In the bathroom."

Zoe's chin quivered. She grabbed her stomach and narrowed her eyes at Renee. "I *told* you I didn't want to remember!" she said, sharply. She sprang from her chair. "I don't want to answer your questions anymore. I want to leave."

CHAPTER 7

WHEN ALLIE TURNED onto their road, she saw Johnny's truck parked next to the house.

She felt her shoulders sag. *Oh—God, no. Not now.*

Sammy's father, Johnny, lived two hours away, in Dallas. Even though he'd texted a few days ago, saying he'd be by soon, Allie hadn't counted on it. She didn't have the mental energy for Sammy's father. She just wanted to be alone with her son. To take a nap. Escape beneath heavy blankets with Sammy and close her eyes for an hour or two.

Bitty stiffened in the passenger seat, but she didn't say anything. When it came to Johnny, Bitty usually kept her mouth shut. Allie was thankful, because any defense she might try to launch for her continued relationship with the man would be a joke.

As they pulled into the drive, Sammy woke up. "Daddy!" he screamed, fumbling with the buckles on the straps of his car seat, anxious to free himself. "Daddy's here!"

After Allie unbuckled the little boy, he scrambled out of his seat. "Daddy! Daddy!" he yelled, flying past Allie, and sprinting to the house.

When Allie got inside, Johnny was on the living room couch, with the television on. Sammy was already in his lap, his little arms wrapped around Johnny's neck.

"I missed you, Daddy!"

"I missed you, too, little man. What's been cooking?"

Allie shrugged her coat off and hung it on the coatrack, then watched the two from the foyer.

At first, Johnny had seemed perfect for her. He was ruggedly handsome, strong, fun, funny, laid back, *completely* carefree. He used to make her laugh, and he held her at night. And outside of her dead brother, Johnny had been the only guy who'd ever been truly nice to her and made her feel wanted. Johnny had been all those wonderful things.

But he was other things, too.

Sammy used to spend a good amount of time standing in the front window of the house, pressing his little hands to the glass, waiting for Johnny. Most of those times had ended in tears because Johnny never showed. Thankfully, Sammy hadn't done that for a while. Over time, he'd seemed to have learned, just as Allie had, that Johnny did what he wanted to do when he wanted to do it—and he often changed his mind without informing anyone.

Bitty and the girls walked into the foyer and hung up their coats. "What do you guys think about resting for a bit? Does that sound good?" Bitty asked the girls, her voice sounding weary.

"Okay," Zoe said.

"Need any help?" Allie asked.

"No, we're fine," Bitty said. "Tend to your company." She planted a kiss on Allie's cheek, and nodded to the girls. "Come on. Let's get you settled in." The old woman and the twins disappeared down the hallway.

When Allie turned back around, she almost jumped. Johnny was standing in front of her, beaming. He was holding a red rose. "This bud's for you, li'l bit," he said, and laughed . . . as always, working his charm.

He opened his arms wide, anticipating a hug.

Lifting an eyebrow, she folded her arms tightly across her chest.

"Well, don't look so enthusiastic," he said, the grin still frozen on his face.

"I'm just tired." Lying was much easier. Besides, he lied, too. In fact, nearly everything that came out of his mouth was a lie. It had simply taken her a while to want to see it. After catching Johnny in his first lie, something broke a little inside of her, and a thin wall went up. When the lies kept coming, the wall grew thicker. Then, without realizing it, her heart had hardened against him and she realized she no longer felt comfort when he touched her.

But still, Allie had clung to her relationship with Johnny out of need. She used to think his deceit was the price she was supposed to pay for him to accept her, because she'd had little self-worth. But she no longer thought that way. As she grew to love and finally accept herself, imperfections and all, her feelings for Johnny had slowly cooled. Now they were iced over.

"Well, aren't you at least surprised?"

"That you showed up? That you finally did something you said you'd do? Uh, yeah. Yeah, I guess I am."

Sammy appeared next to him, clutching two Lego figures. She noticed the boy shifting his weight from one foot to the other.

"Do you have to go potty?"

He shook his head.

But she knew better. She knew he'd rather wet himself than miss a rare moment with his father.

She pointed in the direction of the bathroom. "Go. Now."

"But Mommy!"

She shot him one of her firm mommy looks. He stared at her, weighing how serious she was, then reluctantly darted off toward the bathroom. When he'd disappeared down the hallway, she pushed past

Johnny, into the living room. Her arms folded protectively across her middle, she sat down on the ottoman.

Johnny walked around the ottoman. He placed his strong hands on her shoulders, slid her forward in her seat, and slipped in behind her. "I missed you," he whispered, his breath warm on her earlobe.

He sounded so affectionate.

So genuine.

For years, she craved hearing those words from him, because it was as good as it got.

He pressed his warm lips to her neck and kissed it softly. She breathed in the musky, clean scent of his Cool Water cologne . . . a scent she used to spray on her pillowcases because it made Johnny feel close when he really wasn't: physically or emotionally. Those were the days when every inch of her would ache when she didn't get to see him. The days he made her breathless.

Now it was difficult not to shrink from his touch.

"I need money to take Sammy to the dentist," she said. She used to beat around the bush when it came to the things she needed from him, afraid he would say no. Afraid of rejection. But that had never worked, so now it was time for a new strategy. Besides, Bitty had been having money problems lately, which meant Allie was now pitching in more with the monthly household expenses.

Johnny's mouth was no longer on her neck. "Sorry, li'l bit, but I'm broke. But hey, look, I promise I'll send you some this week." He nuzzled closer to her again.

She twisted on the ottoman. "But you say that every time, Johnny. Don't you realize that? And when . . . *when* do you ever come through for us? Tell me. When?"

Johnny stared at her with the blank look he always got when he didn't know how to answer one of her questions. He stood and returned to the couch. He sat down, the springs protesting beneath his weight.

"Look, babe. I don't want to argue. I came here to spend some time with you and my boy. I just wanted us to have fun. That's all. So please, don't do this."

After returning from the Child Advocacy Center, Carrie crawled into bed and squeezed her eyes closed. She was desperate to find sleep . . . to slam shut the door on the nightmare that her life had suddenly become.

She heard Zoe pacing the floor, humming and muttering to herself. A moment later, she felt Zoe sit next to her on the bed. "Carrie?" she said softly.

Carrie kept her eyes shut.

"I know you can hear me. Look at me."

Carrie reluctantly opened her eyes. Zoe was perched on the side of the bed, her eyes red and full of fear. "They keep saying Dad's dead. Why do they keep saying that?"

Warm tears slid down Carrie's face. They'd already been through this before.

Zoe's eyes were desperate. "Carrie? Why? Why do they keep saying . . ."

Carrie studied her sister, wondering if she really could have forgotten the monstrous things they'd witnessed Tuesday night. "You really don't know, do you?" she whispered.

Zoe shook her head.

Carrie could see that she was telling the truth. "Because he is," Carrie answered. "It's true. He *is* dead."

Zoe gasped. Her eyes filled with tears, then what looked like rage. Her face grew beet red and her jaw tensed—and for a long moment, Carrie thought Zoe was going to hit her. But instead, she buried her face into a pillow and started screaming. She screamed so hard and long, the side of her face grew red and the big blood vessel in her neck throbbed.

Carrie wanted to take care of Zoe . . . to protect her . . . like she always had, but she didn't have the energy to even move. If she had, she'd be searching the bathroom for a razor blade. She'd been cutting for months. Her arms, her stomach, her legs . . . aside from the pills their mother used to give them, it was the only thing that eased the pain when it became unbearable.

And right now, it was unbearable.

But she was so exhausted, just the idea of standing was overwhelming, so she merely closed her eyes . . . and wished for the millionth time that their mother had never met Gary.

Three Months Before the Murders

The night Carrie and Zoe first met Gary, their mother had walked into Zoe's bedroom, holding the brush—and made Zoe sit in front of the vanity mirror so she could brush her long dark hair. The woman hummed as she brushed, a weird, empty look in her eyes.

Every time their mother had something important to say, she'd come in with the brush. And she'd brush their hair way too hard, for way too long, until she finally got around to saying whatever was on her mind. She didn't brush Carrie's anymore. Just Zoe's . . . because Zoe was the confident, stubborn one.

Zoe was also the one she blamed.

In fact, their mother barely addressed Carrie anymore. It was almost as though, over the years, she'd become invisible. But Carrie kind of liked being invisible. Carrie also adored Zoe. She was everything Carrie never would be: beautiful, fearless, funny, confident. While most people starred in the movie of their own lives, Zoe was the star in Carrie's.

She always had been.

Since the death of their little brother, Joey, both of their parents had changed. Their father took more routes as a long-haul trucker, and came home only one or two nights a week. Their mother began using alcohol and pills, and slept during the day and hung out with new male "friends" at night. She met them at the supermarket, at the gas station, the 7-Eleven, the Laundromat. Men were attracted to their mother. She was a beautiful woman.

On the outside.

Over the last three years, many men came and went. Guys with beards, mustaches, goatees, a few with shaven faces. All made their home feel and smell a little different. Carrie and her sister longed for their dad to be home more. They adored him. With him, they felt safe. But he was gone a lot, so most of the time they were alone with their mother.

On the nights their mother went out, she'd drug Carrie and Zoe with Xanax to make sure they slept through the evening and well into the night so they didn't get into any trouble. It was cheaper and more reliable than a babysitter, and she was always able to get more pills from a bald-headed pharmacist "friend" she'd been seeing off and on since Joey's accident. She gave them two or three . . . sometimes even four . . . Xanax that would make them drowsy about fifteen minutes later. Then, often the next thing they knew, it was the following morning. Or afternoon.

Carrie watched her sister from the newly carpeted floor, every nerve in her body standing at attention. She studied the reflection of her sister's eyes in the vanity mirror, wondering how she was going to react. To see if their mother's little visit was going to end up badly.

Zoe had become somewhat of a loose cannon over the last few years—often fluctuating between being really sweet and helpful to their mother, or being mouthy and throwing the woman into a rage.

The brush paused midair, and the humming stopped. Their mother reached for her glass. In two gulps, she finished her drink and set the glass back down, the ice clinking as it settled to the bottom.

She cleared her throat. "I want you girls to meet a new friend of mine tonight. His name is Gary. He's . . . he's different than my other friends."

Carrie saw Zoe's ears redden. Both girls, especially Zoe, hated that their mother had "friends."

"Did you hear me, Zoe?"

Zoe nodded.

Their mother's tone softened and she suddenly laughed. "You know what's hysterical? We met at the Stop n Buy. We were both looking for Bloody Mary mix. It was midnight, and we were both at the store looking for the same thing." She studied her own reflection in the mirror and smiled. "It was like it was meant to be."

Since Joey's death, their mother's moods had become strangely inconsistent. One moment, she treated them like she was a prison warden or simply ignored them. The next, she spoke to them about personal things as though they were close girlfriends.

"Gary . . . he gets me, you know?" she said, her heavily made-up eyes filling with tears.

Both girls were silent.

"And this should go without saying, but you're not to tell anyone about Gary, you hear me? Our friendship is no one's business, especially your father's."

The room was quiet.

"Zoe? I want an answer, young lady."

"Okay."

"Okay what? I want the whole sentence."

"Okay, I won't say anything," Zoe said, angrily. Carrie could see that Zoe was grinding her teeth. Tears suddenly spilled down Zoe's cheeks and she hastily cleared them away with the back of her hand.

Carrie's stomach dipped. Seeing Zoe cry was worse than Carrie crying herself. She hated to see Zoe in pain. She'd rather bear the pain for her.

I know it's hard, but please . . . don't say anything, Zoe, Carrie silently pleaded. *She's almost done. Just keep your mouth shut for a few more minutes, and she'll leave . . . and everything will be okay.*

In the mirror, Zoe's eyes shifted to Carrie's. They narrowed a little and Carrie read the look as *Don't worry. I won't.*

They were good at sending each other silent messages. Their father said it was because they were twins. That it was a gift some twins had that regular sisters didn't. But even though they were twins, they were different in almost every way imaginable. Zoe was the one who had been given all the gifts. Although Carrie had been given nothing special, she'd never felt jealous. Not really.

The doorbell rang.

The brush landed on the vanity with a thud. Their mother fussed with her hair in the mirror for a moment, then leapt off the bed. Straightening her dress, she slipped her feet into her pumps and clapped her hands together. "Okay. It's time. Let's go meet Gary."

CHAPTER 8

ALLIE HURLED LAUNDRY into the washer, taking out her frustration with Johnny on the dirty underwear and socks.

She let the hot water from the fill cycle run over her hand. She was angry. Angry with Johnny for showing up and ruining her day. Angry at herself for not yet ending things with him. For stringing out the relationship for way too long. She knew better than that.

When the spin cycle started, she leaned against the machine, and let the spinning soothe her. She dragged her thoughts to the forty days she'd been on hospital bed rest with Sammy—and how Johnny hadn't visited once. He hadn't been there through any of it: the birth, the ten days that Sammy spent in the neonatal intensive care unit. He hadn't even helped with the expenses.

During the first couple of years, she'd been hell-bent on being the perfect partner to Johnny, thinking that if she was, she'd make herself indispensable to him and he'd finally step up to the plate. Without fail, she put his needs before her own and didn't complain about anything, no matter what he did—or didn't do. But then, one day about a year ago, something Bitty told her really hit home. She'd said that you teach people how to treat you.

The words hit her like a punch to the stomach because it was true. She had taught Johnny that it didn't matter if he was dishonest. That there'd be no real consequence if he didn't keep his word, help with Sammy's expenses, or wasn't there for her when she needed him. She'd taught him that no matter what, she'd still be there.

But that was going to change.

Allie went to the kitchen and prepared lunch. She was carrying a tray of food to the bedroom when she heard the roar of an engine, then tires squealing.

What the—?

She rushed to the front window and pulled back the drapes to see a black truck barreling away, kicking up dirt. Her stomach flooded with anxiety as she watched the truck disappear around the bend.

Could someone just be lost? she wondered. But her gut said no. After all, their house was almost two acres from the closest paved road. And their nearest neighbor was a good quarter of a mile away. You had to really search for their house to find it.

Her mind flashed to the caller this morning, and fear curled in the pit of her stomach.

Could the two be connected?

Could they be connected to the girls?

To their parents' murders?

She walked down the hallway and pressed her ear to Bitty's bedroom door, listening for any signs she was awake from her nap, but there were none. After a quick check of the locks, Allie went to her bedroom and tried to rationalize the situation. After all, it was possible that the person driving the truck had simply been lost. Or, it could've been some kids looking for a place to go four wheeling. The possibilities were endless, really, once she thought about it.

She pushed open her bedroom door. "Who was that?" Johnny asked, propped up against a pillow in bed. Sammy was curled up beside him, clutching Johnny's torso as though if he let go of him, he'd vanish into a puff of air.

"I don't know," Allie answered. "Someone probably got lost."

He flipped through the channels. "Way out here? That's pretty unlikely, don't you think?"

She glared at him.

But even she wasn't buying it.

"What I smell, Mommy?" Sammy asked.

"Grilled tomato sandwiches and cream of chicken soup."

"Mmm!" Sammy released his father and sat up. "Yummy! I want some!"

"Hold on. Let me get a TV tray for you." She went to her closet and reached for one of the folded TV trays. When she straightened, she felt Johnny standing behind her. Before she could move, Johnny's big arms were embracing her. He spoke softly. "C'mon. Relax a little, babe. I came here to have fun. Not fight."

"I *am* relaxed."

He kneaded her shoulders, apparently oblivious to the fact that she was flinching beneath his touch.

"Wow. I can feel your heart racing. You okay?"

"I'm fine," she said, wiggling out from beneath his grasp.

But she wasn't fine. She was worried.

Later that night, after Sammy fell asleep, Allie placed him on a cot next to the bed and covered him with warm blankets. She set Emmet, his favorite Lego man, next to him and kissed him on the forehead.

Sammy had his own bedroom in the five-bedroom ranch-style house, but these days, they used it more for toy storage than anything else. Allie and Sammy had co-slept since he was born, and Allie found it extremely bonding.

Allie crawled back on the bed, next to where Johnny lay queuing up *Breaking Bad* on Netflix. It was one of Allie's favorite things to do with him, and for minutes at a time, she was able to forget about the issues they had—and that she would soon be breaking up with him. Allie concentrated on the program, welcoming the chance to escape for a while. But twenty minutes into their second episode, the phone rang.

She hurried to pick it up before it woke anyone. "Hello?"

She heard silence on the other end of the line. The hair on the back of her neck rose.

What the hell? Again?

She glanced at the caller ID, but the screen indicated the call was coming from a private number. "Hello?" she said louder.

She could hear muffled breathing. Then a man's voice asked, "Who is this?"

She frowned. "Who is *this*? You called *me*."

The man was silent.

A shiver crawled up Allie's back. She instinctively glanced at Sammy. He was still asleep.

She heard more muffled breathing, then the line went dead.

When she hung up, Johnny was propped up on his elbow, staring at her. "Who was that?"

"I don't know. Some man," she said, rubbing her arms.

"Well, what did he say?"

"He asked who I was."

"Really? Well, that's weird."

"Yeah . . . and I think he might've called this morning, too."

He squeezed her shoulder. "You okay? You look a little green."

She *felt* green.

Allie glanced at Sammy again to make sure he was still asleep, then she lowered her voice. "Did you see those little girls who came home with Bitty today?"

46

"Yeah, why?"

"Their parents were killed a few days ago."

"Killed? What? How?"

"They were murdered."

Johnny's eyes widened. "No shit?"

"Yeah."

"Jesus. That's crazy. Who killed them?" Johnny asked.

Allie shrugged. "That's the thing. They haven't caught him yet. He's still out there somewhere."

Johnny let out a low whistle. "Holy shit."

"Yeah, I know. And what if he didn't just want to kill the parents? What if he wanted the girls, too? Or what if the girls saw him the night their parents were killed and now he's after them? I mean, it wouldn't be hard for him to get our phone number. Or figure out where we live." She shuddered, hearing the words leave her mouth.

"Come here," Johnny said, patting the mattress in front of him.

Reluctantly she lay down on her side and let him pull her close. This time she didn't cringe. This time his closeness to her comforted her a little.

They lay in silence, their bodies pressed together for several minutes. Johnny's arms felt safe; she felt protected. She'd always longed for that feeling from a man, but she hadn't felt it with Johnny for some time. For a fleeting moment, she wondered if maybe, just maybe, she could make the relationship with Johnny work after all. Maybe she was being too tough on him, and he could change. Maybe—

She felt him easing down her sweatpants.

She jerked away from him. "Johnny, don't."

"Shh," he whispered. "It'll make you feel better. I promise."

"For heaven's sake, Sammy's right there!" she hissed.

"Then let's go somewhere else. How about the laundry room?"

It's what she'd taught him to expect. That when he visited he would at least get a quickie. In the laundry room. In the woods, in his truck.

"I said no, Johnny!" she said. "Can't you take a freaking hint? My God, I've been hinting all day!"

The desire vanished from his eyes. He sat up in the bed. "Seriously? After I drove all the way out here?"

"Yes, *seriously*. And lower your voice."

"May I ask you why?"

Anger flared in her belly. "I wouldn't even know where to freaking start."

CHAPTER 9

THIRTY MINUTES LATER, everyone but Allie was sleeping peacefully. She was on one side of the bed, with Piglet and Johnny curled up on the other side.

In the darkness, she quietly climbed out of bed, then walked through the house making sure that all of the doors and windows were still locked. She knew that it wasn't logical to keep checking, but it made her feel better.

She went to the girls' bedroom door and listened for movement on the other side. But she heard only silence. She studied the space between the carpet and the bottom of the door for a line of light that would indicate someone was awake. There wasn't one.

She hesitated, wondering if she should go in. She didn't want to invade the girls' privacy, but what if they'd opened their window? She couldn't be too cautious. She quietly pushed the door open and went inside. Moonlight streamed in from the window, bathing the room in murky light, casting dark shadows on the walls.

She crept across the room and checked to see if the window was locked. It was. She let her eyes adjust and searched for the girls in the darkness. After a moment, she could see outlines of their bodies on the bottom bunk. They were huddled together and seemed to be sleeping peacefully.

Next she went to Bitty's room. She knew that the woman had been up earlier that evening, somewhere between Allie seeing the truck and receiving the phone call from the breather. She'd heard her moving around, the sound of dishes clattering in the kitchen. She'd also heard the woman's voice a few times, which meant that she'd been talking to someone, so it was likely the girls had been up, too.

Allie slipped inside Bitty's bedroom and checked the window.

Locked.

Good.

Before leaving the room, she studied Bitty in her bed. For once, the woman was too exhausted to rattle around the house all night like she usually did. But it was a relief to see her getting some well-deserved sleep.

In the kitchen, Allie grabbed one of the dining room chairs to stand on, opened a high cabinet above the fridge, and retrieved a bottle of vodka. She poured three generous shots into a small glass and added a splash of olive juice. Once the chair was tucked back in its place, she turned off the overhead light, bathing the kitchen in complete darkness, and made her way to the kitchen table. She placed her drink on the table and slid the window open a little to enjoy the chilly air.

She sat and took a sip of her drink, enjoying the bloom of heat as it slid down her throat.

Ahhh.

Allie drank only late at night, when the house was quiet. Though life had improved immensely, and she had become much stronger, the constant fear that had become a permanent part of her was still some-times too much to handle without some kind of release.

She needed a way to forget for a few minutes . . . to become numb . . . and the vodka did the job. For a few hours, the alcohol would dull the pain that inflamed her mind. The memories of childhood terror and coldness. Her mother's cruelty. The bad decisions Allie had made both before and after her brother's death. The person she used to be, who still lurked somewhere inside of her.

As she stared out at the chilly darkness of the yard and the encroaching woods, she felt the alcohol hit her bloodstream. The thoughts flashing in her head slowed to a manageable crawl.

She would talk with Bitty in the morning and let her know about the second phone call. Bitty would console her. She'd convince her that there was nothing to worry about. She'd say that someone had simply gotten the number wrong and had tried twice to reach whomever they were trying to call. She'd also explain away the appearance of the truck by saying that another person, someone not connected to the phone calls, had simply gotten lost—although Allie couldn't remember it ever happening before.

Bitty would say that there was absolutely no connection between the calls and the truck.

They were simply coincidences.

That Allie was just being paranoid.

Something in the yard snapped. Allie tensed. She stared out, straining her ears to listen, but the night was still. She waited quietly for another sound, but it didn't come.

After a while, she relaxed. *Of course you heard something, silly*, she told herself. *A bird. Deer. Raccoon, a squirrel. Relax. Seriously. There are literally a hundred things it could've been. Stop being so paranoid.*

Her thoughts shifted to the twins and the terror they'd just experienced. Their parents had been killed on Tuesday night . . . only two miles away. What had she been doing on Tuesday night, the very moment it was happening, she wondered. She thought of how hopelessly sad, confused, and lost the girls must be feeling right now, and felt a lump in her throat.

Stop thinking about them, she told herself, taking a long pull of her drink. *You already have enough to worry about.*

She stared out the window and suddenly shivered. But it wasn't from the cold air trickling in through the window.

It was from an acute sense of being watched.

She swiftly pushed out of her chair and crouched down in front of the window. Her eyes darted back and forth as she checked the yard for movement and studied the tree line. But again, she saw nothing but shadows and trees swaying in the wind. She listened so hard her ears began to ache, but heard nothing odd.

Nails clicked against the wood floor in the distance. Piglet had woken up and was looking for her. The dog walked up to Allie and made grunting sounds like a piglet, hence her name.

Allie looked out at the yard one last time, then lowered the window and locked it. She picked up Piglet, and carried her back to the bedroom. A few moments later, she was beneath the covers again. She closed her eyes and eventually found sleep.

Johnny bolted upright in bed. "What the hell is that?" he asked, his voice husky with sleep.

Carrie was screaming again. Allie jumped out of bed and rushed to the girls' bedroom, but as she neared it, she saw Zoe dart out and run toward the living room. Allie tailed her and flipped on the light. Carrie was standing in the middle of the big room. Her screams were so loud and shrill, they seemed to vibrate in Allie's bones.

Zoe stood frozen a few feet away, her hands clamped against her ears. She walked around in little circles, humming loudly.

Allie heard Johnny's voice behind her. "Holy Jesus. Is she awake?"

Allie wasn't sure. After a brief hesitation, she went to Carrie and wrapped her arms tightly around her. "Shhh . . . Carrie, it's okay," she said, emulating what Bitty had done the night before. "Calm down. Shhh. You're safe."

But Carrie kept screaming.

"Holy shit," Johnny said, running his fingers through his hair.

Allie searched past him and saw Sammy, in his *Lego Movie* pajamas, staring wide-eyed at the screaming girl.

"Take Sammy back to the bedroom . . . please!" she said to Johnny.

After Johnny and Sammy disappeared, Allie turned back to Carrie and held her a little tighter. She could feel the girl's delicate little ribs, her heart pounding beneath them. "Shhh. It's going to be okay," she said again, having no idea if it actually would be, but not knowing what else to say.

Eventually, the screaming stopped and Carrie went limp in her arms. As the girl sobbed against her shoulder, Allie felt something stir inside of her. A warm . . . pleasant . . . feeling.

Zoe rushed in to take her place, and Allie was surprised to find herself a little reluctant to step away.

Hugging Carrie, Zoe said, "It's okay. It's okay. I'm here."

Allie watched Zoe embrace her sister until she again had the strong sense she was being watched.

That they all were.

She stared at the sliding glass doors. But all she could see was her reflection, with the twins, standing in the living room.

"Here, honey. Take a drink," said Bitty, her eyelids heavy, walking in with a glass of ice water. She handed it to Carrie.

The skin on her arms prickling, Allie went to the sliding glass doors, cupped her hands against the glass, and peered out. But aside from a few leaves drifting across the deck, carried by a strong wind, she couldn't see anything.

As Zoe and Bitty led Carrie back to the twins' bedroom, Allie went to her own bedroom to check on Sammy. She heard the bed shift in the darkness.

"Holy hell. This place is a freaking circus," Johnny said, sounding exasperated.

It was one thing he and Allie could agree on.

"Is Carrie okay, Mommy?" Sammy asked from the darkness.

The sky lit up outside the window behind him. Lightning. Yet another storm was on the horizon.

"Yes, I think so. She's just very sad," Allie said.

"I no like her be sad."

"I don't either, honey. Stay here with Daddy. I'll be right back, okay?"

"Okay."

Allie walked into the hallway in time to see Bitty pulling the girls' bedroom door closed.

"She okay?" Allie asked.

"For now," Bitty replied. "You hanging in there?" she asked, fully aware of what loud noises did to her since her brother's suicide.

"Yeah, I'm fine."

"I saw what you did for Carrie," the woman said. "I'm proud of you. I know how difficult intimacy can be for you."

But Allie didn't deserve the praise. She wasn't as proud as Bitty seemed to be of her, because she was pretty sure it had been the alcohol that had allowed her to relax enough to reach out to Carrie.

"I'm sorry, but these girls aren't going to be easy, Allie. And I'm sure this won't be the last of Carrie's night terrors." She looked inquisitively at Allie, as though searching for feedback. To maybe give Allie the chance to ask her to make the girls leave . . . to be placed with another foster home.

But Allie wouldn't—*couldn't*—do that. These girls needed help, and Bitty was the best foster parent for the job. There was no way Allie could deny them that.

Besides, she felt a connection to Carrie. To both girls.

"That's okay. We'll get through it," Allie said.

"Are you sure?" Bitty asked. "Because you and Sammy are my first priorities. If the girls become too much, I want you to tell me—

"I will. I promise."

But Allie wasn't so sure her promise was good.

Bitty studied her for a moment. "I'm going to need a little help with these two. I'd never ask you if I didn't absolutely need it. Again, if it's too much—"

Allie heard herself say: "I'd be happy to. Anything I can do, I'll do it. Seriously."

Bitty's weary face broke into an exhausted smile. "Good. Thank you."

"Have you noticed Carrie's arms?" Allie gestured to the inside of one of her arms just above the elbows.

Bitty nodded sadly.

"She's cutting, isn't she?"

"I'm afraid so. I'm hoping the counseling will do her some good. Both of them."

Allie nodded.

Bitty hugged Allie, then, after a long moment, pulled away. "I love you. Now go get some rest."

A feeling of joy still shot through her every time Bitty told her she loved her. It wasn't every day, but it was fairly frequent—and far more often than her biological mother had said it. In fact, she couldn't remember her biological mother telling her that, even one time. What she *could* clearly recall, though, were the times she'd told her she was ugly and worthless.

Back in bed, Allie let the gravity of her conversation with Bitty sink in. *So much for not getting involved,* she thought.

As Allie tried to find sleep again, she realized her skin was still vibrating from touching the fragile girl. She recalled the way Carrie's little heart had been hammering in her small chest, and something stirred inside of her again. She wondered if she'd really helped Carrie to calm down. If she'd somehow made her feel a little bit safer. Even for just that instant.

Allie realized that she'd agreed to make her world a little bigger, but instead of feeling apprehensive, it felt as though the knot in her stomach had unfurled a little bit. As though helping with the girls was exactly the thing she was *meant* to do.

But then, she reminded herself again, it could just be the vodka talking. She was fully aware that she could wake up in the morning and regret it all. Hoping that wouldn't be the case, she smiled a little in the darkness and closed her eyes.

As she drifted off, she wondered what she'd just gotten herself into.

CHAPTER 10

ALLIE AWOKE SLOWLY, taking a mental inventory of what day it was and what had happened the day before.

It was Monday, the only day of the week she worked from the wellness center. The rest of the week she worked from home. Sammy would be going to preschool for the day, like he did every weekday. The girls were still at the house. Carrie had had another night terror last night. Johnny—

Oh, God.

Johnny.

Is he still here?

Opening her eyes, she turned to find Johnny still lying on the other side of the bed, sound asleep. She groaned. She blinked at Piglet, who lay on her back, her spindly legs pointed toward the ceiling. Her front paws stabbed at the air; she was running in her dream. Allie looked down at the cot and realized Sammy was gone.

She shot upright.

Almost without exception, when Sammy woke up before her, he waited in bed quietly, playing a game on the iPad or with his minifigures. It was rare for him to leave the room by himself before she woke up.

She scrambled out of bed and hurried down the hallway. The living room was empty. The kitchen was empty, too. She could both smell and hear coffee brewing, but where was everybody? Adrenaline flooded her veins.

Where's Sammy?

Catching movement in the backyard, she rushed to the sliding glass doors and quickly zeroed in on her little boy. He was just on the deck. A few feet from him, Bitty walked around, tending plants. Allie exhaled loudly.

Christ, you're going to end up giving yourself a heart attack! Relax. Stop being so overprotective.

Willing her pulse to slow to a normal pace, Allie pressed a palm to the cold glass of the sliding doors and watched her son play. Already in his school clothes, he was lining up Marvel minifigures on one of the deck's wooden railings.

Zoe was in the oversized coat she'd arrived in, standing a few feet away from him. Her lips were turned down, and she was squinting up at the gray autumn sky. Carrie sat, stone-like, in a deck chair, her eyes squeezed shut. She was clutching the stuffed bear she'd arrived with, holding it tight to her chest.

Through the glass, Allie could hear the *slap slap* of Bitty's flip-flops, the shoes the woman wore year-round. The sound soothed Allie because it was so familiar. After a life full of unknowns and inconsistency, familiarity was comforting.

Bitty always took the foster kids outside as much as possible. She said that they needed fresh air, a chance for their bodies to produce vitamin D. She also didn't like for them to sleep late very often. She said oversleeping and a lack of routine fostered depression, something a lot of the kids were already suffering from to various degrees. So she rarely let them sleep past eight in the morning, and she made sure their days had structure.

Allie opened the sliding door and hugged her body against the cool fall air. "Good morning."

Bitty looked up and smiled. "Good morning, sweetheart."

The girls both glanced up at her, their faces impassive. Carrie's eyes looked almost swollen shut from her crying jag the night before.

Sammy saw Allie and his face lit up. "Mommy!" he shouted and ran to her as though he hadn't seen her in days.

When he reached her, she lifted him off the ground and kissed his cool cheek. "Good morning, sweet boy."

"Good morning, Mommy! Look what I do!" He wiggled to get down, then ran to his minifigures. "Mommy! Look what I do!" Sammy shouted again, pointing at his toys. "I orgorize them into good guys and bad guys. See?"

"You did that all by yourself?"

He nodded, beaming.

"Good job, honey! You're a great organizer."

Smiling, he returned his attention to his project.

"Sleep well?" Bitty asked.

"Mm hmm," Allie said, taking a lungful of chilly air. "Thanks for getting him dressed."

"Of course."

Allie stared at the gray, cloud-filled sky, then out at the gloomy woods behind the yard. She remembered the sound she'd thought she heard the night before. The strong sense of being watched.

It was nothing. Just forget about it, she told herself.

She turned to Bitty. "Is Sammy okay out here with you while I get ready?"

"Sure. Go do your thing. He'll be fine."

The hot spray of the shower thundered down, pelting every inch of Allie's skin. She turned to let it hit her face and felt the blood rush to her forehead, her cheeks, her chin.

She thought about this new chapter of her life. In terms of her career, she was following in Bitty's footsteps as a wellness practitioner. She was drawn to the work for many reasons, but mainly because it was so rewarding and flexible. She worked part-time at a wellness center in the next town on Mondays, then took clients in her own small practice over the phone, two to four days a week. She liked the flexibility of the schedule and of feeling she was making a positive difference in people's lives.

Her thoughts went to the girls. She wondered what their lives had been like before their parents' murders. Had they been happy? What had they been like before? Had their parents' murders significantly changed them? Suddenly she had a strong desire to know.

Allie turned off the spray and toweled dry. She dressed quickly, looking in the mirror only to apply minimal makeup. Because of her BDD, her looks had been an obsession for most of her life. Even now, if she wasn't careful, she could easily worry about how she looked for several hours each day. Bitty told her she suffered from BDD for several reasons, not the least of which was because of the lies her mother had told her as a child, seeding thoughts of deficiency in her mind.

Seeds she continued to fertilize as Allie grew older.

Allie could still picture the glaring disapproval in her late mother's eyes. The look of disgust on her face as she'd shake her head.

How I made such an ugly child is beyond me. We're going to have to figure a way to hide those looks of yours, girl.

In fact, up until only six months ago, Allie never would have let Johnny—or anyone, for that matter—see her without a full face of makeup. She could still clearly remember the first day she'd shown herself to him with a completely bare face, almost trembling with shame. She'd fully expected him to look at her with disgust like her mother had often done. But if he noticed anything was different about her, he didn't show it.

It had astounded her.

It had also empowered her, if just a little. But she still had a long road of healing in front of her, so aside from basic hygiene and tidiness, she forced herself not to pay much attention to her appearance. She also took care not to catch her reflection in car windows, rearview mirrors, or the glass of framed photos.

Out of sight, out of mind.

Back in her bedroom, she tiptoed around, gathering her purse and laptop, trying her best not to wake Johnny. But as she started to walk out, she heard him grunt and stir in bed.

"What the hell was wrong with that girl last night?" he asked. "Jesus, I thought an animal was mauling her."

Allie glared at him, then started again for the bedroom door.

"Hey, hey, no. Come back here, beautiful," he said. When she turned, she saw him patting the bed. "Take care of your man's needs," he said in a tone that she supposed was meant to sound playful and sexy but did nothing but repulse her.

"Oh, right. Like you take care of mine?"

Johnny's smile vanished. "Hey. Easy, tiger. Come on, seriously. Get back in bed with me." He rubbed the curly hairs on his chest. "Just for a second."

But she was done dragging out their unhealthy relationship . . . done even talking to him until she was prepared to have The Big Talk . . . after work.

Without a word, she left the room and went to the kitchen to pour herself some coffee.

When Allie reached the kitchen, she found a piping-hot cup of coffee already waiting for her. Sammy's *Lego Movie* lunch box was also beside it. She opened it up to find it was already packed.

Allie smiled inside.

In so many ways, Bitty understood Allie's needs better than Allie even did. *Women should have wives, not husbands,* Allie thought, not for the first time. They just seemed better suited mentally and emotionally. It was too bad she wasn't attracted to women.

Realizing she now had several spare minutes before she had to leave to bring Sammy to preschool, she pulled on her jacket and walked outside to join everyone on the deck.

Since she'd last been outside, the sun had sliced through the gloom. Sammy was in the yard now, pushing leaves around with a toy rake. Zoe was sitting cross-legged on a stone paver in the yard, picking blades of grass. Carrie still sat in the deck chair, her eyes squeezed closed.

Allie sat on a rocking chair and took her first sip of coffee, enjoying its heat as it glided down her throat.

She sipped and kept an eye on the tangle of loblolly pines that bordered the yard as she watched her son play. It was the only part of their home that she didn't trust. Although she'd spent most of her childhood playing in woods just like it, they now creeped her out.

Once their financial situation was healthier, she'd have a fence built. A tall privacy fence so she wouldn't have to look at the trees beyond it. But she needed to focus on just covering the basics for now, because money was tight. From what she'd gathered from recent collectors' calls, Bitty was having financial problems, and Bitty wasn't someone who usually had issues with money. Allie wondered if the financial problems were due to depression. After all, she'd been grieving the loss of a close friend, back in Louisiana, for a long time now. A man whose death she still hadn't seemed to have completely come to terms with, leaving her perpetually sad and somewhat withdrawn.

As Allie turned her attention back to Sammy, she thought she saw movement in the pines behind him. She frowned and leaned forward in her chair. She watched closely, but the only activity she saw was the shivering of pine needles in the cool breeze.

Hardly anything unusual.

Or dangerous.

You're just creeped out because of yesterday, she told herself. *You need to stop.*

Bitty sat down in the rocker next to her.

"How are they doing?" Allie asked, pointing her chin toward the girls, her voice low.

"As well as can be expected, I suppose," Bitty said quietly. "Carrie still hasn't said a word. Zoe speaks only when spoken to."

As they sat, rocking and drinking their coffee, the breeze kicked up, blowing Allie's hair into her face. She closed her eyes and enjoyed the warmth of the sunshine on her eyelids for a while, then decided to take the opportunity while they were alone to tell Bitty about the second phone call the previous evening, and the truck that had been on their property. Bitty rocked quietly for a few moments, listening.

When Allie had finished, Bitty sat silently and sipped her coffee, her face blank of emotion. But Allie could see the wheels in her head turning.

"Think there's anything to be concerned about?" Allie asked.

Bitty shook her head. "Probably not."

Piglet started to howl. Allie opened her eyes to find Sammy shaking a young peach tree, trying to get the dead leaves to fall to the ground. For some reason, Piglet seemed to be frightened of trees, and had the same reaction any time Sammy was near one.

Piglet's howls grew louder, more mournful. "Piglet, stop!" Allie called. The dog turned in Allie's direction and cocked her head to one side.

"I said, stop," Allie repeated.

The dog just stared at her, panting.

Allie turned back to Bitty. "Johnny's still here. But he should be leaving soon," she said, embarrassed to admit he hadn't left yet.

Bitty nodded.

Allie watched her son lose interest in the tree and begin walking around, crunching dried leaves and pine needles under the toes of his sneakers. Every once in a while she saw him steal curious glances at Zoe.

"Want me to pick up anything on my way home?" Allie asked. "Any groceries?"

"Thanks, but I'm taking the girls back to the Child Advocacy Center this morning, then we're going to do some shopping. We'll get whatever we need while we're out."

Piglet began to bark. Before Allie had the chance to look up, a patio chair screeched against the deck and Carrie shot up from her chair. The last vestiges of blood had drained from her pale face, and there was a look of terror in her eyes. She was staring at something in the yard.

"What the—" Allie started. She quickly scanned the perimeter and then she saw what Carrie was looking at.

A strange man was in their yard.

From the very first glance, Allie could see that there was something not right about the man. The unnatural wideness of his eyes screamed trouble. "Sammy!" she shrieked, jumping up and barely noticing the splash of hot coffee across her chest as she darted toward her son.

"Sammy!" she screamed. "Sammy, come here! Now!"

But Sammy just stood, facing the gaunt, scraggly-looking man. The two stood only ten feet from one another—the man would have plenty of time to snatch him up and run off into the woods.

Bitty was yelling for the girls to go inside the house when, to Allie's surprise, Sammy took a step toward the man.

"Hi. What your name?" she heard her little boy ask politely.

Finally reaching Sammy, Allie gathered him in her arms and ran back to the house. She whipped past Zoe, who was standing frozen in the yard, a blade of grass still between her fingers.

"Johnny!" Allie screamed, out of breath. *"Johnny!"*

Allie released a frightened, crying Sammy into the safety of the living room, and turned back to the yard. Bitty, a cell phone pressed against her ear, was now standing between the man and Zoe.

"Don't you dare come any closer," the old woman warned, her palm extended. "Who are you? And why are you on my property?"

From where Allie stood, she could see sweat streaming from the sides of the thin man's face. It was barely fifty-degree weather, and he was wearing only short sleeves, but sweating. He scratched hard at one of his arms.

As a frightened Sammy wailed in the living room, Allie realized she no longer saw Carrie. She stepped back onto the deck and found the girl by the stairs leading into the yard, her back pressed against the house.

Allie yanked her inside, then called for Johnny again. "Johnny, dammit! Are you still here?" Allie yelled again. *"Johnny!"* she called, watching the man in the yard step to one side of Bitty so that he had a direct line of sight to Zoe. He stopped scratching his arm and extended his hands, palms up, as though showing they were empty.

"Hi, Zoe girl," he said, his eyes wild. "Now, now . . . there's no reason to look so scared."

The blade of grass fell from Zoe's hand, and Allie watched her back away from him.

Is that the mother's boyfriend, Gary? Allie wondered, remembering Zoe talking about him with the forensic therapist. If so, she was pretty certain that he was a suspect in the murders. Her chest tightened even more.

"We're at 22741 County Road 447," Bitty said, speaking rapidly into her cell phone. "We have a trespasser who appears to be dangerous. Please, hurry. Three children are in danger."

Johnny finally appeared at the sliding glass door, shirtless, and his hair damp as though he'd been in the shower. "What the hell's going on now?" he asked, fumbling with his belt.

Allie pointed to the man. "There's a man in the yard. Do something!"

"What?" He squinted into the yard. "Who the hell is he?"

"I don't know! And Zoe's out there!"

Johnny stepped onto the deck. "Dude, what do you think you're doing?" he called. "This is private property."

In the background, Sammy began to cry even louder. Piglet, her barks now howls, stood rigid only a few feet from the man. He kicked awkwardly at the dog, but his foot didn't connect, and he stumbled.

"Carrie . . . bring Sammy to my bedroom and lock the door," Allie instructed. "Now!" Carrie silently grabbed Sammy's hand. He screamed as she pulled him away.

Ignoring Johnny, the man continued to talk to Zoe. "Zoe girl. I didn't come to hurt nobody, okay? I just need to know what you told them about me."

Bitty grabbed Zoe by the arm and pulled her back to the house.

"No, don't!" the man shouted. "I need to talk to her!"

But Bitty kept moving. She and Zoe scrambled up the stairs of the deck and to the door.

"Dude! You didn't hear me talking to you?" Johnny asked, finally stepping off the deck and into the yard.

The man's eyes darted from Zoe to Johnny. He blinked and regarded Johnny for the very first time, his eyes bugging out. He reached into his waistband and pulled out a gun. He swung it in Johnny's direction. "Don't you come closer, you hear me?" he warned.

Allie's world went still.

Johnny stopped in his tracks and raised his hands. "Whoa. Easy now."

The man's hands shook as he took a step closer to the house. "I just want to talk to Zoe. That's all. I didn't come here to hurt anybody, okay?" he said, looking frantic. "Now bring her back out."

"Jesus! Put that gun away, dude. Someone could get hurt."

"I said bring her out!" the man screamed.

"Look, I don't know what in the hell is going on, but you don't want to be doing this," Johnny told the man.

"Shut the fuck up!" he roared. Then he returned his attention to the house. "Bring her out, dammit. Bring her the fuck back, I said!"

Allie stepped into the living room, slid the door shut, and locked it.

A long moment passed in silence.

Finally realizing they weren't going to bring Zoe out, the man lumbered toward the house.

CHAPTER 11

AS THE MAN reached the top step of the deck, the screams of police sirens split the cold morning air.

The man paused, his eyes darting from the sliding glass door to the windows of the back bedrooms, then to the sliding glass door again. "Shit!" he yelled. He glanced once more at the house, then jumped from the deck and quickly vanished into the woods.

Her hands trembling, Allie unlocked the sliding glass door and slid it open.

"What the hell?" Johnny asked from the yard, dumbstruck. "This place is insane."

"Come in, and make sure to lock the door behind you," Allie said. Blood still thundering in her veins, she hurried to her bedroom to check on her son.

As she passed the foyer, she saw Bitty at the front door, talking to a uniformed police officer.

"In the backyard," Bitty was saying. "He just took off into the woods. He hasn't been gone two minutes."

"And you don't know who he is?" the police officer asked.

"I have no idea, but he seems to know my foster children."

Zoe unlocked the bedroom door, and Allie rushed inside and folded a crying Sammy into her arms.

"You scared me, Mommy!" he whined, big tears sliding down his cheeks. His blue eyes were wide, frightened. "I no like what you did. Why you scare me like that?"

He sobbed against her chest, his long, damp eyelashes fluttering against her collarbone. She sobbed right along with him. "I'm so sorry, honey," she said, pressing her nose in his hair and kissing his head. "Mommy didn't mean to. I just needed you to go inside the house. But everything's okay now. Everything's okay."

Allie felt the air behind her part. She turned to see Johnny. "Daddy!" Sammy cried. He released Allie and ran to his father.

Allie went to the girls. They were huddled together on the bed. "Are you guys all right?"

"Is he gone?" Zoe asked, her cheeks tear streaked.

Allie heard the blip of a police vehicle outside. "Yes. He's gone."

"Is he . . . is he coming back?"

Allie hoped not, but she didn't know, so she didn't answer. "Was that Gary? Your mother's boyfriend?"

Zoe nodded, her chin trembling.

An hour later, Allie sat in the kitchen with Zoe and Renee, the forensic therapist Zoe had talked with at the Child Advocacy Center.

Because Zoe had refused to go back to the center, Detective Lambert had arranged for the therapist to come to the house to speak to her. He'd also arranged for closed-circuit television gear to be set up so the session could be recorded. Sammy was in the living room with Bitty and the girls' caseworker while Allie sat in the kitchen with Zoe. Throughout the house, the drapes and blinds were all drawn, making it feel much later in the day than it was.

Zoe sat by the bank of windows in the kitchen, hugging her body tightly and rocking. As Allie studied her, Zoe suddenly looked up and their eyes met. Allie lifted her lips into a smile, but Zoe didn't smile back. Instead, she studied Allie with those guarded eyes of hers. Although she'd insisted on Allie being with her during the therapist's interviews, Allie could still tell the girl didn't trust her.

"You okay?" Allie asked, then immediately regretted the question. It was a stupid one. Zoe must've realized it was stupid, too, because she didn't bother to answer.

After talking with Detective Lambert, Renee walked in and took a seat. She was looking very casual again in yoga pants and a long-sleeved T-shirt that read "Calm down. I'm a shrink." She smiled warmly at Zoe and did her leaning-in thing again. "Is there something at the advocacy center that makes you uncomfortable, Zoe? Is that why you didn't want to go in today?"

"I . . . I just wanted to stay home," Zoe answered.

Allie was surprised to hear Zoe use the word "home." She couldn't help but wonder if it was simply a figure of speech, or if Zoe was already feeling a little more comfortable at their house.

"I see. I'll tell you a secret then. I do, too," the young woman said, and winked. "I love being at home. I wish I was able to be there more."

Zoe stared at the woman.

"So, tell me more about this man, Gary, who paid you guys a visit today. Is he the same person you were telling me about yesterday?"

Zoe nodded.

"Do you know what he wanted? Why he showed up today?"

Zoe shrugged. "He said something about wanting to know what I'd told you."

"Did you answer him?"

"No. I didn't talk to him at all."

"Are you afraid of Gary, Zoe?"

Zoe peered down at her hands, pressed together in her lap. "I hate him."

"Why do you hate him?"

"He's weird. He . . ." She lowered her eyes and rocked harder. "Once, he . . .

Allie shifted in her seat.

"What did he do, Zoe?" Renee asked.

Zoe swallowed hard. "I woke up in the middle of the night a couple of weeks ago, and . . . and he . . ." She inhaled sharply and shuddered. When she looked up, her eyes were glittering with tears. "He was standing next to my bed. He asked if he could get in with me and rub my back."

The rest of the morning was a blur. Johnny left for Dallas shortly before Zoe's session with the therapist, and at some point, although she couldn't remember when, Allie had grabbed Sammy and retreated to her bedroom. Now they lay in bed. The morning's excitement had sucked them both dry, physically and emotionally. Sammy was taking his second nap of the day, and Allie was trying to fall asleep, but there was still too much adrenaline in her bloodstream.

As she had sensed, the girls' arrival had changed everything.

It had been fewer than three days since she'd first laid eyes on these girls, and now the whole safe world that had taken her years to build felt as flimsy as a house of cards.

It'll all pass soon, she assured herself. *This, like everything else, will pass . . . and we'll be fine.*

The police had issued an all-points bulletin on Gary and his truck. Detective Lambert was confident that as long as he hadn't already skipped town, they would find Gary quickly. Plus, the twins weren't going to be in Bitty and Allie's care forever. Both situations were only temporary. The detective had also assigned a patrol car to the property for the time being . . . hopefully until Gary was caught.

Bitty had asked endless questions of Detective Lambert, but because Gary was a suspect in an active homicide investigation, the detective was unable to answer a lot of them. Nevertheless, Bitty was stubborn and resourceful. If she wanted to get to the bottom of a situation, she usually did. So she began making phone calls.

Between what the detective and Zoe had told them, and what Miss Bitty had learned on her own, Allie knew that the man in their yard had been Gary Jason Willis. He was thirty-seven years old, a longtime substance abuser, and his current substance of choice was believed to be methamphetamine. He'd worked as an installer for a local granite company for over ten years, but was known to deal drugs on the side. Gary had a long police record, had been charged with two assault and battery charges in the last five years alone, and had three young sons under the age of ten and a baby on the way. He'd also been "dating" the girls' married mother, Julie Parish, for about three months.

After news of the murders had broken, no one had seen Gary—until this morning. Troubled by the length of time he'd been gone, his wife had even reported him missing. A neighbor gave a statement saying that not only was Gary's truck parked in the Parish family's driveway until late Tuesday night, those who saw him when he left said, as Zoe had, that he seemed to be in a big hurry.

Allie tried to process everything she'd learned, but it was too much. Her brain was so scrambled she could barely think. She just knew that she was disturbed. She thought of how easily Sammy could've gotten abducted. How quickly bad things could happen. How, suddenly, everything . . . *everything* . . . could change. It made her realize that she had Bitty and Sammy only temporarily. That one day, both would be taken from her. Whether their bond was broken due to a disagreement or because someone died, a day would come when they'd be separated forever.

A shiver rolled through her.

For God's sake, STOP! You're doing it again.

Forcing herself back into the present, she kissed her sleeping son's soft cheek and watched his tiny hands and stubby little fingers as they rose and fell on his little round stomach. She watched him and tried to convince herself that their life was still easy, safe, comfortable, and secure.

Never mind that a patrolman was sitting in front of the house in case a suspected murderer decided to threaten them again. Or that a few feet away, a child whose parents had both just been murdered was likely, at any moment, to let out a blood-curdling shriek.

At eight o'clock that evening, Allie decided to check on Bitty and the twins. She felt guilty for leaving Bitty alone with the girls, but she'd needed some time to just breathe and get through the emotional trauma of the morning. Besides, it was only for a few hours, and if Bitty needed anything, Allie had only been a few feet and a couple of walls away.

When she stepped into the hallway, the house was dark and eerily quiet. Usually, Bitty would still be up. But right now she was nowhere in sight. Allie stopped outside the girls' room and listened, but all was quiet on the other side.

She poured a drink, then did another quick security check of the house, knowing good and well that Bitty had already done the same. But checking and rechecking made her feel better.

After her drink, she retreated back to her bedroom. Earlier, she'd called her office to tell her boss that she needed the day off for a family emergency. Taking the day off was the last thing she'd wanted to do. Her boss was a very kind man who believed in her. He was one of the very few who ever had. But she couldn't leave Bitty alone with the kids while a murder suspect was stalking them.

She tried to push the financial repercussions of the missed work to the back of her mind. It wouldn't do her any good to try to deal with everything all at once. She rubbed her temples. She couldn't—*wouldn't*—worry about any of that . . . yet. As with everything else, one step forward at a time. *Just move in the right direction and everything will be fine.*

In the bathroom, Allie took her antidepressant, washed her face, and brushed her teeth without even one glance in the mirror. Crawling into bed, she flipped off the lights and stared into the gloomy darkness, trying to get her brain to shut down for a little while. Taking deep breaths, she closed her eyes and waited—for sleep or the screams, whichever would come first.

CHAPTER 12

BUT THE SCREAMS didn't come.

Allie had slept restlessly, and when her eyes fluttered open at three in the morning, her first thought was that something was wrong.

The house was too quiet.

She jumped out of bed and hurried to the twins' bedroom. As she was about to push their door open, she heard Zoe talking in the room. She wondered what the girl was doing up so early.

Was she having trouble sleeping?

She was also curious whether Carrie was responding. Or, if Carrie was mute with Zoe, too. She listened for a moment, but heard nothing but silence. She then realized that maybe they knew she was standing at the door, so she stepped away.

Unable to go back to sleep, she brewed coffee, and sat in the darkened kitchen, staring out into the backyard. She watched the entire tree line and the spot where Gary had emerged from the woods the previous morning. She wondered where he'd gone. And if he was still out there somewhere, watching them.

She peered out the window until the inky sky brightened into smatterings of gray and lavender, wondering how differently things might've turned out if Johnny hadn't been there. The same Johnny who hadn't so much as lifted a finger to send a text or Facebook message after his hasty departure back to Dallas. Her mind continued to slip over the dark possibilities until she realized what she was doing. Then she found the big Stop sign in her mind and waved it in front of her eyes.

Stop! It's okay. Everyone's safe.

She downed her coffee and poured another cup, then crossed the living room and went to the front window. She peered out to make sure the patrolman was still there.

She relaxed a little, seeing that he was.

Allie and Sammy were in the middle of breakfast when they heard a door down the hall click shut, then footfalls heading toward the living room.

Bitty appeared in the entryway, carrying a notebook and her cell phone.

"Grammy!" Sammy squealed. He scrambled from his seat and ran to her.

The old woman's eyes lit up. "Good morning, pumpkin!"

After they said their morning hellos, Sammy walked up to Allie. "May I be excused, Mommy?" he asked.

"Yes, sir, you may."

"Yay!" Sammy shouted. Then he darted from the room, Piglet the Protector at his feet.

"I take it no preschool today?" Bitty asked.

Allie shook her head. She had called Sammy's preschool to let them know he'd be absent a few days. There was no way she was going to let her son out of her sight until she knew Gary Willis was no longer a threat.

"It's probably best," Bitty said.

As Allie cleared their dishes, Bitty told her she was going to make more phone calls and continue to investigate Gary and the girls' family.

Bitty had many gifts. One of Allie's favorites, though, was that she had a special way with people. She had a way of making them comfortable. Of getting them to open up. While Detective Lambert seemed personable, he had a disadvantage in that he was law enforcement. From what Allie understood, the county had recently seen a surge in methamphetamine production, and since many members of the community or their families were connected to the trade in some way, they were hesitant to call attention to themselves by stepping forward. And if they felt forced to talk, the investigators received the bare minimum of what they knew . . . if even that.

A little before eight o'clock, Allie answered the front door to find the girls' caseworker. "I'm sorry to show up so early in the morning, but I wanted to bring these before I got my day started," Miss Judy Marsons said, nearly out of breath. Allie wondered if she was always so harried. Miss Marsons held out two brown paper shopping bags. "It's a few changes of clothes for the girls."

As Allie took the bags, she caught a whiff of an overly sweet and discomfortingly familiar smell: the odor of decomposition. She flinched, and her eyes teared up. It was an odor she'd smelled a few times in her youth. One that brought back awful memories.

"Dreadful, isn't it?" Miss Marsons said. "It was extremely difficult being in the house, so I just grabbed what I could . . . *quickly*. I just hope the smell washes out." She made a face. "The . . . odor . . . from the bodies is still so strong."

Allie nodded. "Did you want to speak with Bitty?"

"Yes. Is she up?"

Allie led the caseworker to the home office, then went to the laundry room and upended the paper bags, dumping the clothes in the washer. She programmed the machine to its hottest setting, then closed the door tightly behind her.

After making breakfast for the girls, she checked the backyard again. Aside from grass and trees, it was empty. In the distance, she saw a dark cloud of buzzards circling high above the woods. There seemed to be at least a hundred of them. They were always lurking over something in the woods. A dead rabbit. A dead deer. Allie cringed at the constant reminders of death, then let her eyes drop back to yard level. She was studying the tree line again when she heard footsteps behind her.

Turning, she saw Zoe lingering in the entryway. She was in her nightgown and looked small and pale.

"Good morning. How'd you sleep?" Allie asked.

Zoe shrugged. "Good, I guess." She stepped hesitantly into the room.

"Is Carrie up?"

"No."

"Well, come sit down. I made breakfast."

A few minutes later, Allie sat across from Zoe. The girl moved her fork around, quietly, picking at her food.

"I can make you something else if you don't like eggs," Allie said.

Zoe looked up. "No, thank you. Eggs are good." She looked down at her plate again and took a small bite.

Not wanting to stare, Allie peered out the window, at the dark clouds floating through the sky. The weather was going to get bad again, and the temperature was expected to drop another ten degrees.

A brisk wind sent orange and yellow leaves dancing across the yard. Allie took a sip of her coffee and glanced at Zoe, and found the girl was watching her intently. Allie wanted to know more about her and her sister, and wondered how forthcoming Zoe would be if she asked questions.

"So, what kinds of things do you like to do, Zoe?"

Zoe chewed her food slowly and continued to study Allie's face through swollen eyes. She was quiet for so long, Allie began to wonder if she'd even heard the question.

"What do you mean?" she finally asked.

"What do you enjoy doing? Do you play any sports?"

Zoe shook her head. "No."

"You like movies? Any television programs?"

"Yeah. I like both. I watch *Modern Family* a lot on the iPad."

"I haven't seen that."

"It's good. It's funny."

"You like comedies?"

Zoe nodded. "But I mostly like it because of the families. Even though they fight sometimes, you can still tell they really love each other."

Allie was encouraged that Zoe was opening up a little. "My brother used to watch old shows like *Leave It to Beaver* for the same reason. The family was totally different than ours."

"Where is he? Your brother?"

Allie's eyes stung. "He died."

Zoe studied her for a long while, then looked down at her eggs. "Yeah. My brother died, too."

They sat, silence growing between them. Allie searched for another question, but came up with nothing. She stood up. "You don't drink coffee, do you?"

Zoe shook her head.

"Okay. Well, I'm going to get another cup. I'll be right back."

Allie went to the kitchen to pour another cup of coffee. She lingered at the counter for a moment, and studied Zoe from afar. Now that she was no longer in the room, the girl was shoveling food into her mouth. She'd been hungry but hadn't wanted to eat in front of her. In that moment she reminded Allie a little of a wild animal. One frightened and far from home. Suddenly Zoe turned and stared into the kitchen—and directly into Allie's eyes.

Crap, busted.

Allie put on another smile, then grabbed her coffee and walked back into the dining room.

Thirty minutes later, Allie pushed open the girls' bedroom door to find Carrie still fast asleep in her bed, tangled up in the covers, the stuffed bear cradled in her arms.

Allie sat down softly on the edge of the bed and watched the girl sleep. It was the first time she'd been able to really get a close look at her. She was a cute girl with almond-shaped eyes, long pale lashes, a snub nose, and thin, pale eyebrows. Aside from a smattering of caramel-colored freckles, her skin was almost colorless, and sallow beneath the eyes. Again, she reminded Allie of a porcelain doll. As she slept, the fingers on her left hand kept twitching.

One of her feet was hanging from the edge of the bed. Allie noticed the top of it, just below her toes, was blistered, the bottom edges a little red. She frowned, then left the room to get the first aid kit.

Back in the room, she touched the girl's arm. "Carrie?"

Carrie's eyes moved beneath their lids. A few seconds later, she inched her eyebrows together, then sniffed and opened her eyes. Allie could see her trying to acclimate herself. Once she did, she sat up and peered at Allie through bleary brown eyes and carefully adjusted the stuffed bear beneath her left arm.

Allie pointed to the blister on her foot. "That looks bad. How did you get it?"

Carrie stared down at her foot, but didn't say anything.

"Mind if I clean it?"

Carrie looked away. Allie took it as a cue that she wouldn't mind, and gently cleaned and bandaged the wound.

When she was done, she sat next to the girl, then giving in to a peculiar impulse, reached out and folded the girl's cool limp fingers into hers.

Carrie didn't squeeze back, but she also didn't flinch or pull her hand away.

Allie felt a warmth pass through her again. Carrie's hand seemed strangely right in hers. Like it belonged. Almost like Sammy's or Bitty's. The fact that it did stunned her.

CHAPTER 13

AFTER CARRIE HAD eaten her breakfast, Allie assigned the girls their chores.

Throughout her years of fostering children, Bitty had learned that many troubled kids had never been given responsibilities, rules, accountability, or even much attention—all important ingredients to raising healthy human beings with good self-esteem. Young people who would be able to function independently in the real world. So Bitty was diligent about giving her foster kids this nurturing.

Allie remembered when she'd first arrived at Bitty's as a sixteen-year-old foster child. She'd been an elementary school dropout and her mother had barely interacted with her, so Bitty's rules were the first she'd ever been given. Allie'd been surprised to find that she liked having rules. They gave her a sense of security. She also enjoyed the new responsibility because it freed her mind from her dark thoughts and worries for stretches of time.

Plus, the accountability had felt good. The fact that someone was actually paying attention to her, actually putting serious thought and time into her welfare for the very first time in her life, made her feel valued.

As Allie gave the twins their chores, Sammy clutched her leg and stared. Allie showed the girls step-by-step how Bitty liked everything done. Both girls dutifully did what they were asked. The only hesitance Allie sensed was when she asked Carrie to put away the stuffed bear while she cleaned. Carrie had frozen a moment, clutching the bear even tighter. She'd peered quickly at her sister, but then eventually did as she was asked.

Allie watched from the living room as she did the week's meal planning, Sammy sat snuggled against her, playing an Xbox Lego game.

Allie realized her attention lingered on Carrie. She wasn't sure why she was so drawn to the girl. Yes, the similarities between her and Carrie were obvious: they were both orphans and their mothers had both been murdered . . . but she had the same thing in common with Zoe, yet she didn't feel quite the same pull toward her that she did with Carrie.

Maybe it was because Allie's and Carrie's personalities seemed more similar? Where she had pegged Zoe to be the confident type, Carrie appeared to be more self-conscious. She also seemed to be the more wounded of the two.

After the girls finished their chores, Allie showed Zoe how to use the Xbox to find age-appropriate programs, movies, and games. Bitty didn't want the girls to have access to local television networks because she didn't want them to see news coverage of their parents' murders.

Network television was rarely watched in the house anyway. Bitty didn't watch television at all, and Allie liked to control what she and Sammy saw. The fewer unrealistic images she saw, the better for her BDD. The fewer unrealistic images Sammy saw, the healthier his expectations would be when he was old enough to be interested in females.

Allie noticed that when the girls were around, Sammy watched them carefully. Sammy had always been an observant child. A spider the size of a small tick couldn't cross the room without him noticing. He'd been that way since he was very young. He also had a strong sense of wonder and curiosity. Allie loved seeing the world through his eyes.

It was almost as though she were seeing things for the very first time again. As though she were reliving her childhood.

But this time around, a normal one.

Sammy liked to be sneaky and spy on people.

But he didn't spy on them to be mean.

He did it because it was fun.

Today he'd been spying on the twins a lot. Quiet Carrie and her sister, Zoe. He thought they were both a little strange. First, Carrie didn't talk . . . *at all*. And she cried a lot. Both of them did, especially when they were in their bedroom with the door closed.

He'd also caught Zoe earlier that morning in his mommy's room, smelling a shirt in her closet. He stood behind her for a while, watching. When she turned around and saw him there, she jumped like she was really surprised. Then she let go of his mother's shirt and without even looking at him, went into her bedroom and closed the door.

He'd also noticed that Zoe stared at his mommy a lot when she wasn't looking. He had no idea why. He just knew it seemed a little weird.

Now his ear was pressed against the girls' bedroom door. He could hear Zoe saying something to Carrie. And she sounded angry. He strained to hear her words, but couldn't. But then, someone started walking toward the door . . . toward him.

And he ran down the hallway as fast as Flash.

Before Allie knew it, the sun was going down. Thankfully, the day had flown by without any sign of Gary or any phone hang-ups or strange trucks.

Over the course of the day, she had washed the girls' clothes in hot water three times, but the dizzying odor lingered, so with Bitty's okay, she ordered the girls each three new outfits online and had the shipping expedited. Bitty would take care of the rest of their wardrobe later at a discount store in Tyler.

She watched the kids in the living room. Sammy was sitting on the floor playing with his Legos, and the twins were sitting on the larger couch. Zoe was reading an old Judy Blume book, one of the many books Bitty kept for the kids, and Carrie was curled into a ball, fast asleep.

Allie went to check on Bitty and found her in the home office, chewing on the end of a pen, staring at something she'd jotted down in her notebook.

"Hey," Allie said. "How's it going?"

Bitty peered at Allie through her spectacles. "Well, it's certainly been interesting."

"Yeah? How?"

"Anyone in the hallway?" Bitty asked.

Allie quickly poked her head out. "No. Why?"

"I just stumbled upon something odd."

"What?"

"Remember how I told you that the Parishes won all that money in the lottery?"

"Yeah."

"Well, rumor has it that a day before the murders, the girls' mother, Julie, wrote Gary Willis a check for seven hundred thousand dollars of it."

"Holy crap! Seven hundred thousand dollars? Why?"

Bitty removed her glasses and rubbed her eyes. "I don't know," she said. "But I certainly plan to find out."

CHAPTER 14

SADNESS HUNG LIKE a thick fog in the truck on their way home from the Parishes' funeral. The sun quickly disappeared behind the dark clouds, and the sky opened up. Rain now pelted the windshield and spilled down the side windows in crooked lines.

Allie navigated the rolling East Texas hills in silence, whizzing past sprawling pastures of lush green grass and countless herds of cattle. No one seemed to have the energy to talk. And Sammy was fast asleep in his car seat, sucking his thumb—something he hadn't done in two years. Allie felt a pang of guilt, worrying that taking him to the funeral had been damaging in some way. Today she'd exposed him to death, something she wasn't sure she was comfortable with him knowing quite yet.

There'd been a small turnout for the service at the funeral home, and an even smaller one at the graveside. Allie remembered the girls' grief-stricken faces as they stared at the polished oak caskets. How Carrie had vomited at the cemetery. A weathered old woman had watched the girls from afar the entire time, but she never bothered to even say hello. Bitty said that she thought it was the girls' maternal grandmother.

At home, Allie tucked Sammy into bed for his nap, then sat at the kitchen table to make sense of her checking account. But she couldn't get the seven hundred thousand dollars that the girls' mother had given Gary Willis off her mind.

Had he killed Zoe and Carrie's parents for the money?

But why kill them after he already had the check in hand?

It didn't make sense. She stared out the window, barely aware of the wind screaming on the other side. A moment later, she heard little feet padding her way. Sammy walked into the kitchen in his white T-shirt and boxer briefs and reached his arms out to be held.

She set her pen down and picked him up.

"Hey, buddy." Allie smiled. "Why are you out of bed?"

"I sad."

"What's wrong?"

Thunder rumbled outside. "I no want to tell you now. I want to watch ants," he said, asking to watch a documentary on ants that they had on DVD. Out of all the movies he owned, it was his favorite, and the one he always wanted to watch when he felt emotional.

The funeral was still affecting him.

It was affecting her, too.

"Okay, baby," she said, smiling at her son. "We can do that."

She carried him into the living room and set him down on the couch, then slid the DVD in the tray. She covered him with a quilt and kissed his forehead.

"Mommy, watch it with me."

All the things she needed to do flashed through her mind. In the last few days she'd gotten behind on so much—updating her checkbook, client scheduling and marketing, figuring out what bills she could afford to pay next—and now she was starting to feel as though the walls were closing in. But Sammy was her priority. She didn't want him to remember her as being too busy. She wanted her son to remember her as an involved mom, a mother who always made time for him.

"Okay, but just for a little while, okay?"

"Okay."

She heard more footsteps. A few seconds later, Zoe appeared in the entrance of the hallway. Her face was washed out from all of the crying, and she'd put her nightgown back on.

"Hey there," Allie said. "We're about to watch a program. Want to watch with us?"

Zoe nodded, then silently took a seat in the recliner.

"How about I make some hot chocolate for our show?"

Sammy's eyes brightened. "Yes! Hot chocolate!"

"Do you like hot chocolate, Zoe?"

Zoe nodded.

"Then three cups it is." Allie smiled.

After serving the drinks, Allie sat on the couch with Sammy and began watching the documentary for about the two hundredth time. The storm had intensified and rain was now pouring from the sky.

She studied the safe, clean, comfortable house she lived in— the high ceilings; polished cherry floors; the big flat-screen television; comfortable, sturdy furniture; the soft, overstuffed pillows; and charming wicker baskets that graced most of the rooms—and was still surprised it was hers. That she lived here now, and not the rundown house of her childhood, or the string of filthy motel rooms she'd spent time in after her brother's suicide. Everything was tidy. Clean. Safe. And it wasn't merely a house . . . it was a home.

She'd gotten lucky. So very lucky.

Lightning slashed the sky outside. "Mommy! Mommy!" Sammy suddenly whined.

Allie turned to her son and saw that blood was gushing from his nose. She grabbed a napkin from the coffee table, pressed it against his nostrils, and applied pressure. "Tilt your head up a little," she said, gently coaxing his chin up with her fingers.

"Can I help?" she heard Zoe say.

"Yes, please get some paper towels from the kitchen."

Zoe took off toward the kitchen. Less than a minute later, she was back with a roll of paper towels. Allie took them from her and switched out the napkin that was now sopping wet with blood.

Thunder boomed in the distance. "Oh my God," Zoe said.

Allie glanced at Zoe. She was staring at the blood-soaked napkin. The color had drained from her face.

"Zoe, it's just a nosebleed. It's okay," Allie said.

Zoe staggered backward. "No, no, no!" she whispered, her eyes brimming with tears. She bumped into the coffee table and nearly fell over it.

Carrie opened her eyes and turned her head toward the bedroom door. Zoe had just rushed in and was sobbing.

"No!" Zoe said. She paced from one end of the room to the other. "No, no, NO!"

"Zoe?" Allie called from the other side of the bedroom door.

But Zoe didn't answer her. Her hands were pressed against her ears and she was humming.

Allie pushed the door open. "Zoe? Are you okay?"

Zoe remembers now, Carrie thought. Now she'll know how it feels to not be able to unsee the terrible things that we've seen. To have to live every day with the memories. But Carrie didn't say anything. She remained silent as Allie walked into the room and tried to calm Zoe down. She was silent when Bitty came in and tried to do the same. She just turned on her side so her back was facing everyone, including her sister. She just focused on the wind rattling the window next to her. Not on Zoe's pain.

Because she could barely live with her own.

The storm had subsided and the afternoon light had just begun to slant down across the room when Allie heard a knock on the front door. She, Bitty, and Sammy were on the couch. She and Bitty had just been discussing Zoe's outburst, and Bitty had called the Child Advocacy Center to schedule an extra counseling session for the girl.

Bitty rose from the couch and went to the front door. A moment later, Allie heard her saying, "Detective. Sergeant. What a nice surprise. Come on in."

Allie's pulse spiked, suddenly self-conscious. She wished she'd known the detective would be coming by. She glanced down at herself: old sweats, a Marvel Lego T-shirt she'd bought for herself because she knew Sammy would like it.

Oh, God.

She sat up straight and ran her fingers beneath her eyes to catch any bits of fallen mascara, then retied her hair into a topknot.

How I made such an ugly child is beyond me.

"Shut up," she whispered, shoving her mother's words away.

Sammy looked up at her. "What you say, Mommy?"

"Sorry, baby. Nothing."

Hopefully Bitty would bring the police officers to her office and not to the kitchen, otherwise they'd pass through the living room.

"Anyone care for some coffee?" Bitty asked, heading to the kitchen.

Allie groaned.

"Always," she heard Detective Lambert say.

She closed her eyes and willed them to pass by without them noticing her.

Sammy's head swiveled as Bitty and the police officers walked through the room. "Hi, policemans!"

Great! Just great!

"Hi. Sammy, right?" Detective Lambert asked.

Sammy nodded, one of his nostrils crusted with dried blood, a big smile on his face.

"Can I get a high five?" the detective asked.

Piglet jumped down from the couch and sniffed the detective's legs, while Sammy gave him a high five.

"And how are you today, Miss Allie?" he asked. He rested a large hand on her shoulder—and her stomach did a somersault.

"I'm fine." Against her will, her eyes flitted to him, and his blue eyes held hers.

"Great. That's really good to hear."

"And you?" she asked, holding his gaze, again determined not to be the one to break eye contact.

"Just fantastic," he answered.

He was wearing plain clothes again. A black V-neck sweater with a black button-down beneath it, dark jeans, black cowboy boots. Identification hung from around his neck. He was beautiful, and she was most uncomfortable around beautiful people. She didn't trust them. Especially ones as handsome as this guy. People like him made her feel uglier than she sometimes already felt. But there was something aside from his looks that made her feel . . . actually, she wasn't certain what she was feeling. All she knew was the room suddenly felt too hot.

"Good afternoon." Sergeant Davis smiled. He was holding his black leather notebook between his palms.

"Good afternoon, Sergeant," Allie said, grateful to have a reason to break eye contact with the detective.

Sergeant Davis winked at her, then his eyes skimmed the living room. He cracked his notebook open and scribbled something in it.

"Allie, would you mind showing Detective Lambert and Sergeant Davis to the dining room table and put on a fresh pot of coffee while I go check on the girls real quick?" Bitty called.

"Yes, ma'am," Allie answered.

As instructed, Allie showed the policemen to the table and brewed a fresh pot of coffee, suspicious as to why Bitty hadn't just asked her to look in on the girls.

When the coffee was ready, Bitty was already sitting at the table, talking with the officers. As Allie served the coffee, she was careful not to look directly at Detective Lambert's face—especially into his eyes, because her body was still buzzing from the last time they'd made eye contact.

Back in the kitchen, she heated up leftovers and prepared a large salad for dinner. She dipped her arms, elbow-deep, in warm, soapy water as she quietly cleaned pots and pans and listened in on the three as they talked at the table. From where she stood, she had a perfect vantage point. She could see Bitty full-on, and Detective Lambert's profile.

After a few minutes of small talk, Bitty took a sip of her coffee, then held the mug between her hands. "Okay, so I have a question for you that I was hoping you could answer."

"What's that, ma'am?" Detective Lambert asked.

"Why on earth would Julie Parish want to give Gary Willis seven hundred thousand dollars of her husband's lottery winnings?"

Detective Lambert choked a little on his coffee. Allie saw his eyes swing briefly to his sergeant's. "I'm sorry," he said. "What?"

Allie could tell he was surprised and maybe even a little impressed that Bitty had unearthed the information.

"Now how did you find out about that when we just found out ourselves not an hour ago?" he asked.

Bitty smiled. She sat a little straighter in her chair. "I know people."

"People, huh?" He narrowed his eyes, but his lips turned up in a smile.

Sergeant Davis was scribbling in his notebook again.

"I hear the manager at Southside Bank in Riverside was pretty shocked when Gary Willis wanted to open a new account with that kind of money," Bitty continued. "And that branch is, what, about fifty miles from town. Doesn't seem like the most convenient place to bank, now does it?"

"Pretty impressive," Sergeant Davis said with a smile, leaning back in his chair.

Bitty shrugged. "It's a small town. Murder is exciting. People are just about busting at the seams, wanting to share what they know about the Parishes. About Gary Willis. To share their theories about these murders," she said. "And I'm not the law, so I don't pose a threat. I'm just a nosy little old lady."

Detective Lambert nodded. "Makes sense."

"Not saying you're not good at what you do, because I know you are. But an extra pair of ears couldn't hurt, could it?"

"It sure couldn't." Detective Lambert traded another look with Sergeant Davis. "Looks like we have another CI on our team. And a damn good one, I'd say."

"Can't beat a good CI," Sergeant Davis said, a glimmer in his eyes.

"I just want the girls to get justice as soon as possible. To stop having to look over their shoulders and get some closure," Bitty said.

Detective Lambert nodded. "I want that, too."

"So do you know why she gave that money to Gary Willis, Detective?" Bitty asked.

Allie knew the question had been bugging Bitty. It had been bugging her, too.

"We have a few theories," said Detective Lambert.

CHAPTER 15

LATER THAT NIGHT, Allie felt the air move. Someone had just walked into the bedroom. A chill crept up her back and crawled across the tops of her arms.

She reached to make sure Sammy was in the bed.

He was.

Her pulse spiking, she quietly rolled over to the side of the bed and ran her hand between the mattress and box spring, her fingers searching for the knife she kept for emergencies.

"Allie?" a soft voice called.

Allie exhaled sharply and sat up. It was just Zoe.

"Yeah?" Allie said, her heart still pounding.

"I'm scared. Can I sleep with you?"

Allie remembered the girl's episode after the funeral. The anguish in her eyes. How she had refused to talk about it or come out of her room for the rest of the day. "Uh, yeah. Sure. C'mon."

She scooted a sleeping Sammy to the side, then slid next to him, leaving Zoe almost half of the bed. Johnny's half when he slept over.

Correction: when he *used* to sleep over.

Zoe crawled into bed and turned on her side, her back facing Allie. "Thank you," she whispered.

"Can I get you anything?" Allie asked.

"No. Thank you," Zoe said, and Allie could hear tears in her voice.

Allie stayed awake awhile, listening to the branches outside tap at the bedroom window, and thought about the girls. She wondered about the circumstances around their little brother's death. And if his death had driven a massive stake through their hearts like her brother's had. She let her mind wander for a little while, then yanked her thoughts to the present, back to the gloomy darkness of her bedroom.

Finally she closed her eyes and drifted away.

Carrie wondered where her sister had gone. Zoe had left the bedroom about an hour earlier and hadn't come back.

Carrie was relieved her sister was gone. Zoe had been crying all day, practically nonstop, which had made Carrie feel even worse than she already felt . . . because for the first time that she could remember, she couldn't help Zoe.

Carrie slipped out of the bed and went to the window. She stared out at the darkness, trying hard to force away memories of the funeral, because every time she thought about it she felt nauseated again.

I miss you, Daddy, she thought. *I miss you so much.*

She cleared her tears away with the back of her hand.

The pain was unbearable.

She slipped out of the room and into the hallway bathroom to look for a razor blade. She'd just make one small cut. Just one teeny one on her arm. That's all it would take to numb the pain for a while. To give her some peace.

She'd begun cutting three months ago when the teasing at school had gotten worse. Both she and Zoe had been teased in elementary school for living in a trailer and not having nice clothes. Even worse, their school clothes were usually soiled when they were younger because their mother only went to the Laundromat once a week. They'd been called the Trailer Trash Twins since the third grade, when a girl in their class, Lucy Santos, first screamed it at them on the playground. And the teasing had only gotten worse this past year when Zoe had sex in the school's bathroom with a boy from their class.

Now not only did their classmates hold their noses when passing them in the hallways and in class, like they'd done for years, they called Zoe a whore and other nasty names. But Carrie knew Zoe wasn't a whore or any of those other names they'd given her.

Zoe just tried too hard, with everyone . . . and it usually backfired.

Carrie knew her sister tried to get people to like her by making them happy. With their mother, she'd done it by being helpful and complimenting her, even when she didn't deserve the compliment. And she had sex with the boy because she thought that would make him happy and like her. But it didn't, at least not for long, because afterward he only laughed at her and treated her worse.

When Zoe told Bitty that they didn't want to go back to school, she said she'd be happy to homeschool them for as long as they stayed in her care . . . which had been a relief because Carrie couldn't even imagine what the kids were calling them now that news had gotten around that their parents had been murdered.

Just thinking about the possible names made her shudder.

In the bathroom, she searched the drawers and cabinets, then the cabinet above the toilet. But she couldn't find any razor blades. She wondered if Bitty hid them . . . and if there were any in another bathroom. She would look when she got the chance.

She considered using a kitchen knife. Chewing on her bottom lip, she thought about it, then shook her head no. It didn't have the same appeal.

She returned to the bedroom and crawled back into bed—and fantasized that none of it had ever happened.

CHAPTER 16

"MOMMY? MOMMY." SAMMY'S little hand tapped Allie's shoulder. He began tapping harder. He was trying to wake her.

Allie opened her eyes to find his face close to hers. Morning sunshine streamed into the bedroom window, directly into her bleary eyes, making her blink.

"Look!" he pointed, his jaw set.

Allie sat up. Zoe was lying next to her, fast asleep, her long dark hair pooled on a pillow.

Allie remembered waking in the middle of the night, surprised to feel Zoe's body pressed up against her back. Like a cat, she'd been curled up into her, one of her small forearms resting gently on Allie's stomach.

Sammy shook his head. "But it's *two* bugs in a rug, Mommy. Not three!" he whined.

A cold front had swooped in overnight, chilling the morning air to a frigid twenty-four degrees, and the local weatherman was predicting snow.

Allie, Sammy, and Bitty sat together in the living room. Sammy was curled up in his grammy's lap reading a book, while Bitty drank a cup of coffee.

Allie sat across from them, putting together her To Do list. She felt hopelessly behind on everything, and anxious, but was determined to start catching up today.

Earlier, she had told Bitty about Zoe wanting to sleep with her. "I mean, isn't that kind of strange that she'd pick me?" None of the other foster kids had.

Bitty shrugged. "She knows you're a nurturer. Children can sense it," she said. "And she sees how you are with Sammy." Bitty set down her coffee mug. "But, of course, you have to have clearly defined boundaries with kids. With anyone, for that matter—so if you're not comfortable with her sleeping with you, you need to tell her. Worse comes to worst, she can always sleep with the old lady of the house," she said with a smile.

"*Two* bugs in a rug," Sammy mumbled bitterly, his eyes never leaving his book. "Not *three*."

Allie smiled at her son. She hadn't even realized he'd been listening. Everything had its place in Sammy's mind. And it was obvious that he didn't think Zoe's place was in Allie's bed.

Bitty peered at her watch. "I have to take two phone clients this morning. Mind keeping an eye on the girls for an hour?"

"Yeah, no problem."

After she was done writing out her To Do list, Allie got to work. An hour later, the dishwasher was humming, the clothes washer was spinning, and a load of laundry was tumbling in the dryer. The house almost seemed normal again with the productive sounds that made Allie feel safe and secure.

She was chopping garlic and onions for red beans and rice, and washing berries to add to an after-dinner dessert, when the phone rang. When Allie answered, she heard a familiar voice on the other end.

"Good morning, Miss Allie. It's Detective Lambert."

Allie's heart fluttered. She quickly cleared her throat. "Good morning, Detective. Bitty is with a client right now, so—"

"That's okay. I can talk to you, if that's all right, and you can relay the message."

"Okay. Sure."

"I'm calling with what *might* be good news."

"Yeah?"

"Yes, ma'am," Detective Lambert answered. "We had some activity on one of Mr. Willis's credit cards in Orlando last night."

"Orlando, Florida?"

"Yes, ma'am. That's the one."

Orlando was hundreds of miles away. Maybe even a thousand.

"Of course, we aren't certain yet it was Gary using the card, but we do have other good reasons to believe Mr. Willis has left town."

Allie processed the news.

"I'm afraid that means that the department can no longer justify round-the-clock patrol of your property after tonight, but I'll make sure someone shows up at least twice a day until the end of the week. Just to have a look around, okay?"

"Okay. Thank you."

"But Miss Allie . . . I'd still strongly recommend you keep everything locked up. And keep your eyes peeled, okay? Until we know for sure, keep taking precautions."

"Okay, we will."

"Good. Once we have more news, we'll either come by or call."

"Thanks. We appreciate that."

But when they hung up, Allie was immediately struck with a sense of unease. Was it because they'd be losing the patrol out front?

Or because her gut was telling her Gary wasn't in Orlando?

That evening, after the kids had their baths and the twins had retired to their bedroom for the night, Allie and Sammy were on the couch, reading the last pages of *Llama Llama Red Pajama*. Before Allie could even get the words "The end" out, Sammy was begging for her to read it again.

"Okay. One more time. But just one, okay?"

"Okay."

As Allie flipped back to the first page, she noticed Sammy squirming.

"You have to go potty?" Allie asked.

He shook his head but squirmed again.

"Go potty, Sammy. Now."

Sammy groaned and darted out of the room. While he was gone, Allie thought about Gary possibly being in Orlando, of the uncertainty that still hung in the air. Then her thoughts shifted again to losing the patrolman in the morning. There was a new knot in her stomach. An even tighter, more distressing one than earlier.

Zoe wandered in, silently, and sat on the couch. She hugged her knees to her chest and looked at Allie.

"Hey," Allie said, smiling at the girl. "Did you need something?"

Zoe shook her head and gazed at the book in Allie's hand. "I could hear you reading to him."

Allie glanced down at the book, then looked at the girl.

"Do you do it a lot?" Zoe asked.

"Yeah. Every night."

Zoe studied Allie with those watchful eyes of hers as if thinking about her answer.

"Didn't your parents read to you when you were Sammy's age?" Allie asked.

Zoe shook her head. Then, almost as an afterthought, she added, "Well, my dad did read to us a couple of times when we were little. The book about the red caboose."

"*The Little Red Caboose?*"

Zoe smiled a little. "Yeah. That was it." She lowered her legs to the floor and pushed a piece of lint on the carpet with a bare toe. "But my dad . . . he really wasn't home much. And when he was, he liked to relax."

"I can understand that."

Allie heard Sammy in the hallway. He was talking to his Lego man, Emmet. He'd gotten distracted, and Allie knew he wouldn't be returning to the living room anytime soon.

She watched Zoe push the lint a little closer to her, then pull it back again with her toe.

"You really love him, don't you?" Zoe asked, staring at the lint.

"Sammy?"

"Yeah."

Allie smiled. "I do."

"You're a good mommy."

"Thank you, Zoe."

Zoe studied her, her green eyes intense. "I like how you love him."

Allie peered at her. "What do you mean?

"You make him feel good. You don't make him guess."

"Guess?"

"You know, he doesn't have to wonder if you love him. He just knows."

The room went silent for a moment.

"Did your parents do that? Make you wonder?" Allie asked.

"My dad didn't. He loved me a lot. More than anything." Zoe looked away, her eyes filling with tears. "Me and Carrie loved him so much. So, so much." Her voice cracked. She folded her arms across her chest and hugged her body.

"And your mother?"

Zoe's eyes were on hers again. "She made me guess. All the time."

"I'm sorry, Zoe. That must've been hard."

Allie thought of her own mother. Her biological one. She'd made Allie guess, too . . . at least when she was little. Toward the end, though, there had been no room for doubt. She knew for certain that she hadn't been loved.

"She never liked to do anything with us," Zoe said, wiping at her nose with the back of her hand. "Not like our dad did. She just wanted us to go away all the time. We were work for her."

Silence fell between them. After a moment, Allie asked Zoe something that she'd been wondering about for days. "Why is it that you ask for me to be in the room with you when you talk with the forensic therapist? It's not that I mind or anything. I'm just curious. Why me?"

"You remind me of her." Zoe's eyes were intense. "When I look at you, it's almost like I'm looking at her."

"Who?"

"My mother."

"Oh." From what she'd heard about their mother, Allie didn't think it was a good thing.

"But you're much better than she was. You're what I *wanted* her to be."

"What do you mean?"

"You're a good mom. She wasn't. And I don't mean only sometimes. All the time. She could be . . . hateful." Zoe's eyes filled with tears.

"I'm sorry she let you down," Allie said.

"It's not your fault."

The room was quiet again. Zoe stood up and sighed. "Well, good night."

"Good night, Zoe," Allie said, softly.

Then she watched the girl disappear from the room.

CHAPTER 17

ALLIE HAD JUST crawled into bed when she heard a knock at the front door. It was almost nine o'clock. Who could it—? But then Allie realized Piglet hadn't even bothered to growl.

She groaned.

She knew exactly who it was. It was the same piece of crap she'd hadn't heard from since Gary Willis showed up in the backyard. He hadn't called, texted—nothing.

Knowing the time had arrived, she crawled out of bed and threw on her robe. She should've broken up with Johnny by now, but she'd gotten sidetracked by Gary.

Bitty was already headed up the hallway when Allie slipped through her bedroom door.

"I've got it."

Bitty looked at her. "Who—?"

"Johnny."

Bitty nodded and turned back to her bedroom.

Allie opened the door, and icy winter air rushed into the house. Johnny stood before her, smiling wide, the way he always smiled when he saw her. But she knew now what she meant to him, and what she didn't. She was just a comfortable place to hide away from his real life.

Nothing more.

Well, he was going to have to find a new place to hide. She welcomed the icy air on her skin for a moment, then moved aside so Johnny could come in.

He looked handsome as always, especially with his cheeks flushed from the wind. He looked well rested, as though he hadn't a care in the world. She closed the door behind him. Slid the dead bolt home.

"What's up with the police officer out front?"

"Um, hell-o? The man in our backyard the other morning."

"Oh, right. You find out who that dude was?"

"The girls' mother's boyfriend."

It took him a moment to connect the relationships. Then: "Wow. No shit?"

"No shit," she said dryly.

"Well, you happy I'm here this time?" he asked, reaching out to hug her.

She kept her arms crossed and took a step backward. "Why didn't you tell me you were coming?"

"What? So I have to announce my visits now?"

"Yes, I wish you would."

"I was worried about you. I thought I should come by and make sure everyone was okay."

"Worried? Seriously? You didn't even remember anything had happened until two seconds ago. And you didn't even stick around after everything that happened . . . or bother to call. I didn't even get a text, Johnny."

"I was busy, hon. You know how it gets for me. Sorry. C'mon, now. Let's not do this again. I just drove all the way—"

"Well, you can drive right back, because it's over. *We're* over."

He stared at her. "You're breaking up with me?"

"Well, if you want to call it that, then yes. But I think that would imply that we've been exclusive all this time, and I highly doubt I'm the only person you've been 'dating.' But that's beside the point."

"You've got to be kidding me," he said.

"No, I'm dead serious. I don't want 'this,' whatever it is . . . this thing we've been doing . . . anymore. It makes me miserable, and it's not good for Sammy to think relationships should be this way."

He ran his fingers through his hair. "Wow. That . . . just wow," he said, shaking his head. "Have you even thought about Sammy? You don't think it's important he has a father?"

"He'll still have a father. That won't change," she said. "Right?"

Johnny kept rubbing his head.

"Sammy loves you more than anything, and he needs a father. This shouldn't change a thing between the two of you. And I hope to God you don't let it."

After Johnny was gone, Allie went to the kitchen to make a drink, an extra-strong one, then quietly let herself out the sliding glass door. She drank the first of the vodka in long gulps, welcoming the heat-laced liquid as it bloomed in her stomach.

She sighed, feeling some of the stress of the breakup instantly fall away.

She knew she'd made the right decision with Johnny. She only wished she'd made it sooner. But still, she had a lump in her throat, knowing it was finally over. After all, they had enjoyed some good times.

Standing against the back of the house, she drank and kept a close eye on the dark tree line. She knew that Detective Lambert suspected Gary had fled town, but she'd still be cautious. If she saw any movement at all, heard anything . . . *anything* . . . it would take her only two seconds to be back inside the house with the door locked.

Warmth from the alcohol spread to her cheeks as she surveyed the yard. She thought about what Zoe had said earlier. *When I look at you, it's almost like I'm looking at her.*

When Zoe had said that, Allie had felt a little creeped out. She wasn't so sure she liked resembling a murdered woman or, worse, a terrible mother.

Shivering from the cold, she drained her drink and went back inside to make another one.

———

A while later, Allie felt someone drape a quilt over her body. She realized she was still on the couch. That she must've fallen asleep. She'd drunk a lot; too much. She opened her eyes and saw that it was Bitty.

Her face grew hot.

She didn't want Bitty to see her this way. She wanted her to think she was strong.

"There's a glass of water right here on the coffee table, in case you need it," Bitty said. "And a plastic bowl next to the couch in case anything comes up."

"Thanks," Allie said, tiredly.

"I'll put Sammy in bed with me," Bitty said. She leaned down and kissed Allie's forehead. "Get some good rest, honey." Bitty headed to the hallway.

"I broke up with him," Allie said. "Tonight. I broke up with Johnny."

Bitty paused. "Want to talk about it?"

"No, not really. I just wanted you to know."

CHAPTER 18

ALLIE AWOKE TO the scent of freshly brewed coffee and the sound of Curious George's squeaky monkey chatter.

She opened her eyes to find Sammy peering down at her. He covered his nose and giggled. "Eww. What that smell? Your breath smell . . . gross, Mommy!"

She wasn't surprised. Her mouth was dry and tasted *terrible*.

She grabbed Sammy and pulled him on the couch. "Well, that's not very nice!" she said and tickled his soft tummy.

"No, Mommy, stop!" he squealed.

"I brought you coffee," Zoe said, her eyes bright. She held a cup of coffee between her small hands. "Two tablespoons of cream, no sugar. Bitty told me."

"That's perfect. Thanks, Zoe."

Zoe smiled proudly.

"Whoa!" Sammy suddenly exclaimed, bouncing off Allie's stomach and running to the sliding glass door.

Allie tensed. Was something . . . some*one* . . . in the yard? She sat up and, a little light-headed, followed him.

"It's snowing!" Sammy screamed. "It's snowing!"

He was right. Big, fat snowflakes were falling from the sky, blanketing the deck and yard.

Bitty walked into the room. "Now look at that."

Sammy jumped up and down, his hands clasped together. "I want to go outside and play in it, Mommy. Please?!"

Allie watched Sammy's eyes dance with excitement—and she knew that she couldn't say no. No matter what her gut had been telling her, Gary Willis was probably long gone. And if they played in the front yard, they could run into the house quickly if they needed to. She would just keep an eye out. She was certain Bitty would, too.

"Please?" Sammy said again. "Pretty please?"

"Okay, but you know the rules, right? If I call you, you come the very first time, okay?"

"I know, I know. I listen the first time!"

Allie bundled Sammy up, and Bitty found extra wool scarves for the girls. Then, as a family, they all went in the front yard and played in the snow.

Despite a slight hangover, Allie felt strangely relaxed all day. Gary did, in fact, appear to be long gone, and she'd finally done the right thing about Johnny. She also had a refreshed determination to do her best by the girls. Both of them. She'd try to be at least a little of what Bitty had been for her during her darkest days.

Therapy sessions at the Child Advocacy Center had been canceled due to inclement weather, and the local schools had closed for the day, so Allie and Bitty decided to treat the day like a snow day, too, and skip homeschooling.

After playing in the snow for an hour, they all took warm baths and changed back into their pajamas. And even though Thanksgiving was still a week away, they pulled out the Christmas music, letting it play softly from the stereo.

The energy in the house had completely shifted. Everyone suddenly seemed relaxed. Even Carrie had stayed awake most of the day. But still, Allie couldn't help but think that her face looked more pale than usual . . . and her eyes maybe a little more vacant.

While Bitty, Zoe, and Sammy played a game of Scrabble Alphabet Scoop at the kitchen table, Allie walked over to Carrie and took her small hand again. She held it and together they watched the snow fall in the backyard for a few minutes. "I'm here if you want to talk," she whispered. "I want to help you. When you're ready, please let me, okay?"

Carrie didn't react. Her eyes didn't even move. She just continued to stare out at the yard. Allie turned her attention to the snow again, wishing she knew what Carrie was thinking. Why she refused to talk. When, and if, she would talk again.

Bitty had told Allie that the head therapist at the Child Advocacy Center had diagnosed Zoe with dissociative amnesia, a neurological condition caused by severe trauma. She had explained that as a result of her parents being murdered, Zoe had repressed some of the events that led up to it as well as some of the events that immediately followed it. But the therapist was hopeful that she'd recover most, if not all, of her memories over time.

Carrie, on the other hand, appeared to have selective mutism, which was thought to have manifested from the same trauma. While most kids who suffered from selective mutism talked again after just a matter of days or weeks—some didn't for several months. Allie hoped that Carrie fell into the former category.

After the game of Scrabble Alphabet Scoop ended, Allie drank piping hot coffee on the recliner and watched Sammy run around the house in a Santa hat and his Batman pajamas. They hung out as a family all day, and it actually did feel a little like Christmas.

Then after dinner, they made homemade hot chocolate, popped popcorn, and slid the movie *Frozen* into the DVD player. Bitty had built a nice fire in the fireplace, and the fire popped and crackled in the dimly lit room as they watched the movie. To Allie's surprise, when the movie started, Piglet jumped into Carrie's lap, scooting the girl's stuffed bear aside with her behind to make room for herself. The dog looked up at Carrie and licked her face, and nosed her arm a couple of times, still hoping to get Carrie to pet her. When she wouldn't, the dog curled up in her lap and closed her eyes.

Zoe shared a blanket with Bitty and pressed her head against the woman's thin shoulder. Halfway through the movie, Sammy fell asleep in Allie's lap, worn out from the exciting day. He was sucking his thumb again.

Allie watched Carrie stare at the fireplace for most of the movie. And she couldn't be sure, but every once in a while when she looked over at Carrie, she thought the girl's eyes were glistening, as though she were crying. Again, she wished she knew what Carrie was thinking, but Carrie was unreadable.

Watching everyone in the room, Allie realized they all seemed content. And that they also looked like a nice little family. For the first time in days, Allie felt happy.

After everyone said their good-nights, Allie took her antidepressant and supplements, brushed her teeth, and slipped into bed next to Sammy. She replayed the day, then took a deep breath and found, for the first time since the girls had arrived, that she had no trouble filling her lungs.

She also realized that in that moment she felt little fear . . . of anything.

She yawned, and as she was drifting off, a voice inside her head whispered quietly: *But how long can it possibly last?*

Allie got her answer a few hours later when her bedroom door flew open and the overhead light slammed on, bathing the room in bright light.

She jolted up and saw Zoe running to her side of the bed. A millisecond later, Zoe was tugging on Allie's arm.

"Carrie's gone!" she said, hysterical. "We've . . . we've got to find her!"

"What's going on?" Bitty asked in the doorway, her eyes still half-closed.

"Carrie's gone!" Zoe repeated. "She's . . . she's not in the house!"

Worry flooded Bitty's eyes. "My Lord. Do you know where she might have gone?"

"Yes, I think so! Just hurry, please! We need to get in the truck. Hurry!"

Allie pulled on her clothes and wrapped a jacket around a still-sleeping Sammy. As she hurried by the girls' bedroom, she caught a glimpse of the stuffed bear in the bed—and found it odd that Carrie would have left it behind, wherever she'd gone.

As she made it to the front door, she realized light was spilling from every room of the house. Zoe must've turned them all on, searching for her sister, before waking her.

"Please! Come on!" Zoe begged, standing in the foyer. "We've got to hurry!"

CHAPTER 19

ZOE INSTRUCTED ALLIE to drive to Sherman's Landing. Once inside the community, they sped past one huge house after another until they reached Zoe's family's house.

Allie swung the SUV into the girls' driveway, and Zoe and Bitty jumped out before Allie could even come to a complete stop. Zoe ran up the driveway to the back of the house and Bitty trailed her.

Allie grabbed a still-sleeping Sammy from his car seat and followed them, noticing fragments of yellow crime tape partially buried in the spotty snow of the front yard. She also saw a set of small footprints.

Carrie's.

They appeared to head in the same direction Zoe and Bitty had gone. When Allie reached the back door, it was wide open. Zoe and Bitty were already inside.

Stepping in, Allie instantly brought her free hand to her nose. Her eyes filled with tears. The odor in the house was revolting—and it beckoned childhood memories.

She shivered.

Someone screamed somewhere deep inside the house. It was Zoe.

"Oh my God, oh my God! Carrie, no!" Zoe screeched.

Allie hurried through the kitchen and into the dark living room, and glanced down the connecting hallway that led to the bedrooms. Light spilled out from a room two doors down. It was where the screams were coming from.

She hesitated to bring Sammy any closer to whatever was happening . . . or *had* happened . . . in case he awakened.

She found a lamp in the living room, and with a trembling hand, flipped it on. She reluctantly set down her sleeping son on a brown leather couch. Sammy stirred a little and made smacking sounds with his lips. But he didn't open his eyes. Instead, he plunged his thumb in his mouth, curled up, and became still again.

Allie's eyes went back to the doorway. She slowly made her way down the hallway, goose bumps breaking out along her arms, not knowing what to expect . . . and not knowing if she was prepared. When she was a few feet from the door, the strong metallic odor of pennies assaulted her nostrils.

Blood.

Her stomach turned.

When she reached the doorway, a curtain of steam assailed her. Bitty was leaning forward on the floor, her hands moving swiftly in front of her. Allie could see Carrie's bare, pale legs on the tiled floor. The bandage on top of her blistered foot. Next to her were several smears of blood on the tile. Blood glistened in Bitty's gray hair. On Bitty's frail, liver-spotted hands.

Bitty's voice was high and tight. "I need something else, Zoe! A shirt, another towel. Now, Zoe. Get them for me. Hurry!"

Zoe pushed past Allie, then ran down the hallway.

"Allie, do you have your phone on you?" Bitty asked.

"No."

Bitty fumbled in her jacket for hers. "Call 9-1-1. Have Zoe give you the address. Tell them to send help fast. Carrie's slit her wrists."

Her pulse thundering in her ears, Allie grabbed the blood-smeared phone and called 9-1-1. She hurried in the direction Zoe had gone, and found Zoe in a bedroom. She was sitting cross-legged on a bed with a pink comforter, her eyes closed. She was rocking and humming.

"What's your address?" Allie asked.

Zoe kept humming.

"Zoe!"

The girl's eyes flew open.

"Your address! Give it to me, now!"

Zoe did.

As Allie spoke with the dispatcher, she found a dresser and threw the first drawer open to find a jumble of panties, training bras, socks. She threw open the second drawer and grabbed a handful of T-shirts.

"Zoe, go in the living room and sit with Sammy."

Zoe didn't move. "Now, Zoe!" she shouted.

Zoe sprang up, her eyes wide . . . as though she was coming out of a trance.

"Now!" Allie said again.

Zoe scrambled off the bed and hurried down the hallway.

Allie returned to the bathroom with the shirts. She dropped them on the floor, and Bitty quickly grabbed one. Allie knelt down and while Bitty retied one of Carrie's wrists, Allie tied the other one.

There was a lot of blood.

Way too much.

Carrie's skin was paper-white and her clothes were sopping wet. Her eyes drooped and her trembling lips had turned blue. Allie's eyes darted around the room, lingering on the crimson bathwater, the fine layer of steam covering the bathroom mirror.

"Allie, find some towels," Bitty said.

Allie opened a cabinet and found two messy stacks of towels. She hurried back to Carrie and leaned down to drape them over her body.

Suddenly Allie heard shouting above her head. Zoe. "You know how freaking selfish that was? Did you even stop to think about me?"

Carrie's eyes searched and slowly found Zoe. She stared at her for a moment, then her voice came out thick and thready. "No, but obviously you did," she said. The girls stared at one another for a long moment. "Everyone always thinks of you. No one thinks of me," Carrie continued. "Just let me go. If you do, your life will be much easier."

"What . . . what's that supposed to mean?" Zoe shouted.

Allie turned to Zoe and yelled: "Go sit with Sammy in the living room, Zoe! Now!"

The girl vanished from the doorway.

"You're going to be okay, sweetie," Bitty said, cradling Carrie's head and shoulders in her lap. "Help will be here before we know it."

Carrie's eyes found Allie's. They looked drowsy and defeated. "You're going to be okay," Allie whispered, squeezing the girl's bare calf. "Just hang on. You're going to be just fine."

Allie wished she was as certain as she sounded.

"Hang on, sweet girl. Hang on," Bitty soothed. "You're doing great. Just great."

Seconds stretched into minutes. Minutes into what seemed like hours. Then Allie finally heard the sirens.

CHAPTER 20

CARRIE LAY CURLED up in her bed at Dallas's Sunny Lawn Child and Adolescent Psychiatric Center, thinking about what she'd done, and wishing that Bitty hadn't stopped her.

She had searched everywhere for a razor blade earlier that day, while everyone enjoyed the snow, played games, and listened to Christmas songs, but she couldn't find one. Then, the more she fantasized about having a razor blade in her hand, the more she realized that she didn't want to just cut herself to soothe the pain for a little while.

She wanted to release it forever.

And as much as she had been afraid to, the only solution had been to return to her house. Thankfully it wasn't very far.

Her mind flashed to the look on Zoe's face. How angry she had been when she discovered that Carrie had simply needed to end the pain for good. She hadn't expected that from Zoe. Actually, she wasn't sure what she'd expected. She hadn't had the energy to think that far ahead. For once in her life she was focusing only on herself.

The staff at Sunny Lawn had given her a sedative much like the ones her mother used to give her and Zoe to make them sleep for long stretches of time, so her thoughts were moving slowly and painlessly—washing over her like pictures that didn't carry any strong emotions.

It was such a relief.

The therapists at Sunny Lawn had tried to speak to her, just like the forensic therapist and counselors at the Child Advocacy Center had. But Carrie didn't want to talk. She no longer felt she had a voice, because she no longer knew who she was. The person she used to be had shriveled up and died the night her parents died. She didn't know how to act anymore, who to trust . . . and now who to even love.

She closed her eyes and let herself remember . . .

One Month Before the Murders

"Oh my God! They're driving me insane!" Zoe groaned, burying her face in her pillow. Carrie frowned, unsure how to comfort her sister. Their mother and Gary were in the master bedroom. They were doing *it*. And they were hardly quiet about it. Carrie figured Gary must be good at *it*, because he wasn't very smart, and he wasn't nearly as good-looking as her father.

When Gary and their mother weren't having sex, they were doing drugs, but Carrie suspected the drugs were different than the ones her mother had taken before Gary, because practically overnight her mother had gone from lazy to jittery, and had lost a ton of weight. And now she was a beanpole wrapped in raisin-like skin, just like Gary.

Out of all of her mother's friends, so far, Gary had stayed the longest. And instead of "friend," their mother was now calling him her boyfriend . . . which bothered her sister a lot.

Although Zoe would never admit it, Carrie knew she still wanted their parents to love each other again. Zoe also wanted a close relationship with their mother. She needed their mother's love probably more than she needed anything else in the world. But Carrie knew beyond a doubt that their mother would never love Zoe again.

Because she blamed Zoe.

She blamed Zoe for all the pain she'd suffered over the last three years. For Joey's death, and her marriage falling apart. She blamed Zoe for everything.

But Zoe didn't get it.

Or maybe she did.

In any case, Zoe still tried . . . most days. She'd care for their mother when she was out of her mind from the drugs and alcohol. She'd pick her up off the floor and drag her into bed. She'd clean her and feed her. When Zoe wasn't hurt or angry, there wasn't anything she wouldn't do for their mother.

"It's okay. They'll be in the shower soon," Carrie said to her scowling sister. That was their routine. They'd be quiet for a while, then they'd start doing *it*, then they'd both shower. Some nights that's all they heard. Other times, they did *it* several times, but there was always a shower in between. Their mother and father did all the same things in the exact same order. It was pretty gross.

Zoe finally emerged from the pillow, her face red, her eyes desperate. "I hate her sooo freaking much. I really wish Dad was home and that jackass wasn't in our house. He bugs the shit out of me." She hurled her pillow across the room.

Carrie was usually able to drown out the sex noise by reading. Either that or by going deep inside her head. She could go inside her head for hours and just think. And lately, if their mother's activities were making her feel especially bad, she was able to drown out all of the bad feelings by cutting herself.

Zoe, though, *couldn't* escape it.

Carrie hated to see her sister so upset. She wanted Zoe to be happy. And if anyone knew how to make her happy, it was their dad.

More loud noises erupted from the master bedroom. The sound of a headboard slamming into a wall. Laughter. Before Carrie knew what she was about to do, before she could clamp a hand over her sister's mouth, Zoe suddenly screamed at the top of her lungs: "Shut *up!*"

Carrie's heart nearly stopped.

Oh, shit!

The noise in the next room stopped. The whole house seemed to go still.

"Well, at least they stopped," Zoe said, her voice tough. But her lips trembled a little, giving away her fear—because she knew as well as Carrie did that the next few minutes weren't going to be pretty.

A door clicked open down the hallway, then footsteps approached. A moment later, their bedroom door flew open. Their mother appeared in a short, yellow silk robe. Her hair was disheveled, her eye makeup badly smeared. A strong, musky, perfumey odor floated through the air and into Carrie's nostrils.

"What the hell is *wrong* with you, Zoe?" she barked.

Zoe glared at her mother. "*Nothing* is wrong with me," she said. But her lips were trembling even worse now. She was definitely frightened . . . as she should be.

"Don't you ever do that again, little girl. Do you hear me? You're embarrassing me in front of Gary . . . and you *don't* want to do that."

Zoe narrowed her eyes. "I hate you," she mumbled under her breath.

"I'm sorry. What did you just say?" their mother asked.

Zoe's chin was trembling now. Her words came out wobbly. "I said I hate you."

The woman's eyes darkened. "Well, I hate you, too, kid. So I guess we're even."

Zoe drew a sharp breath of surprise, looking as though she'd been kicked in the stomach.

The woman turned to leave.

"And I'm going to tell Dad . . . *everything*," Zoe shot back, her eyes shining with tears.

The woman froze in the doorway. "Oh, you will, will you?" Their mother turned, and in a flash, she was in front of Zoe, slapping her hard across the face. Before Zoe could even bring her hand to her cheek, she slapped her a second time. A trickle of blood bloomed on Zoe's lower lip—and Carrie could taste the tang of blood in Zoe's mouth.

Carrie jumped off the bed and wedged herself between the two of them.

Her mother chuckled and gazed at Carrie as though she pitied her. "Oh, little Carrying Carrie. Always protecting your sister. Not like she'd ever protect you."

Carrie refused to look her mother in the eye. She just wanted her to go away. Unlike Zoe, Carrie's heart had hardened against the woman. Inside it now burned a hatred she had no idea she was even capable of feeling. Her mother had lost her love—and much of her power over her—three years ago . . . exactly two weeks after Joey died . . . when she'd done something completely unforgivable to Zoe.

Something Carrie would never, ever forget.

The woman's steely eyes bore into Zoe's. "That was just a little preview of what you'll get if you tell your father. You tell him, and you'll be sorry. And I mean *really* sorry. You'll never be allowed back in this house again. In fact, I'll send you to live with your grandmother."

Carrie gazed at her sister's tear-streaked face. There was pain in her eyes. Her nose was running and a small trickle of blood was oozing down her chin. But she didn't seem to notice.

"See, if you tell, I'll know I can't trust you anymore. So off to Grandmother's you'll go. Now you wouldn't want that, would you?"

It was the threat their mother had always hung over their heads so that they wouldn't tell anyone her secrets. Still, Carrie shuddered, thinking about the possibility. It was miserable living with their mother, but Grandmother? She wasn't just mean, she was plumb crazy. All their lives their mother had told them stories about the awful things their grandmother had done—some of which, now that Carrie was older, she realized probably hadn't been true—and they'd always been frightened of her.

"And if you think you're miserable now with me, wait 'til you live with her. I did, and I barely got out alive."

Zoe shook her head. "No, we'd live with Dad."

Their mother chuckled. "They never give children to their daddies. Don't you know that? Plus, that dad of yours would never take you in, even if he could. He's not cut out for kids. His time alone on the road is way more important to him than you two. More important than anyone. One day you'll come to realize that, and you'll stop looking at him that stupid way you do. Like he's some goddamn hero."

A man's deep voice traveled from down the hallway. "Julie? You comin' back, hon?"

Gary.

After their mother left the room, Carrie was able to relax again. She turned to her sister, who had gone to the window and was staring out. Carrie placed a hand on her back and realized she was trembling. "You okay?"

Zoe shook her head. When Carrie's eyes met Zoe's, she saw not Zoe's usual strength and sass, but emptiness. It was as though the light that had always been there, that seemed to be flickering—barely holding on—for as long as she could remember, had finally been snuffed out.

Allie stood in the doorway of the small room at Sunny Lawn Child and Adolescent Psychiatric Center and watched Carrie lay on her back, blinking up at the ceiling. Bitty, Zoe, and Sammy were waiting in the lobby.

Allie was so relieved the girl had pulled through. They were told in the emergency room that if it had taken just a mere ten minutes longer for help to arrive, she probably wouldn't have.

The center was a two-hour drive from their house, and Carrie was expected to stay for a minimum of five days. She'd already been there for three. Bitty and Zoe drove back and forth each day, but this was Allie's first visit.

"Hi, Carrie," she said, stepping into the room.

Carrie turned her head and looked at Allie, her face blank. Then she returned her attention to the ceiling.

Breathing in the scent of antiseptic, Allie remembered Carrie's words at the Parishes' home while she'd lain trembling on the bathroom floor:

Everyone's always thinking of you. But whoever thinks of me? Let me go. If you do, I promise, your life will be much easier.

She'd been wondering about those words for days. What had they meant? Allie had put a lot of thought into Zoe's strange reaction to her sister's suicide attempt, too. How she'd responded when Bitty had asked for help. How cold she had been . . . expressing no compassion, only anger at her sister.

Bitty had explained that Zoe had been in shock. That her reaction wasn't abnormal. Allie remembered her own shock when her brother had killed himself when she was fifteen. Maybe if she hadn't blamed herself so much for his suicide, she would've been angry at him, too. Thinking back on it, she was pretty sure she would've been.

Yesterday, they'd celebrated Thanksgiving without Carrie. It had just been a quiet dinner. Bitty and Zoe had been tired from their trip to Dallas . . . and even Sammy was quieter than usual. He'd asked a million questions about why Carrie would have to stay in a hospital for so long just because she was sad, and hadn't seemed satisfied with her answers, which of course skirted around the disturbing fact that she'd slit her wrists.

Allie took a seat on the side of Carrie's bed, then, careful not to touch the bandage around her wrist, reached for the girl's hand. It felt smaller, cooler, and more limp than before. Carrie didn't react at all to the touch. She just kept staring at the ceiling.

Swallowing back tears, Allie looked around. The floors were all pristine white tile, and the walls were a soft shade of green. The same shade of green many of the hospital's personnel wore. As she'd walked to Carrie's room, she'd passed several signs that contained sunny pictures and positive affirmations of hope. Sunny Lawn seemed like a really nice place. She had no idea that places like these even existed.

"We miss you at the house," Allie said, studying the bandages on Carrie's wrists. She remembered the deep cuts Carrie had made in her wrists. They'd been a clear sign that Carrie hadn't simply been crying for help.

She had wanted to get the job done . . . and quickly.

Carrie peered back at her, her brown eyes unfocused, probably due to the trazadone Bitty said they had put her on to help with the anxiety.

"I was an orphan, too," Allie said. "I bet you didn't know that. I never had much family. Just a mother and a brother. But they were really sick, and both were dead by the time I was fifteen." Carrie's eyes remained on Allie's, as though maybe she was listening. "After they died, I tried to kill myself, too. But I didn't do a very good job of it. Well, *obviously*. I'm still here." She swallowed, remembering the filthy motel room. The dirty bathtub. The bottle of pills. The unbearable loneliness. The sheer terror and desperation. "Sometimes I think that I lived because I was meant to be here, you know? Just like you are." She shook her head. "It would've been awful if I would've died back then, because I'm so happy now. Back then I had no idea being this happy was even possible."

She looked at Carrie, and saw the girl's eyes were shimmering with tears.

"Anyway, I know what it's like to hurt really, really bad, and to feel like it'll never get better. To feel completely hopeless. But there's always hope. And it does get better. It really does . . . especially with good people like Bitty in your corner. She can teach you things. Help you think differently. Help you heal. You just have to let her."

They sat in silence for a long moment. "Did you make that up? The stuff about your family?" Carrie asked, her voice hoarse.

Allie felt a powerful tide of emotion pass through her. *Carrie just spoke to me!* She tried to stay calm, not to show her surprise . . . how excited she was about finally getting through to the girl. "No," she answered. "I didn't make it up. Any of it. But I *wish* I had."

CHAPTER 21

WHEN THEY RETURNED home from Dallas, Johnny's truck was parked in the driveway. Allie's face grew hot. Johnny wasn't free just to drop in anymore. Didn't he know that?

She threw the truck into park and glimpsed Johnny sitting on the porch, shielding his eyes from the bright beams of the headlights. She asked Bitty to unbuckle a sleeping Sammy from his car seat and put him to bed, then she stepped out into the chilly night and marched up to Johnny.

When he saw her, he stood and opened his arms. "Hey, li'l bit. Welcome home."

"What do you think you're doing?" she demanded.

"Well, I didn't think it would be a good idea to go in, so I just waited out here."

"That's not what I meant," she snapped. "I meant what are you doing *here*? At my house?"

"Whoa, there. I just came here to see my boy. And you, too, of course."

"Yeah? Well, when did you get here?"

"I don't know. About twenty minutes ago? Thirty? Why?"

Just as she suspected. "It's almost ten o'clock and you're telling me you came to see Sammy, who has an eight-thirty bedtime? Who's had an eight-thirty bedtime for almost three years now?" She stared at him, incredulous. "That's bullshit, Johnny. You didn't drive here to see your son, and you know it."

He shrugged. "I would've been here earlier, but you weren't answering my texts."

Since Allie'd seen him last, she'd received about fifty texts. All *I miss you*s and *I love you*s, and *let's work this out*, but he hadn't mentioned Sammy once. That fact hadn't been lost on her then, and wasn't lost on her now.

After Bitty, Zoe, and Sammy were safely inside and had time to clear the foyer, Allie led Johnny into the house, but stopped him as he tried to walk into the living room.

"Look, we need to have a talk. A serious one," he said. "I've been thinking about things. *A lot* of things."

"What things?"

His brown eyes held hers. "Let's move in together," he blurted out. "Get a place of our own. I want to give you and Sammy that. You guys *deserve* that."

It was too little, way too late. She was done with Johnny as a boyfriend . . . or whatever it was that he'd been the last several years. Ending things with him had been the right thing to do. She only wished she'd done it sooner.

Now he was just Sammy's father. The only serious discussions they would need to have would be centered around Sammy and Sammy only.

Johnny's mouth spread into a smile. "So what do you think? Wouldn't that be nice? A place of our own? A safer, calmer place for Sammy to live? Just think, having Sammy around weird kids like those little girls all the time can't be good, Allie."

Anger flared in her belly. *"Weird kids?"*

A floorboard creaked. Allie turned and saw Zoe peeking from around the corner.

"Is everything okay?" Allie asked. "Do you need something?"

"Sorry," Zoe said. "I just wanted some water, but I didn't want to . . . disturb you."

"I'll get it for you."

Zoe shook her head. "No, I've got it." The girl's eyes quickly flitted to Johnny as she hurried to the kitchen, and Allie wondered if she'd heard what Johnny had said. She hoped not.

"Well, can I sit down?" Johnny asked.

"No," Allie said firmly. She held her hand out, palm up. "I want your key."

"What?"

"Your key. *Now.*"

"Hold on. Did you hear what I just said? What I just . . . *offered* . . . you? We could do it fast, too. Fast enough to be settled in by Christmas. Think about it. We can spend our first Christmas together . . . as a family."

He had no idea how badly she used to long for that scenario. Her, Johnny, Sammy, and Bitty together for the holidays. Johnny had never spent the holidays with them. Not even one.

She waited until Zoe left the kitchen and she heard the bedroom door click, indicating she was back in her room.

"Did you hear me?" Johnny asked.

"Yes, I heard you," she barked. "But let's get a couple of things straight. First of all, don't you ever, *ever* call anyone in this house *weird* again. And I mean *ever*. Do you understand me? Those kids have gone through things you could never imagine. Stuff that I'm pretty damn sure you'd never survive."

Johnny lifted his palms in mock surrender. "Sorry, I didn't mean anything. It's just that kids who scream—"

"And secondly," she interrupted, her words coming faster, her tone sharper. "You and I are over. What do I need to do to get you to understand that?"

He stared at her in silence.

"I tried for years to make you happy, Johnny. To get you to take Sammy and me seriously . . . and you didn't give a shit. But, you know what? I finally pulled my head out of my ass and did what was right for us—and I am so happy I did. I only wish I'd done it sooner."

His shoulders slumped as the realization that she was serious finally dawned on him.

"So from here on, you are Sammy's father. That's it. When you're ready to be a father to him, give us a call. Otherwise I have nothing to say to you."

She swung the door open, and the chilly night air flooded in. "Now give me the goddamn key, because you really need to go."

After Johnny left, Allie went to her bathroom to take her medicine and wash up. When she was done, Zoe was standing in the doorway.

"Hey. What's up?" Allie asked.

"Nothing really."

She noticed Zoe had changed clothes since they'd been home. She was now wearing another of Allie's T-shirts, for the third time this week. Allie wondered why, since Bitty had just filled their closet with a new wardrobe.

"Don't you like your new clothes?" Allie asked.

Zoe looked puzzled, then she glanced down at the shirt. Her face reddened. "Oh, sorry. I was helping with the laundry and I liked it, is all, so I pulled it out. I guess I should take it off and give it back to you?"

"No, you don't need to do that. It's okay." Allie smiled so that the girl truly knew it was.

"So, uh . . . are you leaving?" Zoe finally asked.

"Leaving?"

"Yeah. I wasn't trying to eavesdrop or anything, but I heard your boyfriend ask you to move in with him."

"He's not my boyfriend. And no, I'm not leaving. I'm staying put right here."

Zoe's eyes widened. "Really?"

"Really."

Relief washed over the girl's face and she smiled.

Allie smiled back at finally being able to offer the girl some relief. God knew she needed it. She just wished she could do the same for Carrie.

And she would.

Somehow.

She was as stubborn as Bitty, and she'd find a way. But right now, she was exhausted and just wanted to unwind.

"Okay, well, good night then," Zoe said and walked from the room toward her own.

"Good night," Allie said, pretty certain that it was just a pretense. That Zoe would soon be in her bed. She'd been sneaking into it late every night, ever since Carrie's suicide attempt.

But Allie didn't blame her. She knew if she had gone through everything Zoe just had, she wouldn't want to be alone either.

CHAPTER 22

"MOMMY, I NO want Zoe to sleep with us anymore, okay?" Sammy said from the backseat as they were pulling onto Main Street the next afternoon. It had been a long day, and Allie wanted nothing more than to be back home. Wind whipped at the Tahoe as she pulled off Main Street and onto the dirt road that led to the house.

She glanced in the rearview mirror. "It bothers you, doesn't it?"

"Yes. I no like it. Two bugs, not three."

"Okay, I'll talk to her."

A few minutes later, Allie pushed the front door open and Sammy rushed past her into the foyer. "Carrie's home! Carrie's home!" he squealed, seeing her on the couch. He darted through the foyer and into the living room, then came to a screeching stop right before he reached the couch where Carrie lay.

"Why you got owies on your arms?" he asked.

"Sammy, honey! Come here and say hello to Grammy!" Bitty called from the kitchen.

"Grammy!" Carrie's bandages already forgotten, he dashed to the kitchen.

Allie could smell something cooking. She guessed it was Bitty's famous chicken potpie. She shrugged off her coat and walked into the living room. The white bandages on Carrie's arms had been replaced with smaller, flesh-colored ones. Allie also noticed the stuffed bear was no longer at Carrie's side. She hoped it was a good sign. That maybe she didn't need it anymore to feel safe at their house.

"I'm happy you're home," Allie said, sitting next to her. She took Carrie's hand in hers and squeezed gently. And this time, to Allie's surprise, she squeezed back.

Allie's pulsed quickened. First Carrie talking to her at Sunny Lawn. Now squeezing her hand. Both were major, completely unexpected victories.

She was getting through to her.

Allie caught movement out of the corner of her eye and glanced up. Zoe was standing at the edge of the living room, frowning at them. Allie saw something flash behind her eyes, then she turned and fled down the hallway.

A few seconds later, a door slammed.

Carrie yanked her hand from Allie's, then lay down, her back to her.

"Zoe?" Allie called at the twins' bedroom door.

Silence.

She knocked twice on the door. "Zoe? Mind if I come in?"

More silence, then: "Whatever. It's *your* house."

Allie let herself in and found Zoe on the upper bunk, leafing through a magazine. She had earbuds in her ears, and an iPod rested on her stomach.

Where did those come from? She wondered if Bitty had bought them for her . . . or had arranged to get them from her house. She'd have to ask. "What's going on? Why are you so angry?" she asked.

Zoe pulled an earbud from her ear, letting it dangle against her chest. "Who said I was angry?"

"No one, but you look and sound angry, so I'm guessing you are." Allie studied the girl. "Is it that you're still angry at Carrie? For what she did?"

Zoe didn't respond.

"Look, I know you're hurt. And you have every right to be. But she's hurting, too. So don't you think we should all support her?"

Zoe didn't respond.

"Zoe?"

Zoe ignored her.

Allie sighed, knowing that she'd have to wait for the girl to calm down before they could have a real conversation. As she started to leave the room, she remembered the promise she'd made to Sammy about talking to Zoe about the sleeping arrangements. She really didn't want to bring it up now while Zoe was already upset, but she also realized there'd be no comfortable time to discuss it, because no matter what, she was going to feel rejected. Allie hated that, but her son's feelings were important.

"I also wanted to talk about . . ." She hesitated, trying to figure out how to string the words together the right way.

Zoe's eyes were now on hers, searching. "What?"

"Well, since your sister's back, you should probably start sleeping in here again."

For a brief moment, Zoe looked hurt. But then she quickly rolled her eyes. "Okay, fine. Whatever."

"Does that make you angry?"

Zoe didn't say anything.

"It's just that . . . Sammy doesn't sleep well when you sleep with us. I think he might be a little jealous. Before you and Carrie, it was just him and me. And that's what he's used to, you know?"

Silence.

"Plus, there's nothing to be scared of now. Gary's far away from here in Florida. He can't hurt anyone. You know that. Right, Zoe? There's nothing to be afraid of."

Zoe turned away from her and shoved the earbud back into her ear. "Whatever. I didn't want to sleep with you anymore anyway."

CHAPTER 23

THAT EVENING, THE doorbell rang. Allie peered through the peephole and was surprised to see the old lady from the funeral standing on the front porch. The one who had watched them, but hadn't approached to say hello to the girls.

Bitty appeared behind Allie, wiping her hands on her apron. "Who is it?"

"That strange old woman from the funeral. The one who kept staring at us."

Bitty frowned. "Let me get it."

Bitty went to the door and pulled it open. "May I help you?" she asked, the odor of stale cigarettes and mothballs floating in on frigid wintry air.

"Are the girls here?" the old lady asked, her voice gravelly, as though she were a smoker. She wore her gray hair up in a '50s beehive hairdo and looked like she could've been beautiful once. But her blue eyes had a hard, glacial quality to them, and her skin was tinged with gray, as though she were unwell.

Bitty's frown deepened. "I'm sorry. You are?"

"I'm Ruby Duvall. I'm Julie Parish's mother. Those kids you have living here are my grandbabies. Go tell them Grandmother is here to see them."

Hearing Ruby's voice, Carrie jerked into a sitting position on the couch, tense as pulled wire. Allie had never seen the girl move so quickly.

Bitty invited Ruby into the foyer, but stopped her with the motion of the palm of her hand before she could go any farther. The woman had a frenetic, nervous energy about her that made Allie uneasy. Allie knew Bitty noticed it, too.

"I'm sorry. But to what do we owe the pleasure of this visit?" Miss Bitty asked, her voice not holding its usual warmth.

Ruby's eyes darted around the foyer and past Bitty. She stood on her tiptoes to see over Bitty's shoulder and into the living room. "You people and your fancy houses," she muttered, shaking her head.

Bitty repeated her question, but it went unanswered.

The old woman stopped looking around and focused on Bitty with her cold eyes. She looked distrusting. "I've changed my mind about taking the girls," Ruby said.

Allie and Bitty traded glances.

"I see," Bitty said. "Well, that's something you need to take up with Child Protective Services and the judge. I'm in no way involved with guardianship decisions."

"I'm planning on doing just that. But right now I'd like to see my grandbabies."

Allie turned to look at Carrie again, but the couch was empty.

"Have CPS call and tell me it's okay, then we'll talk," Bitty told the woman.

"Are you kiddin' me? You're sayin' you won't let me see my own grandbabies?"

"Yes. That's exactly what I'm saying."

Ruby twisted her mouth, as though she'd just sucked on a lemon. She stared at Bitty for a long while, then: "Let me see them or I'm going to call the cops."

Bitty's hands went to her hips. "Go ahead. Call them."

Ruby's eyes widened. She thrust her bag off her shoulder and made a big show of digging around in it for her phone. As she pulled a scratched flip-top cell phone out, she lost hold of the bag and it tumbled to the floor. "Aw, shit, look at what you gone and made me do!"

She planted a scabby, veined hand against her thigh and groaned, then bent to retrieve her things. Bitty knelt down to help. Scattered all over the ceramic tile were used tissues, a tube of off-brand petroleum jelly, empty gum wrappers, pencils, and a pen.

Bitty grabbed the gum wrappers and the pencils. Then her hand paused on the pen and she stood up again. She rolled it around in her hand. Allie could see the words printed on the side: Ed's Granite Show House. She recognized the name, but couldn't immediately place it.

Ruby finished throwing everything back into her bag and, with another groan, stood.

"You get granite work done lately?" Bitty asked.

Ruby looked confused. "Granite? No. Why would you get a fool idea like that?"

Bitty held out the pen. The older woman squinted, her eyes running over the words on the side, and slowly, realization bloomed in her eyes.

The tension in the air seemed to thicken.

"Why, I have no idea how that even got in there," she said, twisting her wrinkled mouth again and revealing two rotten bottom teeth. She snatched the pen from Bitty's hand. "Just want to keep takin' what isn't yours, do ya?"

Allie racked her brain trying to figure out why the granite company's name sounded familiar, but it still wasn't coming to her.

"So . . . I'll just come out and ask," Ruby said. "You gettin' my daughter's money?"

"Absolutely not," Bitty replied.

Ruby snorted, and her beady eyes traveled to Allie's. "Does it look like I was born yesterday? I don't believe that for one second."

"I don't get a penny of your daughter's money."

The woman seemed to be considering whether Bitty was telling her the truth.

"I hear you're talkin' to a lot of folks around here. That they're talkin' to you."

Bitty crossed her arms.

"And I heard Julie gave that Gary fella most of her money. See, my daughter was never the sharpest knife in the drawer, but she'd have to be a real buffoon to give that money away, especially to an old burnout like Gary Willis." Ruby stared at Bitty, expecting an answer. "Well, did she?"

"I wouldn't know."

"Oh, I don't believe that for an instant," Ruby growled.

Bitty went to the door. "I think you should go."

Ruby quickly stepped sideways so that she stood between Bitty and the door, and the odor of mothballs intensified. Her words came quicker, and now sounded desperate. "Just give me a little. Just a little of that money. I sacrificed a lot bringin' my daughters up. Now I'm barely gettin' by. I deserve that money. Give me a little and I'll let you keep the rest. And I won't take the girls away. That's a promise. I'll never even bother you again."

Bitty pushed past the woman and swung the front door open. A rush of frosty air flooded in. "Like I said, contact CPS. And until then, do not come here again."

Ruby furrowed her brow and lifted her chin. She gave Bitty a thorough once-over. "You must think you're high cotton, lady. But you don't look like it to me. I'll be back. You can bet on it."

Bitty watched Ruby march out into the evening and plunge her thin body into an old rusted Dodge Charger.

"What's Ed's Granite Show House?" Allie asked as they watched the woman fire up her car.

"It's the company where Gary was working when the Parishes were killed."

Now the pen made sense.

As soon as Ruby pulled away from the house, Bitty had her phone in her hand and was making a call.

"Calling Detective Lambert?"

"Damn right. Over my dead body will that crazy old woman get custody of those girls."

———

Shortly after putting Sammy to bed, Allie went searching for Bitty, hoping to find out what Detective Lambert had said about the grand-mother's visit and her likelihood of being awarded custody of the girls.

As she headed to the kitchen, the girls' bedroom door flew open. Zoe stepped out and grabbed Allie's arms. Her cheeks were streaked with tears. "I'm *so* sorry for the way I acted earlier. I was rude, and I'm *so* very sorry. I shouldn't have behaved that way. I promise I won't do it again. But please," she pleaded, wearing the same look of horror that Allie'd seen when Gary had shown up in the backyard. "*Promise me* you won't let her take us! Please, Allie. We—"

"Zoe, calm down."

The girl's grip tightened. "No, you don't understand!"

Allie frowned. "Zoe, let go. You're hurting me."

Zoe released her hold on Allie's arms. "Oh, God. Sorry." She pressed her hands together and held them under her chin. "Please. Don't make us live with her. She doesn't want us, she wants the money. Promise me?" she begged.

"It's going to be okay, Zoe."

She shook her head quickly back and forth. "No, don't you see? It *won't* be okay. It won't! Not if we have to live with her. Please, you're not promising me!" Her eyes were desperate. "I can help around here. I can watch Sammy all you want. I can clean, cook. I can—"

"Mommy?"

Allie turned. Sammy was in the doorway, his brow creased with worry.

"What wrong, Mommy?"

"Nothing. Zoe's just a little upset right now."

"She sad?"

"Yes. Go back to bed. I'll be in there in a few minutes."

"She going to the hospital?"

"No. Sammy go back to—"

"But I sawed a shadow."

"That's okay. Shadows can't hurt you."

"But I scared, Mommy!" he whined.

"Turn on the lamp and wait for me. I'll be right there."

Sammy disappeared back into the room.

Allie turned back to Zoe. "I'll talk with Bitty, but I really don't think a judge would grant guardianship to a woman like your grandmother."

Zoe looked doubtful. "But you're not sure, are you?"

"No, I'm not. But I'll talk with Miss Bitty, okay?"

The answer didn't seem to comfort Zoe much. But still, she backed away. "Thank you. Please do whatever you can. And I meant what I said. I'll help out a ton around here. I'm a really, really hard worker. I can make your life easier. I can help . . . if you just let me."

———

After Sammy fell asleep, Allie found Bitty in the kitchen, just finishing up a call on her cell phone.

"I just talked to Detective Lambert."

"And—"

"I've got good news and bad news."

Feeling her chest tighten, Allie sat down. Bitty explained that the detective had reassured her that it was very unlikely that the grandmother would get custody of the girls. He'd told Bitty that Ruby had a police record that included a conviction for drug charges. He'd also told her there were probably a dozen good explanations for Ruby to have had the pen with Gary's workplace printed on it. It was a small town, and things like pens with names of local companies monogrammed on them just had a way of getting around. Also, Ruby's younger daughter, Sandy, was a known meth user. Ruby was suspected of it, too. Gary had probably been their dealer, or maybe Gary, Ruby, and Sandy had shared a dealer. But even with the myriad of possibilities, Detective Lambert promised he'd follow up on it.

"And the bad news?"

Bitty sighed. "The bad news is that they found Gary's truck in the woods today."

"The woods . . . *in Orlando?*"

Bitty shook her head. "No. The woods here. Just a quarter mile away from our house."

Allie glanced at the kitchen window and the dark yard beyond it. "But I thought he was in Florida?"

"There still hasn't been confirmation yet that it was Gary using his card in Orlando. Someone could've stolen his card and tried to use it. But it's also quite possible that it *was* Gary using the card in Florida and he just left the truck behind before leaving town. The truck could've easily been sitting there, abandoned, for the last few weeks, and simply gone unreported until now."

Allie replayed the times she thought she saw and heard something in the backyard. Had she? "So, what does this mean?"

"Well, I hate to say it, but I think we need to behave as though he's out here . . . someplace nearby, until we know more. Better safe than sorry."

CHAPTER 24

IN THE MIDDLE of the night, Sammy got up to use the bathroom.

After flushing the toilet and washing his hands, he realized his throat felt dry, so he went back to the bedroom and picked up the glass by the bed. But it was empty. He reached out to wake his mommy, but stopped when he heard a noise.

He froze. *What was that?!*

He looked at his mommy again to see if she had heard, too, but she hadn't. She was still asleep. Piglet was asleep, too, on her back with her toothpick legs up in the air.

He heard the noise again.

His heart thumping against his rib cage, he tiptoed to the bedroom door, opened it, and peeked out. The noise was louder now.

It was coming from the girls' room.

He tiptoed down the hallway and pushed open the girls' bedroom door a little bit. Enough to see Carrie on the bottom bunk bed, her face buried deeply in her pillow. She was crying really hard. He wondered why. Maybe because Zoe had been mean to her earlier. He knew she had, because he'd heard.

Grammy had made a special welcome-home dinner for Carrie: chicken potpie with a chocolate cake dessert. And after dinner, because he'd been feeling sneaky, he'd pressed his ear against the girls' bedroom door and heard Zoe say: *What exactly were we celebrating at dinner, Carrie? Welcome-home-from-the-loony-bin?*

Although he didn't know what a loony bin was, he knew it wasn't something good by the way Zoe's voice sounded when she said it. He didn't like that she'd been mean to Carrie. Carrie seemed nice.

Right now Carrie's shoulders were jumping up and down. She was having a big cry, like his mommy sometimes did when she wasn't happy with his daddy . . . or when she woke up from a scary dream.

He opened the door wider and took a step into the room, and a floorboard creaked.

Uh oh.

Carrie's crying stopped. She raised her face from the pillow and looked at him, then turned over so he couldn't see her face anymore.

He stepped into the room. "Carrie? You okay?" he asked.

She didn't say anything. But he hadn't expected her to. She *never* said anything. "Why you crying? Your arms hurt?"

She lay still as though she hadn't heard, although he was pretty sure she had.

He shivered, even though he was wearing his favorite *Lego Movie* pajamas and they were very warm.

It was just soooo cold in the bedroom.

Why?

He received his answer as a gust of wind blew in through the window, making the curtains jump out at him. His eyes went big.

The window.

It wide open!

His mommy would not like that. She liked all the windows closed and locked at all times, especially since the day that scary man had shown up in their yard. He could see that it was really dark on the other side. He didn't like the dark because he knew that monsters lived in the dark, even though his mommy had told him several times over the years that the only monsters that really existed were bad people.

He started for the window, to close it, but then he heard a bump that made him hop backward.

A backpack flew into the room and hit the floor.

Whoa!

It had just flown into the room. *All by itself!* Even Carrie looked up.

Sammy inhaled sharply. He didn't know backpacks could do that!

Suddenly, he saw legs swinging over the window ledge. Then Zoe was inside and replacing the window screen.

As she pulled the window closed, he stood there, frozen, wishing he wasn't in the room, because he had the feeling she wouldn't like that he was there, watching her do this naughty thing. He thought about running, but before he could get his legs to move, she looked up and saw him.

Her mouth dropped open. "Oh, shit."

"That a bad word. You no should say bad words," he said, in case she didn't know.

She rolled her eyes. "Well, no shit."

He stared at her, wondering why she'd said that bad word again. "My mommy likes the windows closed and locked," he told her, in case she didn't know that either. But he was pretty sure she did.

She flipped the lock on the window, then turned to him. "Where's your mommy, Sammy?"

"She sleeping."

"You sure?"

"Uh-huh."

"So she doesn't know I was gone?"

Sammy shook his head.

Looking as though she felt a lot better, Zoe smiled, then went to the bedroom door behind him and gently closed it. She came back and knelt down on her knees. "You can keep a secret, can't you?"

He blinked at her. Of course he could! He loved secrets! And he had a bunch. Probably more than she had. His stomach suddenly growled, and he realized that he wasn't just thirsty, he was a little hungry, too. Maybe he'd have to wake up his mommy after all.

"Sammy? Did you hear what I just said?"

He blinked, realizing Zoe was talking to him and he'd forgotten to listen. "Huh?"

"I said . . . big boys. They keep their friends' secrets. You're a big boy, right?" Zoe asked.

"Yes."

"And you and me. We're friends, right?"

He didn't think so. Well, maybe. He wasn't sure.

"Now, don't tell your mommy that you saw me coming in the window, okay? Because that's my secret."

"Why?"

"Because she wouldn't like that I went out the window, and I don't want to worry her."

"But why you sneaked out? That naughty."

She smiled. "Because I wanted to get you and your mommy a surprise.

Surprises were even better than secrets! "A surprise?" he said, a little wary. "For me?"

"Yep. And for your mommy, too. Want to see?"

He nodded.

She grabbed her backpack and started to unzip it.

He held his breath, wondering what it was going to be. The Lego Batman 3 game for Xbox? A new Lego figure for his collection? A Mr. Freeze minifigure?!

Just as she was about to reach in, her hand stopped, and she looked up at him.

She wasn't smiling anymore. She bit down on her lower lip. "Okay, now you're going to have to promise me that you'll keep my secret, okay?"

"Okay."

"I'm serious, Sammy."

He put on his most serious-looking face. "Okay. Me, too."

She stared at him. "Say the whole sentence."

"What sentence?"

"I promise I won't say a word."

"Okay. I promise I no say a word."

She smiled again and pulled out the surprises.

He smiled, and jumped up and down.

CHAPTER 25

ALLIE LEFT THE preschool, Sammy in tow. She'd received a call from the school's secretary saying he'd vomited in class—no doubt having caught the twenty-four-hour bug that had been making its rounds.

As she turned onto the main road, she glanced into the rearview mirror to find Sammy dozing. She turned her attention back to the road, and her thoughts drifted to Gary's truck being found only a quarter mile from their house. Her hands went clammy as she wondered if Gary had been watching them this whole time. If so, why? What was he planning to do?

And, if he did have plans, what was he waiting for?

She realized she was white knuckling the steering wheel. *Calm down, Allie,* she told herself. *Don't get all worked up. There's a good explanation for the truck. Gary probably just abandoned it, then skipped town. Seriously . . . a truck is hardly anything to be frightened about.*

As soon as they got home, Allie tucked Sammy into bed and queued up *Lego Movie* on the television, then went to the kitchen to warm some soup and brew him some tea.

Bitty and the twins were sitting in the kitchen, books and note-books spread across the table, finishing up their homeschooling work for the day.

"Little man pick up a virus?" Bitty asked.

"Yeah . . . I think so."

"Fever?"

"No. Thank God. At least not yet."

"You going to work from the home office?"

Allie knew it would be tricky trying to work with clients while Sammy was home. She'd attempted to before and it hadn't gone smoothly. Not even close. "I'm going to try. I have three more clients on today's schedule."

"Carrie has two appointments in town this afternoon, but I can reschedule if you need some help with Sammy."

"No, you don't need to—"

"I can help," Zoe volunteered. Her eyes darted from Allie to Bitty. "I'll watch him. It's not a problem. I don't have any appointments today . . . and I wanted to stay home anyway."

Allie considered the offer. Zoe seemed capable, and if they needed anything, Allie would only be a few feet away.

This is just what you need. Don't be so overprotective.

"I'm good with little kids," Zoe said. "I used to watch my little brother all the time."

Sammy didn't feel sick to his stomach anymore. In fact, his stomach didn't hurt at all. He felt almost as good as he always did, so he didn't want to stay in bed for the rest of the day. Plus, his mother said Zoe was going to watch him for a few hours. And maybe playing with Zoe would be fun.

His mother was in her home office working . . . and Grammy and Carrie had just left the house. Zoe had smiled at them when they left, then locked the door behind them.

She turned around and opened her mouth to say something. But before anything could come out, he asked: "You got more gummy worms?" The gummy worms had been his surprise. Five of them! All red and green—and even though they smelled a little weird, they were so tasty! His mommy didn't let him have store-bought candy very often—she and his grammy were always busy trying to make healthy desserts—so the worms were a real treat.

Zoe grabbed his hand and pulled him to the living room, to the leather couch that Carrie usually lay on. She knelt down and whispered, "You didn't tell your mommy, did you? About our secret?"

He shook his head. "I kept our secret."

"Good. Thank you. I just don't want her to worry, okay?"

"Okay."

"Pull out your Lego figures, and I'll get you two worms."

"Three."

She stared at him. "Okay, three. What colors do you want?"

He thought about it carefully. "Red and green."

"Okay, I'll be right back."

Sammy pulled out his blue canvas basket where he kept all his minifigures and picked out his favorites.

When Zoe came back, he ate his worms really slowly so he could taste every bite. Zoe lay on her stomach on the floor, resting her face in her hands, and watched him. When he finished eating his worms, she listened patiently as he named each and every one of his forty-one figures . . . then started naming them all again. When he was done, he looked at her and saw that Zoe was frowning.

"Why you looking like that?"

She shrugged. "You just remind me of my brother."

"You have a brother?"

"I did."

"Where is he?"

Her eyes got shiny. "He's dead."

Goose pimples popped up on Sammy's arms. "Dead?"

"Yeah. He died."

Dead, died. Those words made his stomach feel yucky. Just like it had at preschool right before he vomited in Miss Tina's class while he was building his purple birdhouse.

He didn't want to talk about her brother anymore.

"Guess what?" he said.

"What?"

"After preschool, I going to kindergarten."

Zoe's sad face turned a little happier. She sniffed and sat up. "Well, that sounds exciting."

He yawned and felt his eyes droop a little.

"Are you tired?" Zoe asked. "Want to lay in bed and watch a movie?"

He nodded. "I want to watch ants."

"Okay." Zoe picked him up and carried him to his mommy's bedroom. Then she covered him up in his mommy's bed just like she was a mommy and played the ants documentary on the television. As she cleared away his used tissues and refilled his crackers, his eyes got even heavier.

"I like ants," he said.

"You do?"

He nodded.

"Do you like *me*, Sammy?" she asked.

He thought about it. "I think so."

She smiled.

"But it two bugs in a rug. Not three," he said. He didn't want Zoe, the wanna-be bug, to sleep with him and his mommy anymore. He didn't like it. Not one bit.

Zoe's smile slipped off her face. Her dark eyes got shiny again and little pink circles popped up on her cheeks. "It can totally be three bugs, you know. It doesn't have to be two."

"Yes it do."

"No, three's better. I mean, really. *Everyone* knows that."

He shook his head.

"It is. You can be okay with that, right, Sammy? With three?" She raised her eyebrows high, and made the face Piglet made when she wanted a dog treat. "Please?"

"Two," he said, using his most serious voice.

Zoe's eyebrows fell back into place. "Whatever. You'll change your mind."

"No, I not."

She looked away from him, and they watched the ants documentary together, but after a little while, he felt his eyes close.

When he woke up again, Zoe, the wanna-be bug, was lying next to him, reading a book and wearing one of his mommy's blue T-shirts.

"Your mommy was just in here checking on you, but you were asleep. She said she'd be back in twenty minutes."

He yawned and stretched his arms.

"Would you like more soup, honey?"

He stared at her. His mommy and Grammy called him honey. But he thought it was kinda silly for Zoe to call him that. He didn't really know why, he just did.

He shook his head. "I not hungry."

"Okay, well, let me know. Want me to put something else on? *Curious George*?"

"Okay."

She found the disc on his mommy's bookshelf and slid it in.

"Why you wear my mommy's shirt?" he asked.

She picked up her book again and glanced at him. "Why not? Mothers and daughters share, silly. Didn't you know that?"

"Huh?" he said in surprise.

She stared at him for a moment, then smiled. "I'm just kidding. I know she's not my mother."

But for some reason he didn't think she'd been "just kidding."

"But we do look a lot alike, don't we?"

"What?"

"Me and your mommy. We look a lot alike. Don't you think?"

They both had the same long dark hair. The same big eyes. Except his mommy's eyes were gray like a wolf's . . . and Zoe's were green like a . . . like a green gummy worm. Zoe was even wearing her hair in a ball on the top of her head like his mommy did. So yes, they did look alike. But he didn't want to tell Zoe he thought so.

"Well, do we?" Zoe asked. "Look alike?"

He shook his head. "No. Uh-uh."

"Yes, we do," she insisted. "We could totally be mother and daughter."

"No." He shook his head.

"Whatever," she said, gazing down at her book. "We do," she whispered. "And one day we will be. She'll be *my* mommy, too."

He crossed his arms. "No, she not."

Zoe's eyes went small. "Why do you think we're here then?"

"You just here for a little while. Not forever."

"Whatever, Sammy. You're wrong. Just wait and see."

Allie pushed away from her desk and rubbed her eyes. It was after nine o'clock, and she had just processed a huge stack of paperwork.

With Zoe's help that afternoon, she'd gotten through all of her remaining appointments without any distractions, which was a huge relief. Sammy was now in bed fast asleep . . . and, hopefully, would sleep through the night and feel even better tomorrow.

Zoe poked her head in. "Are you busy?"

Allie smiled. "Nope. I'm done for the day. What's up?"

Zoe hesitantly stepped into the room. Her hair was in a messy topknot and she was wearing a pair of new red-and-white polka-dotted pajamas. "I just wanted to tell you good night."

"Good night. And thanks again. You helped a lot today."

The girl beamed. "You're welcome. Anytime you need me to watch Sammy, I'm more than happy to help. My schoolwork takes me all of an hour or two to do. Then I just have my chores . . . and I can do them pretty fast."

"Well, how about watching him tomorrow? I'm not going to send him to preschool, and I have five clients on my schedule."

"Yes!" Zoe said, happily. Then her eyes widened. "Oh! Wait. I have something for you! Just wait right here. Don't move!"

Less than a minute later, she returned with her hands behind her back. "Guess which hand," she said, looking giddy.

"The left one."

She made a face. "Aw, dang it. You guessed right." She reached her left hand out and revealed a glass heart. She held it in front of Allie. "Ta-daaaa!" she said.

"It's for me?" Allie asked.

Zoe nodded, smiling.

"Thank you," Allie said. She turned the delicate, handblown heart around in her hands. "Where did you get this?"

"It's mine. I've had it for a long time. But I want you to have it now." Zoe's eyes sparkled the way Sammy's did when he was excited.

"It's . . . beautiful," Allie said, setting it on her desk. "I'll put it right here."

Zoe gazed at the heart on the desk, then turned her attention back to Allie. "Do you know what it is? The heart?"

"What?"

"It's *my* heart. And I just gave it to you."

———

A little while later, as Allie checked in on Sammy, she couldn't get Zoe off her mind.

It's my heart. And I just gave it to you.

Zoe's words made Allie feel uncomfortable. She needed to talk with Bitty. To find out where the heart had come from. She realized she'd forgotten to ask about the iPod and the earbuds, and would have to ask about them, too.

The phone rang.

Allie jumped, then frowned at herself because she had.

My God! Get ahold of yourself.

When she reached the kitchen, she found Bitty sitting silently at the table with a cup of tea between her hands. Allie didn't like the look on her face. She almost didn't have to ask.

"Who was on the phone?"

Allie could tell Bitty was hesitant to answer her question. "I don't know. The call came from a private number . . . and whoever it was hung up."

Allie felt her shoulders sag. "Oh, God. Not again."

"Yeah, I'm afraid so," Bitty said, her voice weary.

"It was Gary, wasn't it?" a soft voice asked in the distance. "On the phone?" Both women turned and were surprised to see Zoe standing at the mouth of the hallway.

The girl's forehead furrowed with worry. "I heard you say he might be back. Is it true? Is he? Is he back?"

CHAPTER 26

EARLIER THAT AFTERNOON, Carrie had lain on the couch, her eyes closed, but not all the way. Through her eyelashes, she had watched Sammy carefully organize his minifigures.

Sammy reminded her so much of Joey it hurt. And it wasn't just his age either. It was some of his features and mannerisms: the thoughtful, careful way he lined up his toys, the way he squinted and held his mouth when he was really focused—which he seemed to almost always be.

Now Carrie lay in the bottom bunk. It was in the middle of the night, and like most nights, she couldn't sleep. She turned on her side and sighed, watching the shadows dance across the bedroom walls.

Zoe was snoring in the bed above her. Carrie was surprised she hadn't been sleeping in Allie's bedroom lately. Since they'd been living at the Callahans', she'd watched Zoe's fascination for Allie grow. Zoe wanted a mother badly, and Carrie could tell she had her sights set on Allie.

Earlier that night Zoe had snuck out the window, probably returning to their house to get more of her things. She'd done it twice before. The first time she said she'd walked. The second time she'd hitchhiked with a teenage boy. Both walking and hitchhiking were very dangerous. Normally Carrie would have tried to stop Zoe from doing either, afraid for her safety, but nothing was normal between her and Zoe these days. Carrie wondered if things would ever be again.

She thought about Gary and shivered.

Zoe had told her that he might be back in town. The very thought horrified her. She didn't think she could handle seeing him again. She pushed thoughts of Gary to the back of her mind and turned her thoughts to Joey. She'd loved Joey so much. They all had. He had been the baby of the family, and definitely the golden child of the three.

Until fairly recently, her family had lived in a trailer just past a sharp bend in the road. The neighbors had repeatedly complained about the sharp curve and the roadside oak in full leaf, whose limbs were in bad need of trimming. There'd already been three accidents on that very turn that year, one fatal, and many more close calls.

The family trailer itself sat only a couple of hundred feet away from the road, down a short, cracked concrete slab that they used as a driveway. It wasn't out of the ordinary to bolt awake late at night from the blare of honking horns, the loud squealing of brakes, and, if the windows were open—which they often were—the odor of burning rubber.

One summer afternoon, three years ago, Zoe was playing hopscotch in their driveway while their little brother, Joey, toddled around, carrying a kitten their father had brought home from a truck stop.

Their mother had been sunbathing on a bath towel in the grass. She stood up and readjusted her bathing suit. "Zoe. I'm going in for a second. Keep an eye on Joey?" their mother asked.

"Okay!" Zoe called.

Carrie had been sitting in a lawn chair, closer to the trailer, reading a book. Knowing her sister could be a little scatterbrained, every once in a while she'd look up and take her own accounting of their brother.

A few minutes after their mother had gone inside, she happened to look up to find the kitten bounding off toward the road, and Joey running after him. "Joey, no!" Carrie screamed. "Zoe! Get him!" she yelled. Her eyes flew to her sister, who was much closer to Joey than she was. But Zoe just sat, unmoving, gazing at him from her place on the driveway, holding a pink hopscotch chalk midair.

"Zoe!" Carrie screamed again. She scrambled from her chair and took off after him. "Joey, no!"

She heard the door to the trailer slam open. Then out the corner of her eye, she saw Zoe jump up and run after Joey, too. But they were too late.

He'd had too much of a head start.

He didn't look either way when he ran onto the blistering asphalt. His eyes were focused directly ahead on the kitten.

"Joey!" their mother screamed from someplace behind them.

A truck flashed around the bend in the road. But by the time the driver saw Joey, he didn't have the chance to stop. Carrie still remembered the squeal of brakes. The acrid odor of burnt rubber. The soft thump. She could still hear her mother's hysterical screams.

She remembered how hard their mother had slapped Zoe across her face after the ambulance left with Joey's body. And the words of blame that she would serve like poison over the next three years.

Carrie remembered it all like it had just happened yesterday.

Their mother barely left her bedroom in the two weeks after Joey died. But when she finally did, their father was already on another long haul. In fact, he left the evening after Joey's funeral.

Their mother walked out of her bedroom one afternoon with a strange look on her face and alcohol on her breath. She clutched a bottle of baby shampoo and told Zoe to get in the bath so she could shampoo her hair. Carrie remembered thinking something was very wrong. Their mother hadn't shampooed their hair for years. Carrie stood outside the bathroom door, listening in.

"I'm sorry, Mom. I'm *so* very sorry," she heard Zoe say. But if her mother replied, Carrie didn't hear it. The knob on the bathtub faucet squeaked and bathwater roared into the tub. Carrie heard Zoe's voice again. She was probably still apologizing, but Carrie couldn't make out her words over the rush of water.

Carrie leaned against the door and continued to listen. A few minutes later, Carrie heard the thrashing of water and her mother's loud grunts. Panicking, Carrie tried to open the door, but it was locked. She rammed her body into it. "Zoe? Mother? What's going on? Open the door!" But no one answered, and the thrashing and grunting continued. Carrie kept ramming and ramming until finally, the bathroom door swung open.

She ran to the tub to find her mother leaning forward, tears streaming down her flushed cheeks, both palms flat against Zoe's chest. As she tried to pull her mother's arms away from her sister, Carrie could see Zoe's face beneath the water. She was looking up in horror, her dark hair swimming around her face.

"Stop!" Carrie screamed, the sound of blood rushing into her ears. She tried to yank her mother's arms away from her sister as hard as she could. "Mom, stop!" she yelled. After a long moment, the woman, her face a crumpled mess, finally released her grip and Zoe shot up, sputtering and crying.

Their mother claimed it was an accident and warned them not to say a word about it to their father or anyone. And Zoe never did say a word.

Neither of them did.

CHAPTER 27

THE NEXT morning Allie woke up to Sammy playing with his mini-figures in bed.

"How are you feeling, honey?" she asked.

"Fine."

It looked like the preschool's secretary had been right and Sammy had just had a twenty-four-hour bug—one that, thankfully, hadn't even lasted that long.

She yawned. "Did you have fun with Zoe yesterday, honey?"

"Uh-huh. Zoe fun," he said, adjusting a leg on one of his minifigures.

"Good, because Mommy has to work again today and you're going to play with Zoe again. All right?"

"Okay."

He set his toy down and curled into her. She squeezed her eyes shut and held him tight, enjoying his warm little body in her arms.

"But . . . but Zoe say something weird," Sammy said.

Allie opened her eyes. "What did she say?"

"She say you will be her mommy."

"She did?"

He twisted around and searched her eyes. "But you're not, Mommy. Right?"

"No, I'm not," she said, softly.

Allie thought of the glass heart.

It's my heart. And I just gave it to you.

Having someone's love was a big responsibility . . . one Allie wasn't ready for. She had all the love she could handle. Allie sighed. The girl was twelve years old and had just lost everything. She needed someone to reach out to, who could give her what she needed.

"That what she say. I tell her you are *my* mommy. Not hers."

"We need to try to be nice to Zoe. She just misses her mommy."

"Because her mommy will not ever come back?"

"That's right."

After breakfast, Zoe cornered Allie, wanting to know everything about the phone call the night before. If Allie thought the person had been Gary, and if she thought Gary was back.

Allie told her that there was nothing to tell. The caller hadn't said anything . . . and yes, it was *possible* Gary had been the one who'd called and hung up, but that they couldn't know for sure.

It could have been anyone.

Allie didn't say anything about his truck being found. There was no point in worrying the girl any more than she already was.

Before heading to the home office, Allie showed Zoe how she liked everything to be locked up, then she showed Zoe how to mix Sammy's vitamins and add them to an oral syringe to help him drink them down. Since he'd been six months old, Allie had prepared his vitamins in the same manner, careful to combine pleasant flavors like citrus-flavored vitamin C with not-so-pleasant flavors like cod liver oil, in order to get Sammy to get everything down without much complaint. She found that when she closely followed the regimen, Sammy rarely got sick. And when he *was* sick, that the regimen decreased the severity of the illness and shortened its duration.

A few minutes later, Allie was at her desk when Bitty appeared in the doorway. "You have a minute?" she asked.

"Yeah, sure."

Bitty came in and closed the door. She looked like she wanted to talk about something serious.

Allie felt her palms go moist.

"I just spoke with Detective Lambert," Bitty said. "He followed up on the phone calls made to the house, and he said they both pinged from a cell tower nearby." She exhaled wearily. "Which I'm afraid means it's very likely Gary's back in town."

Allie felt a crawl of dread in her stomach. This was worse than the truck being found abandoned near the house. Far worse.

"And he's positive the calls came from Gary's cell phone?"

"No, apparently Gary hasn't used his phone in quite some time. The calls came from Julie Parish's cell phone. She had accounts with two providers. The phone that was used seems to have been a personal phone Julie kept exclusively for communicating with Gary."

"And assuming Gary has the phone in his possession, which it's likely he does, he was nearby when he made the calls."

Sweat pooled in Allie's armpits. It seemed they were getting more bad news every day. *Seriously—how much worse can this get,* she wondered, then immediately shook the thought from her mind. She didn't want to know.

"We'll just keep doing what we're doing and stay aware. Okay, honey?"

Allie nodded. "Yeah. Okay."

Bitty stood to go. "The good news is that Detective Lambert said he now has approval to put more manpower behind finding Gary. So if he *is* local, chances are they'll find him."

The doorbell rang.

Bitty looked at her watch. "Hmm. I wonder who that is? The girls' caseworker isn't due for another hour."

Allie followed Bitty out of the room and checked on the kids. Sammy and Zoe were in the living room playing Ms. Pac-Man on the Xbox, and Carrie was sitting on a chair in the kitchen, staring out the window into the backyard. Allie wondered if she was looking for Gary.

Allie stepped barefoot on the cool ceramic tiles of the foyer to see who Bitty had opened the door for. It was a woman she'd never seen before.

"Please? I just need some answers," the woman was saying to Bitty. She sounded desperate.

"Okay, come on in," Bitty said and gestured for the woman to enter the house.

"This is my daughter, Allie," Bitty said.

The woman looked very nervous, frightened. She was also very pregnant. She nodded a hello to Allie.

"And Allie," Bitty continued. "This is Laura Willis. Gary Willis's wife."

———

Allie set up the Xbox in the girls' bedroom. She made sure the window in the room was locked, then told the kids to stay in the room until they were told otherwise. When she returned to the kitchen, she found Bitty and Laura sitting at the kitchen table. She sat down and listened.

"I haven't seen him in nearly three weeks. Since the eleventh. I'm worried. If he was okay, he would've called," Laura was saying. "I just know he would have. I *know* Gary."

Allie did the math in her head. Gary had shown up in their yard on the twelfth, so if Laura was telling the truth, they'd been the ones to see him last. Not her.

"I'm worried. He suffers from depression. That's why he uses, you know. But he gets . . . he's tried to kill himself before. And with all the stress this is causing . . . I've got three kids . . . and another on the way." Her voice trailed off as she wiped tears from her cheeks. "Look, I'm not gonna sit here and pretend he's a good man. He's done his share of bad things. But I just can't see him hurting people like that. Like he supposedly did with the Parishes. I don't think he's capable of that."

Allie thought it was interesting that the woman had chosen the word "hurt" and not "killed." Her mind flashed back to Gary holding the gun in the backyard. Waving it around. Pointing it at Johnny. Obviously she'd seen a side of Gary that Laura never had.

"I understand your distress. Have you talked with Detective Lambert about this?" Bitty asked.

"I have, but it didn't do any good. I wanted to know if it was true that Julie Parish had given him money before she . . . died. But the detective wouldn't tell me anything." She sniffed, her eyes glittering with more tears. "It's not that I wanted it. The money. But if she had . . . I mean, they'd have to have really been serious for her to give him money like that." The woman paused. "Plus, I'm not sure why they even suspect him in the first place. I feel like I'm the only person who has no idea what's going on here."

"I can understand that," Bitty said. "How far along are you?"

Laura laughed nervously. "My due date was yesterday."

Bitty nodded. "Okay, what do you want to know?"

CHAPTER 28

HIS HEART RACING, Sammy darted into the foyer and crouched down. He and Zoe were playing hide-and-seek. Zoe was *it* and was counting in the living room.

Playing with Zoe was fun, even if she said weird stuff sometimes. Earlier, while they were finger painting, she told him again that one day she'd be his sister. But he didn't believe her, of course. Not after talking to his mommy. He knew Zoe just said things like that to make herself feel better.

"Twenty-five! Ready or not, here I come!" Zoe called from the living room.

Sammy was hiding next to the front door, his body folded as small as he could bend, his fingers covering his eyes.

He heard her footsteps get closer.

His body tensed and he giggled. He spread out his fingers a little and peeked through them.

Zoe was standing right in front of him.

"Just because you can't see me doesn't mean I can't see you, Sammy," Zoe said. "You know that, right?"

He giggled again.

"I thought you were a big boy?"

He got to his feet. "I *am* a big boy."

"Well, you sure don't hide like one."

"Yes I do!" he argued. Then suddenly he had a thought. He knew *exactly* where he wanted to hide! Definitely a big-boy place.

"You *it* again, okay?"

Zoe shrugged. "Sure." She headed back to the living room and started counting loudly.

He ran to the junk drawer in the kitchen and found a flashlight. Then he headed to the girls' closet. He moved a bunch of stuff—clothes, a box, some luggage, more clothes—so that he could hide in the corner.

But then . . . he saw Zoe's backpack.

He wondered if more gummy worms were in it, and his mouth started watering.

He quickly unzipped it and rummaged around. He didn't see any gummy worms, but he did see the ears of Carrie's big stuffed bear peeking out. He hadn't seen the bear for a long time. He wondered if she forgot she put it in there.

He tried to pull it out, but couldn't.

It was heavy.

He turned the bag on its side and shook it out. Then he picked up the stuffed bear and ran toward the living room, his legs pumping as fast as they could go. The house was quiet. All he could hear was the soft squishing of his running pants.

He'd give the bear to Carrie and make her very, very, very happy, *then* he'd hide in his cool spot! As soon as his feet hit the living room carpet, Carrie looked up.

He smiled big. "Here your bear, Carrie! I find it for you!"

Carrie's eyes got wide, like maybe she was about to smile. But then an arm reached out and ripped the bear from his hands.

He stopped in his tracks.

Zoe was clutching the bear and glaring at him. "That's *not* yours!" she hissed, holding the bear. He watched a muscle jump in her cheek.

He took a step back. "That . . . that . . . not very nice," he said, his face burning.

The way her green eyes were staring at him made him feel sweaty. His lower lip jutted out and he could feel his eyes filling with tears. "Just wanted to give to Carrie so she be happy."

When Zoe got mad, she got mad different than anything he'd ever seen before. Much more mad than his mommy ever got. His mommy only got disappointed mad, which wasn't really mad at all. But Zoe was *mad* mad. He stared at her and could swear there were snakes squirming around in her hair. Just like that Medusa monster from the movie *Clash of the Titans*.

He got a bad feeling in his tummy. He didn't want to be around her anymore. He didn't want to see those green monster eyes of hers. "I no like you no more. I telling," he said, and turned for the hallway. "Mommy!" he called.

Zoe dashed in front of him, blocking his way so that he couldn't go any farther. She knelt down. "Shh! Don't do that. Look, I'm sorry. I didn't mean to grab it like that. It's just . . . it's just that it's Carrie's, and it's special to her."

He crossed his arms and gave her his maddest frown.

"Seriously, I'm so sorry," she said. "Can you forgive me?"

He shook his head.

"Come on, Sammy. Look, I'll kick your butt at the *Lego Movie* game, okay?

"No. I no want to play with you."

Her eyebrows shot up. "How about some more gummy worms?"

He was just about to shake his head when his mouth started watering. "How much?" he asked.

"You mean 'how many.' And I can give you five."

He thought about it. "No. One hundred."

"Ten."

"Okay," he said, quickly.

As he followed her to her room, he pretended he wasn't mad at her anymore so he could get the gummy worms . . . but he was. As he stepped into the doorway of her room, he suddenly remembered he'd also seen something else very cool in her closet.

He smiled.

When Zoe, the fierce wanna-be bug, wasn't looking, he was going to go back in there and get it.

And she couldn't stop him.

———

All day, as Allie worked, she kept trying to push thoughts of Gary away, but they kept returning.

She wondered if Laura Willis had been telling the truth. That she hadn't heard from Gary, and didn't know where he was. And again, she wondered if it were possible he'd been hiding in the woods in the back of the house this entire time.

Just watching.

Waiting.

Her stomach twisted just thinking about it.

Throughout the day, Allie had checked on the kids several times—both during and between clients—and had been relieved to see that not only was Zoe taking good care of Sammy, he seemed to be having a lot of fun.

After Sammy was asleep, she went into the family room with a drink. A few minutes after she'd sat down, Zoe poked her head into the room. "Hey, do you have a second?"

"Yeah, sure. What's up?"

Zoe sat on the couch next to Allie. She looked nervous.

"What's wrong?"

Zoe shrugged.

"What's going on? You can tell me."

Zoe shook her head. "I'm just . . . I don't know. I . . ."

The room was silent.

"I guess I'm just really scared," she said, her eyes filling with tears.

"Of what?"

"Of Gary maybe being back. Of Grandmother . . . of not knowing . . . not knowing *anything* for sure." Her voice trailed off. "Of not having my dad to talk to."

"I understand," Allie said, reaching out and touching her shoulder.

Tears rolled down Zoe's face. "What's going to happen to me?" she asked, wiping them away.

"You've been talking with the therapist, right? Your caseworker? Bitty? What do they say?"

Zoe sniffed and nodded. "They just say they don't know yet." She wiped more tears with the heel of her hand.

Allie felt terrible for the girls. The only life they'd ever known had just been ripped out from underneath them. But Allie didn't have any answers.

She wished she did.

"Is there anything I can do to help?"

Zoe studied her. "Yes," she said, seeming reluctant.

"Okay. What is it?"

"I'm afraid to ask."

"It's okay. Just ask."

Silence fell between them. Allie could see that Zoe was studying her carefully. Zoe took a deep breath, and snaked an arm around her middle before finally speaking again. "Allie, will you . . . will you adopt me? Please?"

Allie's breath caught in her throat. She was completely blindsided. She thought that Zoe was going to ask her to sit in on more therapy sessions . . . or maybe even sleep in her bed again. She had no clue she was going to ask *this*.

Zoe watched her, a hopeful expression on her face. She looked as if she was holding her breath. Allie didn't know what to say. Of course, her answer was no, but it wasn't like she could just *say* no. She liked Zoe, but she couldn't adopt her. She was struggling to just take care of Sammy, Bitty, and herself.

She'd also noticed Zoe hadn't asked her to adopt both her and Carrie. Just her. The girls hadn't appeared as close since the suicide attempt. They slept in different beds, sat on opposite sides of the couch. Zoe seemed to pretend Carrie no longer existed. It was probably another protective mechanism that Allie just didn't understand.

Allie's heart broke for the girl. No one had a clue where she or Carrie would end up. Bitty had learned from a source inside CPS that their grandmother had never even put in a request for custody. She'd probably never intended to. The last thing a drug user like her wanted to invite was the close scrutiny of the law.

Zoe swallowed hard, her eyes still glued to Allie's. An optimistic smile flickered over her face. "You'll be so happy you did. I promise. Like I said, I can help you a lot. I mean, a *ton*. With Sammy. With the house. I can cook. I'm really good at a lot of things. And I learn new things super fast."

"Zoe—"

The girl's face fell. "You're going to say no," she whispered.

"I'm only twenty-two. I'm way too young. And I'm not married. You need someone more experienced at being a mother."

Zoe raised her eyebrows. "No, I don't. You are such a *good* mom. You are the best mother to Sammy. I've never seen a better mom."

"I don't even think they'd let anyone in my situation adopt a child."

Zoe's eyes glistened with need. "You could at least try. Try, please?"

"Zoe, I'm sorry, I can't. But you'll find a home. A good one. Much better than what I could give you."

Zoe's mouth turned down at the corners. She shook her head. "No. I don't want a new home. I want to be with you."

Allie was at a loss for words.

The two stared at each other for a long moment. Then Zoe's eyes darkened. She inched backward on the couch, away from Allie. "You don't love me," she said. It came out like an accusation. Allie watched a muscle jump in her cheek.

"It's not that, Zoe. It's just that adopting a child is a huge responsibility."

"Not a child like me. I could take care of you as much as you'd take care of me."

Allie was silent.

Zoe's eyes darkened even more . . . and Allie thought she could feel a chill in the room. "Never mind. Just forget it."

"Oh, Zoe."

Zoe jumped up and stalked out of the room. And Allie didn't try to stop her, because she had nothing reassuring to say.

CHAPTER 29

TWO MORNINGS LATER, Allie plunged her hands in warm, soapy water and scrubbed dishes left from the evening before. She'd woken up feeling exhausted.

Her body was tired.

Her mind was tired.

She felt as though she'd had no sleep at all, although she'd had a full seven hours. The fear surrounding Gary . . . the conversation she'd had with Zoe earlier in the week and Zoe's resulting anger . . . the unpaid bills . . . it all felt like too much. Her simple life had grown very complicated in a matter of weeks.

Bitty had also talked with Zoe about the conversation she'd had with Allie, but it hadn't gone any better. The girl was upset, and Allie didn't blame her. She was going through a very dark time. Through things no child should ever have to deal with.

To top everything off, Bitty had come down with the bug that had been going around, and had been in bed close to twenty-four hours. And Bitty never got sick.

Tears welled up in Allie's eyes, and she quickly wiped them away. Forcing the thoughts into the back of her mind, she ran a soapy cloth against the kitchen table, then dried her hands and grabbed the grocery list from the fridge. They were out of a lot of supplies. She'd have to make a trip to the supermarket this morning.

"Want to go to the store in a little while?" she asked Sammy.

"Yes, Mommy," he answered, his face a mask of concentration as he quietly lined Rescue Bots figures across the bar.

Allie walked to her office to look at her checking account balance, but when she passed through the doorway of the room, she was surprised to find something glittering on the floor next to her desk. It appeared to be shattered glass.

Something had broken.

She bent down to get a better look, and realized it was the glass heart Zoe had given her.

Had it fallen off the desk? It was unlikely.

Did Zoe do this?

Sammy?

And, if so, had it been on purpose? Whoever it had been hadn't even bothered to clean it up . . . had probably *wanted* her to see it . . . so Allie suspected it had been intentional.

Sammy *had* acted a little weird when he first saw the heart on her desk. Like he wanted to say something about it but decided not to. Now thinking back on it, his reaction seemed odder than it had before.

He wouldn't break it because he'd been jealous, would he?

She sure hoped not, because that would be a problem.

Taking a deep breath, she cleaned up the mess; then returning to the kitchen, she tossed the bag of glass into the kitchen trash can.

"Sammy?"

"Yes, ma'am?" he said, not looking up from his toys.

"Did you accidentally break that glass heart in my office? The one Zoe gave me?"

He looked up. The expression on his face looked a little weird again. But he shook his head. "No, I not break it."

"Okay, thank you."

She poured a cup of coffee, then knocked gently on Bitty's bedroom door.

"Come in," Bitty called, her voice weary sounding.

Allie carried in a cup of coffee. "You awake?"

"Barely," the woman grunted. "I think a train ran over my head. *Twice.*"

Allie held out the tray. "Want coffee?"

"I'd *love* some."

Bitty sat up in the bed and Allie handed her the tray.

"I'm heading to the supermarket in a few minutes to pick up some things. Need anything special?"

"No, thank you," Bitty said. "Just some coffee and a little more sleep."

"Umm, do those even go together?"

Bitty winked. "This morning they do."

Zoe appeared in the doorway, in her pajamas, her long, dark hair pulled into a high ponytail.

"Good morning, Zoe," Bitty said, appraising the girl. "I don't know where you got your excellent nursing skills of yours, but I really appreciate all the pampering. You're making me feel like a queen."

Yesterday, Zoe had waited on Bitty hand and foot. It was true; she was an excellent nurse.

"Thanks," Zoe muttered, still looking melancholy.

The glass heart flashed into Allie's mind, but she decided to wait until she and Zoe were alone to ask her about it. "Good morning, Zoe," she said.

"Good morning." The girl smiled, but it wasn't one of her usual smiles. Since Allie had told Zoe she couldn't adopt her, she'd felt something shift between them. She knew Zoe felt rejected, and Allie hated making her feel that way. She knew from experience that rejection felt awful.

After two cups of coffee, Allie bundled Sammy up for the supermarket and shrugged on her winter coat. Zoe leaned against the foyer wall, watching them, sullen faced, as if she was waiting to be invited, too.

"Where are your gloves, honey?" Allie asked Sammy.

"My room."

"Go get them."

Sammy darted off to his room.

"I'd invite you to go with us," Allie said, "but Sammy and I really need a little alone time. It's been—"

"It's okay. I need to take care of Bitty anyway."

"Okay, thanks," Allie said. But she could tell Zoe was lying. That not being included bothered her.

"Just make sure to keep everything locked up, and no going outside, okay?"

"Okay."

"And make sure to tell Carrie, too, when she wakes up."

"All right."

———

Before heading to the supermarket, Allie brought Sammy to the local park. The cool air, as always, made her feel a little better, but she still felt exhausted. Thankfully, not many people were there. Just another mother and a little girl. When Allie wasn't assisting Sammy on the monkey bars or teeter-totter, she sat bundled up on a park bench and watched him happily play with the little girl, racing up the ladder to slide down.

She marveled at how easily he fit in with other kids, relieved that he didn't have the issues she'd had fitting in—and she hoped he never would. She wondered how popular the twins had been in their school, and if they missed their friends. She was a little surprised that Zoe never mentioned anyone. Surely she had friends?

On their way home from the supermarket, she remembered that she'd forgotten to stop by the health food store for more supplements. Tears sprang into her eyes for the second time that morning. She wiped them away, surprised at how quickly they'd come.

Wow. Why am I so emotional this morning?

A reason flashed through her mind—and she quickly forced it away.

Don't even go there. It's just exhaustion.

When they pulled up to the house, Johnny's truck was there. Allie groaned and banged her head against the steering wheel. Johnny *still* hadn't gotten the point.

"Daddy! Daddy's here!" Sammy yelled.

Allie's head pounded as she unbuckled her son. She'd need to get Johnny alone for a quick moment and make sure he didn't say anything about the breakup to Sammy.

Not yet.

She hadn't had the time to shape the conversation yet in her mind. To figure out how to tell Sammy in the least painful but most honest way she could.

When she walked into the house with the first bags of groceries, Sammy was running up the hallway.

"Where Daddy?" he asked.

"I don't know. Did you check the bathroom?"

"Yes."

"My bedroom?" Although, certainly, he knew he wasn't welcome in there anymore.

"Yes. Daddy not in there."

"Johnny?" Allie called. She walked through the living room, the kitchen. She looked out the sliding glass doors to the deck and backyard.

But she didn't see him.

In fact, she didn't see anyone.

The house was completely quiet.

Confused, she knocked gently on Bitty's bedroom door, but she didn't get an answer. She pushed the door open and saw Bitty sound asleep in her bed.

Deciding it was best not to wake her, she went to the girls' bedroom. Both girls were asleep in their bunks. Allie looked at her watch. It was thirty minutes until Sammy's nap time. And during his nap, the girls—especially Carrie—often went to their room to either lie down or read.

Zoe raised her head from her pillow, her voice heavy with sleep. "Is something wrong? Did you need me?"

Allie went to the bunk and lowered her voice so she wouldn't wake Carrie. "Sorry to wake you, but have you seen Johnny?"

Zoe blinked, her eyes red rimmed as though she'd been crying. "Your boyfriend?"

"He's not my boyfriend," Allie said again. "But yes, him. Sammy's father."

"No, why?"

"It's nothing. Sorry, go back to sleep."

Allie left the girls' room and called Johnny's cell phone, but the call went straight to voice mail.

Thirty minutes later, after putting away all the groceries and calling Johnny's cell phone at least half a dozen times, Allie looked out the back windows one last time. She turned to Sammy, who had long given up searching for his father and was now sitting on the couch playing an Xbox game. "Maybe he just took a walk," Allie suggested, thinking it was a long shot, but wanting to comfort her son. She knew there was a logical reason for him not to be there when his truck was, but her mind was too worn out to try to figure it out right now.

They'd find out when he showed up.

"Let's go take a nap," she said, yawning. "Mommy's really tired, honey."

"Okay, Mommy," Sammy said hesitantly, taking one more look out at the backyard.

CHAPTER 30

WHEN ALLIE'S ALARM woke her an hour and a half later, she was still exhausted. But when she noticed the bed was empty, she sprang up.

Sammy wasn't in the room, although she'd told him not to leave the bedroom without her. Then it hit her: Johnny had probably shown up and they were in the living room together.

But when she reached the living room, she found Sammy and Zoe alone on the floor, playing with minifigures. She was grateful to see that even though she'd upset Zoe, the girl was still willing to help out with Sammy. It showed maturity on her part. And maybe that she was starting to come around again.

"Have you seen Daddy?" she asked Sammy.

He shook his head.

Allie checked her phone and saw that Johnny had not texted or called back. She looked out the window and saw his truck was still there. Confused, she decided it was time to wake Bitty.

When she pushed open Bitty's door, the woman was curled up in bed.

"Bitty?" she said, gently.

The woman's eyes opened.

"Sorry to wake you, but have you seen Johnny today?"

"No. Why? Is he here?"

"His truck is . . . but I haven't seen him." She explained everything to Bitty. When she finished, Bitty immediately climbed out of bed and called Detective Lambert. He and Sergeant Davis showed up ten minutes later.

After Allie answered the officers' questions, Detective Lambert told her to sit tight and went outside to speak with a few other officers who had shown up.

Sammy was getting antsy, so Allie asked Zoe to play with him. Thankfully, Zoe said yes, but Allie noticed her skin was pale, as though she, too, were beginning to feel ill. "You feeling okay?" Allie asked.

"Yeah, I'm fine," Zoe said. But there were dark crescents beneath her eyes.

Allie made her way to her bathroom. Her mind was foggy, and she was experiencing what felt like tiny spasms in her brain. It was one of the withdrawal symptoms she always got when she forgot to take her antidepressant.

But she'd taken it, hadn't she?

In the bathroom, she twisted open her prescription bottle and took double the capsules she usually took. Just for now . . . until they were on the other side of some of the chaos. After she checked on Sammy and Zoe, who were playing in the family room, she bundled up and went out on the deck, watching uniformed and plainclothes cops walk around the perimeter of the house and into the woods. Every once in a while, someone would call out Johnny's name, and she'd hear the static and high-pitched beeps of police radios going off.

She shivered against the brutal cold, but at least she knew if she were outside, she'd be able to stay awake.

Well, maybe.

Bitty appeared with two steaming cups of coffee and sat down beside her. She still looked awful.

"You should be in bed," Allie said.

"There'll be time for that later." Bitty squeezed Allie's hand and offered her a weak smile. Allie held the woman's hand tightly and watched the police work.

———

They sat outside for several minutes before the frigid weather forced them back indoors. While Bitty was putting on a fresh pot of coffee, there was a knock at the front door. Allie lumbered across the living room, as though wading through mud, and looked through the peephole.

Detective Lambert stared back from the other side. She opened the door and let him in. His cheeks and nose were red from the chilly air.

His blue eyes held hers, and she could tell from the expression on his face, he had bad news.

Her blood ran cold.

Deep voices chattered from his radio, and on the radios of a few of the other officers who were standing on the side of the house. "I'm afraid I don't have good news."

Bitty joined them in the doorway just as a siren sounded in the distance.

Sammy came running. "I hear ambwance!" he shouted, excitedly.

Detective Lambert looked down at Sammy and his eyes softened. "Hi, buddy."

"Hi."

Detective Lambert's eyes were on Allie's again. "Do you have someplace where we can talk in private?"

Her breath left her with a jolt. "Yeah."

She turned and saw Zoe standing against one of the foyer's walls. "Zoe, can you play with Sammy for a few more minutes?"

"No, I want to see the ambwance!" Sammy whined.

Allie went to Zoe and whispered in her ear, "Please help distract him a little longer, okay?"

Zoe frowned. "Yeah, sure. But why's there an ambulance here? What's going on?"

"I don't know yet," Allie said. "But please . . . bring him to my room and close the door. Take his basket of minifigures. Please take Carrie in there, too."

"Okay."

_____

As detective Lambert, Allie, and Bitty walked into the living room, a cacophony of sirens sounded outside as police, fire, and medical vehicles arrived.

Bitty took a seat on the couch, but Allie remained standing.

"You might want to sit, too," Detective Lambert said to Allie.

Allie didn't want to sit. "What's going on?" she asked, pretty sure she didn't want to know.

He stared at her for a moment, his lips pressed into a line. "We'd usually first notify the next of kin in a matter like this, but given your situation, and the fact that Mr. Thompson's truck is parked right outside . . ."

Allie couldn't breathe.

"I regret to have to tell you this, but we just found Mr. Thompson's body in the woods."

Allie's arms broke out in gooseflesh.

"What? What in God's name happened?" Bitty asked.

Adrenaline exploded through Allie's veins, and she suddenly felt more awake than she had for hours. "Body? What? Are you trying to say Johnny's dead?"

"I'm sorry. It appears he suffered multiple gunshot wounds."

White noise roared through Allie's ears. Now she needed to sit down. She felt Detective Lambert's hands on her shoulder as he helped her to sit.

Her mind went to Johnny's face the last time she'd seen him. His big smile. His offer for her and Sammy to move in with them. Her pulse pounded in her ears. *Oh my God. How . . . how am I going to tell Sammy?*

"And you're sure it's Johnny?" Bitty asked.

"His wallet was in his back pocket. His identification's in it."

Allie swallowed back the bile that had slid up her throat.

"Where? Where did you find him?" Bitty asked.

"In the woods. Just a few yards from your property, I'm afraid."

"Was it Gary?" Bitty asked.

"It's too soon to know."

Thoughts flooded Allie's mind. Had Johnny shown up, waiting for her and Sammy to be back home, and seen Gary? So Gary shot him?

And if so, how did no one hear?

She tried to process the fact that Johnny was gone. *Dead.* She just couldn't wrap her head around it.

Tears rolled down her cheeks as she remembered being unkind to him the last time she'd seen him. Taking his key. What if she hadn't taken it—and he'd been able to come inside the house?

Would he still be alive?

As though she knew what Allie was thinking, Bitty squeezed her hand. "Don't blame yourself . . . *for anything*. You hear me? This isn't your fault."

Bitty gave Allie a Valium, and almost instantly, Allie felt like a zombie. She lay in bed with the lights off, floating in and out of consciousness.

Sammy came into the bedroom at one point. She wondered if he knew something bad had happened . . . surely he did . . . but he didn't ask any questions, or request to see the ambulance again, or the police officers, who she could still hear crawling around their property.

Bitty and Zoe appeared every once in a while, to make sure she had everything she needed. At one point, just as it was getting dark outside, Zoe whispered in her ear: "I'm not mad anymore."

The last thing Allie remembered before fading away for good was a ruckus coming from the back of the house. Police officers yelling excitedly to one another.

She tried to stay awake for a little longer, to figure out what was going on.

But her eyes slammed shut.

CHAPTER 31

SAMMY SAT CROSS-LEGGED in the family room, playing a Marvel memory game with Zoe.

He was having a hard time concentrating. He couldn't stop thinking of his daddy. He didn't understand why his truck had been parked in their driveway but he wasn't there. Why the policemen had come. The ambulance. Why his mommy and Grammy had cried. He knew something bad had happened. Something very bad.

And now his daddy's truck wasn't there anymore.

The policemen had towed it away.

He had lain in bed with Mommy for a long time, wanting to ask her what was going on, but he decided not to because he was afraid. So he'd gotten up and went to talk with Grammy, but she was still talking to the policemen, so now here he was, playing with Zoe again.

He had a yucky feeling in his stomach. Like maybe he was going to throw up.

"It's your turn," Zoe said.

He looked up. "Oh, sorry."

He stared down at the cards, but couldn't remember what any of them were. He sat looking hard at them, thinking that maybe if he stared hard enough, he would be able to see the pictures on the other side.

"You move so slow I can feel my hair grow," Zoe complained.

He looked up at her. She had the same too-white skin and dark shadows beneath her eyes his mommy and Grammy had. He didn't like everybody being sick and tired—and not knowing where his daddy was.

"Come *on*," she said. "Seriously. I think I just got my first gray hair."

Zoe had been acting different since he'd found Carrie's stuffed bear. He didn't understand why it had made her so mad at him, but it did. Her moods seemed to change a lot, too. She was nice one minute, mean the next. It was really weird. "That not very nice," he said.

"*That not very nice,*" she mocked, making a face and using a baby-sounding voice. She squinted her eyes. "News flash: Not everyone is *nice*, Sammy. Some people just fucking suck."

His jaw dropped. "That a bad word, Zoe," he said, his eyes wide. "A *really* bad word."

Zoe laughed, but it sounded mean. "God . . . you're such a retard," she said.

"A what?" he asked, suspicious. He didn't know what that word meant, but it sure didn't sound good.

"Um, I think you just proved my point."

Zoe was making his stomach feel even worse. He gathered his cards, trying to get them away from her.

He didn't like her anymore.

And this time he wasn't going to change his mind. He was going to not like her *forever*. That would show her. "I play all by myself."

"Whatever. Go nuts, dude."

Zoe stood up and looked out the window.

"Go nuts"? What that mean? Sammy wondered. She was saying all kinds of stuff he'd never heard of before. It was making him feel like a baby. And frustrated.

He crossed his arms and was about to tell Zoe that he was going to tell his mommy the things she was saying, and the bad word, too, when he noticed something crawling on the hard wood floor. He bent over and saw it was an ant.

An ant! He *loved* ants. He didn't think they came out in winter, but maybe they did. Because one was right there! He lay on his tummy so he could see the ant better. "Oh, hello, ant! Hi, friend!" he said.

The ant was carrying a little speck of something white. Probably something for his home. He wondered what it was. A piece of bread? No . . . it looked too round. A tiny bead? He bet Zoe didn't know that this ant could carry things fifty times his weight. And she certainly didn't know that ants were alive when dinosaurs were.

See, he wasn't a baby. He *knew* things.

He used his hand to block the ant, so it couldn't get closer to the wall and disappear. He wanted to watch it a while longer. When it reached his hand, it stopped, then changed directions. He blocked its path again with his other hand. The ant changed directions again. He smiled. The ant was fun.

All of a sudden, Zoe's bare foot shot out. She stepped on the ant and ground the ball of her foot into the floor, hard, side to side.

"No!" Sammy screamed. He looked up in disbelief and saw a nasty look on Zoe's face.

Tears stinging his eyes, he peered down at the ant's little broken body. It was now in pieces. About a million of them. "You killed it!"

Zoe stared down at him. "So what? Ants are bad."

"No they not," he said, his cheeks wet with tears.

"Yes, they are. They sting you."

Sammy stared at the squished ant on the floor again. "But he no sting you, Zoe."

"Well, how do you know it wasn't planning on stinging me tomorrow? Or maybe in five minutes?"

Sammy didn't have an answer for that.

"God, you're so cheesy," Zoe said, rolling her eyes and leading Sammy to believe it wasn't good to be called that either.

He stared at her.

"What? I'm playing! C'mon, it was a *joke*." She reached out to ruffle his hair.

But he shrank away from her.

CHAPTER 32

ALLIE WOKE UP at five the next morning, still very groggy. She thought of Johnny and instantly felt sick and confused. It just seemed so surreal that he was dead.

Trying not to disturb a sleeping Sammy, she slipped out of bed and went to the bathroom to take her meds, doubling her dosage again.

She trudged to the living room. The sun was rising, painting the sky in shades of gold and pink. She blinked as she noticed yellow police tape cordoning off the area where the backyard met the woods.

"Good morning," Bitty said softly from the kitchen table.

Allie went to the table and sat down. Bitty still looked terrible. Her eyes were watery and framed by heavy bags. The tip of her nose was red and chapped. Her hands hugged a mug of tea.

"You look awful," Allie said.

"Why, thanks." Bitty smiled. She reached for a tissue and sneezed into it three times. "I haven't been this sick in over ten years. I'm having a tough time kicking it." She studied Allie, her watery eyes filled with concern. "How are *you* doing this morning, honey?"

"Better . . . I think," Allie said, not wanting to worry the woman. The truth was that she was still wading through a fog, and she couldn't think clearly about Johnny or anything, really. "Did Sammy ask any questions last night?" she asked.

"No. But he knows something's happened. I think he's just afraid to ask."

"I'll tell him today. I just . . . I still can't believe it."

"Me, either, honey," Bitty said. "And Allie. Something else has happened."

Allie vaguely recalled the ruckus she'd heard the prior afternoon. The din of men talking. Of more emergency vehicles outside the house.

"They found another body last night."

Allie drew a sharp breath of surprise. "What? Who?"

"They're trying to figure it out. But they think it's Gary."

Gary? But how? And what does she mean by "figure it out"?

Bitty scanned their surroundings to make sure they weren't being overheard. She lowered her voice. "The body was hanging from a tree. An apparent suicide, they say . . . but it appears as though it's been there for at least a couple of weeks." Bitty's face looked pained. "Enough time for buzzards to have eaten away any facial features."

"Holy shit," Allie said, a wave of nausea sweeping through her. "But why Gary? Why do they think it's him?"

"There are tattoos still visible on his left hand. They think they match Gary's. Laura Willis is going in to try and identify the body this morning at the morgue in Tyler."

A few hours later, Allie sat at the dining room table, listening to Bitty announce that Laura had confirmed the body was Gary's.

Gary was dead.

The worst was *supposed* to be over.

But Allie didn't feel any relief. She actually felt worse. Now there were new questions. The most important of which: If Gary had been dead for at least two weeks, who killed Johnny?

If Allie had the energy, she knew she'd feel angry. Angry at not knowing what the hell was going on. Angry at still feeling withdrawal symptoms even though she had been doubling her antidepressant—something she knew she shouldn't do without her doctor's okay. Angry at being so damn exhausted. Angry at not being mentally strong enough to fight off depression.

It was time she was honest with herself.

As much as she didn't want to face it, she was falling into a depressive episode.

Dark thoughts were now rattling around in her brain, and she stank because the very thought of taking a shower was completely overwhelming.

When Bitty told the girls the news about Gary, Zoe squeezed her eyes closed in an expression of relief. Carrie, on the other hand, burst out in tears.

She must have been relieved.

Or horrified.

Probably both.

Earlier, Allie had also discovered that the landline had been disconnected. It was one of the bills Bitty usually paid. Allie didn't have money in her account for it, but she had an emergency credit card. She'd have to call the phone company and get it turned back on as soon as possible. But first she went into the kitchen to prepare some supplements. She needed to up her nutrition. To do *everything* she could to beat this depression . . . so she could think clearly again and could properly care for her little boy. She couldn't let things spiral completely out of control—like they had for her mother and brother.

But when she got to the kitchen, she remembered she'd forgotten to go to the health food store, and she was out of three of the supplements she needed. The most important ones. And it was Friday. She looked at the clock on the wall. Their local store was open only for three hours on Fridays.

She'd have to go now.

———

A wave of nausea slammed through Carrie's body when she'd heard Gary was dead.

In the bathroom, she blasted the faucet, then knelt down and hugged the toilet. She retched until there was nothing left in her stomach. When she was done, she rested her forehead on the toilet seat and squeezed her eyes shut, trying to gather her breath.

When she opened her eyes again, she noticed something: a tiny white bead on the tile in front of her knee. She reached for it and rolled it between her fingers.

Her breath hitched.

She'd seen beads like these before, back when they lived in the trailer. She and Zoe had had quite the education in drug paraphernalia over the years from watching their mother. She was pretty sure they could correctly identify most of the drugs—prescription and otherwise—making their rounds across the state of Texas. They also knew what most of the drugs did just by watching their effects on their mother.

She lowered herself to her hands and knees, and found two more beads beneath the counter. She picked them up, beads so tiny, a hundred of them—maybe more—could probably fit in a teaspoon.

A chill ran up her spine as memories flooded her mind. She knew exactly what the beads were.

Oh no.

She hurried to her bedroom and closed the door. Then she threw on her shoes and her coat, and removed the screen from the window. A minute later, she was outside and running toward the main road.

It was time.

She was going to do something horrible, something the old Carrie never in a million years would've done.

Something completely unforgivable.

Something she should've done weeks ago.

———

Allie went to Bitty's room to tell her she was heading to the health food store, but she found her curled up beneath her covers, sound asleep. Bitty had asked for an hour to rest, but of course, Allie would let her sleep all day. Whatever Bitty needed, she would get. Allie would just have to muscle through on her own for now.

She went back to the living room and pulled on her shoes.

"Mommy, where you going?" Sammy asked.

"To the store real quick to get some medicine."

"I want to go."

"No, not this time. Stay here and help Zoe take care of Grammy. I'll be right back."

"But I no like Zoe. Zoe mean."

"Sammy, you know that's not true. Why would you say that?"

He folded his arms over his chest. "She killed my ant!"

"Your ant?"

He nodded.

"Oh." Allie knew how Sammy felt about ants.

"Yes. She mean, Mommy!"

Zoe, in her pajamas, walked into the room. "I'm so sorry. I didn't realize it would upset him. I saw it in the family room and I just didn't want him to get stung."

"I understand," Allie said. She turned back to Sammy. "I'm sorry she killed it, but some people don't love ants the way we do. She was just protecting you. She wasn't trying to be mean."

"Yes, she was!" he said.

Trying to stifle another yawn, Allie finished tying her shoe.

"You no listen to me, Mommy!"

She looked up at a red-faced Sammy and placed her hands on his shoulders. "Look, honey. Mommy's not feeling very well, and Zoe's helping a lot. I really need her help right now . . . until I feel better. And I need you to listen to her."

"But Zoe mean!"

"Sammy, that's not very nice to say. She's been very good to you. To all of us. Look, let's talk about this when I get back, okay?"

CHAPTER 33

HEAVY RAIN CLOUDS blackened the afternoon sky as Allie climbed into the truck. Shivering, she turned the ignition, and the engine roared to life.

She hadn't wanted to leave Sammy, but she'd had no choice. The weather was supposed to get bad, and she was feeling awful. It was definitely best that he stay home. But it would only be a twenty-minute round trip. She'd be back soon.

Power through this, she told herself.

Take control.

You've got this.

She drove past the patrol car that was parked outside of the house, her breath coming out in moist clouds, but she didn't bother to switch on the heater because she knew it would only shoot freezing air until the engine had a chance to warm up.

Raindrops began pelting the windshield, and suddenly tears were streaming down her face. She'd drunk a whole pot of coffee earlier, yet was still tired. It was also impossible to think a positive thought and actually believe it. And she couldn't twist the negative thoughts into positive ones no matter how hard she tried.

Anyone would be having trouble coping in your situation, she told herself. *Not just me . . . not because I am predisposed to extreme mental illness.*

"Right?" she asked aloud. "Right," she answered, trying to bolster her confidence.

But then those ugly words crawled in, her mother's prophecy and her worst fear:

You'll turn out no different than me, Allie Cat. Wait. You'll see.

"Shut up," she said through gritted teeth. "I will *never* be you. I'm *nothing* like you."

She shivered, wondering who she was even talking to. Was it really her mother, or was her brain just playing tricks on her?

Bitty had once told her that only a fine thread separated the spirit world and the physical world, and very few really knew for sure what was real or imagined anyway. With the voice coming and going like it had been, she really needed to believe it.

She felt her eyelids get heavy again. She stretched her eyes open wide and concentrated on the dirt road as it curved sharply in front of her.

Depression was treatable.

Millions of people suffered from it.

Allie just feared where it could lead. That it was just one small step away from slipping into something not so easy to treat . . . *or reverse.*

Slick asphalt shone ahead. As she pulled onto the paved road, she flipped the heat to its highest setting and tepid air blasted through the vents. About a minute later, she felt warm. But the warmth, along with the steady squeak of the windshield wipers as they crawled back and forth, was making it extremely difficult to stay awake.

Her headlights drilled through the darkness as she sped down the rural road. She yawned, and focused hard on staying between the lines on the road. The sooner she had the supplements and was headed back to the house, the better.

But just as she turned onto Main Street, a curtain of rain blanketed the windshield. The storm had escalated and the rain was now pouring from the sky. She couldn't even see an inch in front of the windshield.

Her hands strangling the steering wheel, she tapped the brakes as gently as she could, trying not to hydroplane. As soon as the shoulder came into view, she carefully pulled over and eased the truck to a stop.

The rain had turned into a torrential downpour. She had no business driving right now. She'd end up killing herself. Or someone else. Listening to the windshield wipers march across the glass and the roar of the truck's heater, her mind flickered with confusion.

She watched as rain streamed down the side windows, and waited.

She could feel her eyelids drooping again. The fight was draining out of her. She flipped off the windshield wipers. Barely feeling the tears roll from her eyes, she watched the windows fog up around her . . . and let her eyes close.

CHAPTER 34

CARRIE WAS GOING to do something awful, the second scariest thing she'd ever done.

It had taken her forever to get to the paved road. Now she stood on the side of the road, shivering. It was freezing out. She saw the glow of oncoming traffic. She blinked owlishly in the bright light and waved her hand in the air.

A truck passed her, splashing up muddy water in its wake. She dodged the onslaught just in time, then blinked rain out of her eyes and started walking again.

She noticed the brake lights glow red, then the vehicle reversed. When it was alongside her, the driver's window slid down.

A plump middle-aged woman was in the driver's seat. "What in God's name are you doing out here in the rain, honey?" she asked, concern creasing her face.

Tears and rain rolled from Carrie's eyes. "I'm lost. Can you help me?"

The woman nodded. "Yes, of course. C'mon. Get in."

A few minutes later, Carrie was sitting in the woman's truck, completely soaking the leather passenger seat. After asking a few questions, the woman had gone quiet. But Carrie could see her shooting sidelong glances at her every few seconds. The radio was turned low to some man preaching. The trees whizzed by as she got closer to her destination.

Last time, she'd snuck out the window to get back to her house. But this time she was going somewhere different—and would do something much more difficult.

Carrie closed her eyes and remembered the feeling of Allie's hand in hers. Allie's soft, nurturing hands, knowing that after today she'd never feel them again.

She was going to do something that would make Allie very angry. Something that would make a lot of people very angry.

She closed her eyes and tried to breathe.

One Week Before the Murders

Time always crawled on the days that their father was supposed to return home.

Carrie's father had bought a lottery ticket at a local gas station a couple of months earlier and had won $1.2 million. It had enabled their family to move from the trailer where the girls had been raised to Sherman's Landing, a neighborhood Carrie had never seen before. The house was about ten times the size of the old trailer, if not more.

It was a big, beautiful house her mother didn't seem to have the inclination or know-how to fully furnish. Right now the living room furniture just consisted of a leather couch, a side table with a lamp, and a big-screen television.

The house was so sparsely furnished, if someone yelled loud enough their voice echoed. But the girls didn't want to yell, not when their mother was around, because she used anything she could as an excuse to slap them, scream at them, call Zoe names . . . basically just make their lives miserable.

Her family was living proof that money didn't buy happiness, because they weren't even close to being happy. In fact, Carrie was pretty sure that since winning the money, her parents fought even more.

The only thing her parents still seemed to do together was *it*. And when they weren't doing *it*, her dad slept in a separate bedroom on a mattress while her mother slept in the master bedroom on a brand-new bed.

That evening, Carrie was surprised when she saw headlights splash across the ceiling of the girls' bedroom. She looked out the window and recognized the truck that had just pulled up. It belonged to one of her dad's coworkers, who usually dropped him off after he returned from a run, because he wasn't allowed to park his rig in the neighborhood.

She and Zoe were in bed. Zoe sleeping, Carrie reading.

"He's home!" Carrie squealed, shaking her sister, but Zoe didn't move.

"Zoe, it's Dad." Zoe grunted and turned over. Usually Zoe was the first one to be out of bed and flying out the bedroom door to see him, but not tonight. She hadn't been acting like herself at all since the day their mother told Zoe she hated her. Carrie was worried about her. But she didn't want to think about that now. She wanted to see her father. She was so happy he was home.

A few minutes later, Carrie and her dad sat on the couch in the living room together. It was rare to get the time alone with him. As much as she loved her sister, Zoe always hogged up the little time they had.

He'd started a fire in the fireplace and they sat together, Carrie eating raisins while her father drank beer. She liked the smell of beer on his breath. Both girls agreed it was one of their absolute favorite scents because it made them think about their father.

Carrie wasn't blind. She knew that her father had faults. He didn't spend nearly enough time with his family. Didn't always say the right thing. Didn't always obey the law. Sometimes he did violent things out of plain meanness, like shoot at wild pigs in the woods for sport—something that had always turned Carrie's stomach.

But she preferred not to think about those things. She just wanted to enjoy him. Their father was the only safe place in their life. He wasn't perfect, but she didn't need him to be.

Unlike their mother, their father never raised his voice—or his hand. He was kind to her and Zoe . . . and she loved him, unconditionally. She and Zoe both did. When he was around, he usually liked to take them places: car shows, tractor pulls, rodeos, shooting clay targets and at beer cans on tree stumps.

When he was home, both of them would fetch him beers. Make nachos for him by layering American cheese on tortilla chips and microwaving them. Pull his shoes and socks off and replace them with his favorite slippers. Their mother did nothing for him. She hadn't even bothered coming out of the bedroom since their father had gotten home, but he didn't seem to care.

Her thoughts went back to Zoe. How odd she'd been behaving. Glassy-eyed, distant, exhausted. Much, much quieter than usual.

"We really missed you."

"I missed you, too, darling. Sorry I have to work so much."

She stared at the wood crackling in the fireplace. "But we're millionaires now, right?"

He grinned. "That we are."

"Then, why are you still working?"

He took a long sip of his beer. Stared at the fireplace. "Well . . . I guess there are certain things that make a man feel like he's a man, sweetheart. Working is one of those things for me. It's really all I've ever known. But I promise, I won't be working as much after this next run, okay, baby?"

Tears stung her eyes, because she hoped with all of her might for what he said to be true.

"Hey. Don't cry."

She was upset at herself for crying. She wanted to just focus on enjoying him while he was there. She forced herself to smile.

He pulled the tab off another beer. "My li'l Carrying Carrie . . ." he said. "Mama Carrie . . . your sister's keeper."

He'd called her those names for years.

She felt her smile falter a little. "Yep."

Instead of the nicknames being good things, right now they felt like they limited her. Like they put her in a straitjacket and she could be nothing else. Was her life just about Zoe? Or could it be something more? Did she dare wish it could be? And why was she even thinking these questions? She never had before. Was it because Zoe had been acting so strange?

She looked up and saw her father was staring at her. "What's wrong?"

She wasn't sure how to tell him. Or if she even wanted to. She doubted he would understand. "Nothing." She smiled big, so he'd believe her.

He smiled back at her, then opened up his arms. They sat holding one another in front of the fire for what seemed to be a long time. She breathed in his cologne. Felt the roughness of his skin.

Her dad took his last sip, then crushed his beer can. "Let's play a game," he said. "Think of all the cool stuff you'd like to buy now that we have money . . . and I promise, when I get back, we'll go shopping. We'll get some nice stuff for you and your sister. Maybe even a few things for your uncle Tommy."

"What did you just say?" someone asked.

Both of them turned to find her mother wearing a flimsy nightgown. She'd been eavesdropping and was now glaring at them.

"Go back to bed, Julie," her father said gently.

The woman's hands were on her hips. "That brother of yours isn't getting one red cent of that money. You understand me?"

Carrie's mother hated Uncle Tommy. Always had. Carrie didn't understand why. She barely knew her uncle. She'd seen him maybe three times her whole life. But her father was the one who had won the money. So shouldn't he be able to decide if Uncle Tommy got any gifts or not?

"You didn't answer me," she said, her voice hot.

"I don't have an answer for you."

"Tell me Tommy will not get any of that money. Tell me, Buddy!" she yelled.

Her father kissed her cheek. "Why don't you go to bed, Carrie?" he said, softly. "I need to talk to your mother."

Carrie did what her father had told her to do. She crawled into bed and listened to the two arguing in the distance. They argued for several minutes, then everything went quiet. A few minutes after that, she heard her mother's headboard hitting the wall. Then the pipes clanked, indicating that they'd gotten into the shower.

It was a routine very familiar to her. *Too familiar.*

She turned on her side and tears began falling across her nose and down her cheek. She wasn't sure why she was crying. She didn't feel any worse than she usually felt. Maybe she feared her father wouldn't keep his promise. That he would continue to work just as much.

Or maybe she was afraid that her mother would eventually drive him away forever.

CHAPTER 35

ALLIE HEARD A tapping noise next to her ear. She tried to ignore it, but then she heard it again.

She opened her eyes and tried to get her bearings.

Where was she?

Slowly, she realized. She was in the truck, on the side of the road. She'd fallen asleep . . . but for how long? She shivered, although she was sweating. The vent was still blasting heated air.

She heard the tapping sound again.

Louder.

Then a muffled voice. Someone was knocking on her driver's side window. She turned and was able to make out Detective Lambert through the foggy glass. She clicked the unlock button on the driver's door.

He opened the door and concern flooded his eyes.

"Allie? You okay?"

She stared at him, her eyes fighting to focus. His face was hazy, as if she were seeing it through water.

She was seeing two of him.

One of him.

"I thought I'd be fine to drive," she said, her words coming out garbled.

He frowned. "Have you been drinking?"

She shook her head. "No . . . Of course not." Her words came out wobbly again. Even to her they sounded as though she'd pounded some serious alcohol.

"I need help," she said. "I . . . I can't drive."

"Let me take you home."

He helped her out of the vehicle.

A thought flicked quickly across her mind . . . of how awful she must look. But the concern melted away almost instantly. She didn't have the energy to care right now. She just needed to preserve the little bit of energy she had to make sure she got back to Sammy and let Bitty know what was happening to her so she could help her get well again.

Detective Lambert walked her to his Crown Victoria and helped her into the passenger seat. Then he reached across her and fastened her seat belt. When he shut the door, she rested her head on the back of the seat. The car smelled nice. Of leather conditioner and coffee.

The driver's door clicked open and Detective Lambert climbed inside. The dash radio let out two quick beeps and a voice covered in white noise blared in the closed space.

"Detective Lambert," a disembodied voice called. "Sergeant Glass here."

"Yes, Sergeant."

"We need you back at the station. A young lady is here, asking for you. One of the Parish twins."

Allie's eyelid twitched. Obviously her mind was playing tricks on her, because she could swear the man had just said one of the Parish twins was at the station. She let out an uncontrollable yawn.

"Is Bitty Callahan with her?" Detective Lambert asked.

"That's a negative. The girl came alone. She hitchhiked here."

She *had* heard right. Adrenaline shooting through her bloodstream, Allie opened her eyes. She and Detective Lambert traded a look.

One of the girls was at the station? What? Why?

"Zoe?" she asked. "She's at the police station?"

"Is it Zoe Parish?" Detective Lambert asked.

"Negative. She said her name is Carrie."

Allie frowned, knowing it couldn't be Carrie.

"Are you positive? Carrie Parish doesn't even speak," Detective Lambert said.

"Well, apparently she's started."

The hairs on the back of Allie's neck rose. She straightened in her seat.

"Get in touch with Miss Callahan and tell her Carrie Parish is there and we need her at the station, stat," the detective instructed.

"Affirmative," the voice replied.

"And call CPS and tell them we need Judy Marsons immediately. We'll also need Renee from the Child Advocacy Center. You getting all of that?"

"Affirmative. One other thing."

"What's that?"

"The young lady asked for Allie Callahan. She said she won't talk unless she's here."

"Well, we're in luck. I've got Allie Callahan right here. Fill everyone in. We're about a minute away."

Detective Lambert pressed a button in the console, and the scream of police sirens filled the air. He whipped the car around and sped toward the police station.

———

Sammy sat pouting in his mommy's room, holding the Incredible Hulk and Flash. His ants program was on, but he didn't want to watch it. It reminded him too much of the little ant that Zoe squished. He still felt sick thinking about it.

He'd wanted to go out with Mommy, *not* be left home with Zoe. He didn't like Zoe anymore. And he was mad that Mommy hadn't even listened to him when he was trying to tell her about all the mean things Zoe had done.

He was lonely, too. Mommy was gone and Grammy had just lain down for a nap because she wasn't feeling well.

But then he remembered the secret he'd seen in the girls' closet earlier in the week. He scrambled out of bed and ran down the hallway. He stopped right before the end and peered into the living room. Zoe was lying on the couch, covered up with his mommy's favorite blanket, reading a book. She looked comfortable, like she was going to sit there for a while.

Good! he thought, because he needed time to get the secret thing out of the closet without her knowing. His heart beating loudly, he ran to the girls' room and quietly slinked in. Then he opened the closet door and quickly rooted around behind a bunch of things for the backpack. It took a while, because there were lots of things covering it this time. More stuff than even before.

Then there it was.

Right in front of him!

He grabbed it, then ran to his mommy's room and closed the door. He jumped into bed and burrowed under the covers and turned it on.

Its light illuminated the dark space. He smiled, searching for game apps—and wondered why Zoe was keeping the phone such a big secret in her backpack. As he flipped through the different icons, looking for something fun, the blanket suddenly flew from over his head.

Zoe stared down at him. Her green eyes looked suspicious. She saw the phone, and her mouth opened wide. "Oh my God! Where'd you—?"

Before he could get a tighter grip on it, she snatched it away just like she had grabbed the stuffed bear.

"That not nice," he tried to say, but his words came out quietly because he really didn't like the look on her face.

"You snooped in my closet again!"

Piglet stepped in front of Sammy and barked sharply at Zoe.

"Shut up, you stupid dog!" she said, and shoved Piglet off the bed.

She stared at the phone again, and the muscle in her cheek jumped. She looked at him, then made a frustrated noise. Then she walked to the bedroom door and closed it. He watched as she walked to the window . . . the bedroom door . . . the window . . . the door.

Back and forth.

She dragged her hands through her hair, making it stick up funny. "Shit, shit, shit!!!"

Sammy backed away from her, until his bottom hit the bed's headboard.

Zoe sat on the bed and gazed at him, then quickly sprang up again. She looked like she had ants in her pants.

A moment later, she looked at him hard. "Don't you *dare* tell your mommy about this," she hissed.

The way she was looking at him made him shiver.

"Don't you dare. Don't you dare say *one* freaking word. Not one! Do you understand me?"

Snakes squirmed around in her hair again. He looked away from her and picked up his Flash and Incredible Hulk.

"It a secret?" he asked.

"Yes."

"I can keep secrets."

"Oh, sure you can! Oh, God!" She threw her hands up in the air, then jumped up and started walking around again. She shook her head and mumbled to herself.

"You no allowed to have phone?" he asked.

"God!" she said, not answering his question. "What am I going to do?"

He was scared. Zoe, the wanna-be bug, was acting crazy.

He closed his eyes, willing her to disappear in a puff of smoke.

She go away if I no look.

"I can still see you, dumbass," she said.

He opened his eyes.

She gave him a mean look. "Shit! Shit, shit, shit, *shit!*" she hissed again.

He'd never seen anyone so angry, except maybe the Hulk, but he could tell she was trying hard to keep her voice down so Grammy wouldn't hear. Maybe he should go get Grammy, because he didn't like the way Zoe was acting.

But Zoe was standing between him and the door.

And he didn't want to be any closer to her.

She leaned close to him, her face red as a tomato. "God, why do you have to be *so* jealous of me? You just want to ruin everything, don't you? And I was so nice to you!"

"Huh?" He didn't understand. He wasn't even sure he knew what "jealous" meant. "Sorry, I didn't knowed."

He really wished his mommy was there.

Zoe paced some more, then suddenly froze, her back to him. She stayed like that for a long moment. Then when she turned, she smiled like suddenly everything was okay.

She knelt down in front of him. "Sammy, would you like some gummy worms?"

No! he thought.

Oh no. Hard question.

Maybe.

Yes! Yes, he did.

"I'll make you a deal. I'll give you ten gummy worms if you drink something for me."

"Twenty."

"Okay, twenty."

Twenty? Twenty gummy worms?!

"Drink what?" he asked, his mouth watering.

Her smile grew wider. She wasn't mad *at all* anymore. Her moods changed way too fast. It made him uncomfortable.

But he *really* liked gummy worms.

"It's something tasty. I promise," she said. "Just stay right here, okay? Don't move an inch."

CHAPTER 36

BETWEEN THE INVESTIGATING officers and Bitty, a lot had been uncovered, Carrie thought. The only thing they hadn't figured out yet was the truth.

The police station smelled like the Child Advocacy Center . . . of coffee and lemon disinfectant. Carrie sat, soaked, her clothes clinging to her, in the small room she'd been told to wait in. She'd draped thin blankets over her shoulders and lap but was still shivering.

She was finally going to tell the truth. Keeping the secrets had been ripping her apart. She'd made the decisions she'd made because Zoe meant everything to her . . . and she'd been trying to please and protect her. She also thought she was saving Zoe's life. But now she realized that it was unlikely Zoe could be saved.

Something inside her sister was very broken.

The door opened and the young police officer who'd given her the blankets poked his head in. "Sure you don't want something to drink? We have Dr Pepper and Coke."

"No, thank you."

"All right then," he said. "The detective will be here any minute."

"Thank you."

The door closed again.

She stared at the scars on her wrists. *The truth will set you free,* she told herself. *The truth will set you free . . .*

Zoe was going to lose her mind when she found out, but Carrie had to be okay with that. Still, it would be difficult. She had loved Zoe more than anything all her life. All, except for the last few weeks: since their parents had died.

Because Zoe had changed.

During the weeks at the Callahans', Carrie had tried to see the Zoe she'd once adored, not the Zoe she'd become. But Carrie was frightened of Zoe now. Not for herself, but for Allie, Bitty, and Sammy, because she now knew exactly what Zoe was capable of.

For weeks, she'd watched as the lies just spilled out of Zoe's mouth so effortlessly. *How long had she been lying like this?* All along, and she just hadn't noticed? Or just since that night?

It didn't really matter now. She could never forgive her. The bond they'd once shared had been shattered beyond repair. For as long as she lived, Carrie would always remember Zoe's coldness that night in the bathroom as she lay bleeding on the floor.

You know how freaking selfish that was? Did you even stop to think about me?

Yes—and that's where Carrie had gone wrong.

Zoe didn't love her at all. Zoe didn't know how to love. Not a healthy love, at least. Her love was obsessive, selfish.

Dangerous.

Hearing footsteps approach, Carrie bravely lifted her head and took a deep breath.

The door opened and Detective Lambert walked in. Allie walked in behind him, her face a mixture of surprise and concern. Seeing her, Carrie shuddered. She tried to be strong, to keep it together. But her face crumpled.

Allie crossed the room and knelt beside her. She took her hands.

"What's going on, Carrie? Why are you here?"

"I'm sorry. I'm so sorry," she choked out.

"What are you sorry for?" Allie asked, her beautiful gray eyes as kind as always. But they were also red and swollen.

Carrie knew she was to blame. She shook harder. "You shouldn't be so nice to me. I don't deserve it."

Allie cocked her head. She studied her, a questioning look in her eyes. "Yes you do," she said, but she sounded uncertain.

The door clicked open and her caseworker appeared. Then right behind her, the forensic therapist, Renee, and Sergeant Davis.

Detective Lambert sat down, and said softly: "Carrie, I'm going to have a short talk with Renee, then she'll be in here to talk with you, okay?"

Carrie shook her head. "No . . . I can't . . . I can't wait. I need to tell you now." Her eyes swung back to Allie's.

"Is this about Johnny, Carrie?" Detective Lambert asked.

Carrie listened to the low-pitched hum of the fluorescent lights above her. Tears clouded her eyes as she tried to get the words out, but they were stuck in her throat. "Part of it."

"It's okay, Carrie. Whatever it is, it's going to be okay," Allie said.

She shook her head. "No. It isn't."

Carrie wasn't sure where to start, so she just began talking. "I didn't want to make her mad," she said. "I *never* . . . wanted to make her mad."

———

Sammy waited for Zoe in his mommy's bed. When she came back she was wearing boots and holding a cup and a syringe. She kept pushing at, squishing, crushing, something at the bottom of the cup with the syringe. She looked like she was in a big hurry.

"You spilling on Mommy's bed," he said.

She didn't seem to hear him. She just kept crushing. And spilling.

"You spilling, I said."

Zoe set the cup on his mommy's dresser. "Don't worry. I'll clean that up in a little while."

"What in the cup?"

"Medicine," she said. "*Yummy* medicine. I'll be right back," she said and rushed out of the room again. Seconds later, she was back, her hands full of gummy worms. She threw them on the bed in front of him. He reached for one, and she slapped his hand away.

"Hey!" he said, his hand stinging.

"You have to take your medicine first. You know that."

His eyes locked on the colorful worms.

She picked up the cup and filled the syringe. Then she pressed the syringe to his lips. "Go ahead. Make sure to drink it all."

He did. It tasted like orange juice and something bitter, like the orange peel he had tasted once. It was a big yucky taste. Not tasty at all.

"Focus, Sammy," Zoe said.

He got it all down, then reached for the gummy worms again. She pushed them away. "No, you're not done." She swirled the medicine around in the cup and eyed it. "You have one more to drink."

Sammy noticed something poking out of Zoe's pocket. Grammy's cell phone in its green case.

"Why you got Grammy's phone?"

Zoe ignored him and handed him another syringe filled with medicine. As he tried to get the next syringe down, Sammy stared at Zoe and noticed all the sunshine—every bit of it—had gone from her eyes. Now they reminded him of the fish he caught with his mommy at the lake. It made him sad to see those fish flopping around in the ice chest. It was fun to catch them, but it was sad to know they were going to die when they—

"*Focus,* Sammy," Zoe barked, making him jump. He felt some of the medicine trickle onto his chin. "Drink the rest of it, dammit. C'mon, hurry."

"You say a bad word," he said.

She rolled her eyes.

Even though he wondered why she was in such a big rush, he did as he was told. When he was done, his tummy suddenly felt very full. He cupped his hands to it and heard it gurgle. As he reached for the worms again, Zoe shoved them to the floor.

"No fair! I dranked all my medicine!"

Zoe turned her back to do something, and he noticed she'd left one gummy worm clinging to the end of the bed. A red-green one. His favorite. He grabbed it and held it tight.

His stomach gurgled again. It was starting to hurt.

He wanted his mommy.

"I no feel good. I . . . need Mommy."

Zoe turned around. "Well, you're not *getting* your damn mommy," she snapped, looking mean again. Even meaner than before.

"I think I have to go potty."

"You don't have time for that." She picked him up, her dark hair brushing his cheek. With his head above her shoulder, he could smell the scent of his mommy's shampoo. It was a sweet tangerine smell. But Zoe also smelled like stinky sweat.

Breathing hard, she dashed out of the room and into the living room. With every one of her steps, he felt the medicine slosh around in his tummy, and he felt even sicker.

Zoe went to the sliding glass door and slid it open. She stepped outside and the freezing air made him shiver.

"But I no have coat on," he said. "Or shoes." He was just in his Spider-Man pajamas. "Where we going?"

But she didn't answer him.

His tummy gurgled again. A bigger, more painful, gurgle.

He moaned as he bounced up and down in her arms, across the yard, her shoes making sucking sounds in the wet grass with every step.

She was heading to the woods.

CHAPTER 37

THE INTERVIEW ROOM was silent, which only made Carrie feel more uncomfortable.

"You didn't want to make who mad, Carrie?" Allie asked. "Your mother?

Carrie shook her head, then stared down at her wrists. "No. Zoe."

Everyone in the room waited with bated breath. The silence in the room was deafening. Carrie knew that once she told them, she wouldn't be able to take the words back . . . and that scared her.

But she had to tell them.

She *had* to.

Finally, she took a deep breath, then let it out. "Johnny came by the other morning," she started. "Zoe told him you had gone to the supermarket with Sammy."

Allie nodded for her to go on.

"And he said he'd wait outside for you."

Carrie finally managed to get the words out. She told them how she'd been on the couch in the living room when Johnny had stopped by. And how she'd managed to catch most of their conversation, before retreating to the bedroom to lie down. Bitty hadn't been feeling well and was taking a nap, so Carrie saw it as an excuse to go to sleep, too. Sleeping, when she could manage to do it, was the only time her mind could relax. But she wasn't in her bedroom for a minute when the bedroom door slammed open.

Sitting up in the bed, Carrie watched Zoe rush in, her eyes wild. She crossed the room and threw open the closet door. Then she hurried out of the room, the stuffed bear in her hands.

Her heart pounding, Carrie slipped out of the bed and followed her. She heard her tell Johnny that Piglet had just run off into the woods and asked him to help find her. A moment later, Carrie watched them disappear into the woods together. She remembered her breath catching because she knew what Zoe was planning to do. And how guilty she felt later when she discovered she actually went through with it.

Carrie felt Allie's hand go limp inside her own.

"Are you saying Zoe killed Johnny?" Detective Lambert asked.

Carrie nodded. "Yes."

"She has a gun?" Allie asked, her face white.

Carrie nodded again. The gun was inside the stuffed bear. There was a deep pocket in its tummy, a zipper down its back. Plenty of room for the gun and silencer. Their father had a silencer for all of his handguns, because one of his favorite hobbies had been shooting wild pigs, and doing so in the manner he had wasn't exactly legal. Zoe had been convinced that if the gun was hidden anywhere else, or buried in the woods, it would be found. But who would check a stuffed teddy bear? At least that had been her logic. "Yes. In the stuffed bear."

Allie's hands flew to her mouth. "Oh my God."

Suddenly something occurred to Carrie. "Where's Sammy? Is he here?"

Allie shook her head. "No, he's at home with Bitty and Zoe."

Carrie knew Zoe would be pissed when she found out her sister had left again. She'd be afraid that Carrie was going to tell. And what would that lead her to do? Carrie hadn't thought about that until now.

"Why, Carrie? Tell me. You're frightening me," Allie said.

"I don't think Sammy should be around Zoe right now," Carrie said. "She's jealous of him, and she's going to be so angry when she finds out I left—"

Before she could finish her sentence, Detective Lambert was already out of his chair, ushering her and Allie out of the room and barking orders for everyone to follow him to the Callahans' house.

Within seconds, Allie, Detective Lambert, and Carrie were in the detective's vehicle, leaving the station, police sirens screaming above them. Everything felt more surreal to Allie by the minute. Nausea swept through her body at the possibility that Sammy could be in danger.

"There was a police car at the house when I left," Allie said.

"The patrolman had to leave before shift change. His wife was involved in a car accident during the height of the storm. His relief is on his way to your house now."

Allie's fingers were shaking so badly, she kept pressing the wrong saved numbers on her keypad, trying to reach Bitty. When she finally got the number right, her calls immediately went to voice mail.

Beside her, Detective Lambert barked orders through his police radio . . . *Not sure what we'll be dealing with . . . County Road 447 . . . Paramedics . . . Stat.*

A cool sensation crawled through Allie's body as she stared out the side window at clusters of trees.

"Are you okay?" Detective Lambert asked.

She shook her head no, and conjured up Sammy's handsome little face in her mind's eye. The feeling of his little arms wrapped tightly around her. "Mommy's almost home," she said quietly, hoping he was sitting safely on the couch with Bitty, playing a game or playing with his minifigures.

That their rushing to the house was just a precaution—unwarranted fear.

Her thoughts flew to Zoe killing Johnny. She could hardly believe it. Yes, Zoe was clingy . . . maybe even a little obsessed.

Yes, *definitely* obsessed.

And confused—yes, that, too. But she was also a very sweet and helpful girl.

How could she possibly be so dangerous? And if she was, how could Allie not have seen it?

And she'd left Sammy with her.

Oh my God. If anything happens—

She didn't let her thoughts go there. *If you think a thought long enough, and with enough emotion . . .* She stared out the front window. Rain was falling in sprinkles. She was functioning on her last spurts of adrenaline. But she had to keep going until she knew Sammy was safe.

In the distance, she heard the wails of other sirens. Detective Lambert placed a hand on top of hers and squeezed as though trying to offer assurance. But he didn't offer up any words.

Is it because he can't . . . because he thinks something bad has happened? That Sammy might not be okay?

The three minutes they'd been in the car had felt like hours.

Finally they pulled off the paved road onto the dirt one.

Carrie sat in the backseat of the police car, staring through the bars. She had more to tell them. Much more.

"I think I know why you've been so sick," she said to Allie, wanting to free herself of as many secrets as she could.

Detective Lambert glanced at her though the rearview mirror.

"I think Zoe's been drugging you," Carrie said.

"Drugging?" the detective asked. "What do you mean?"

Allie turned in her seat.

"I didn't see her do it, but I think she emptied out your antidepressant capsules and filled them with something else. With the pills our mother used to give us to make us sleep a long time. They're called Xanax."

"Why would she do that?" the detective asked.

"I think she wanted Allie to need her. She did it to our mother last year for the same reason. She took the little beads out without her knowing. The beads were supposed to make her happier, and when she took them out, she got really depressed. And the Xanax made her so tired she could barely get up some days.

"When she was sad and tired, she'd let Zoe help her do things. I think Zoe felt if she helped her enough that our mother might change her mind and love her again. And I'm pretty sure that's what she's been doing to you."

"Why do you think that?" the detective asked.

"Because I found beads in the bathroom. The beads that are supposed to be in the antidepressant. If you open the capsules too quickly, they spill out really fast. But unless someone's been opening the capsules, you never even see the beads." Seeing the tears in Allie's eyes, she swallowed hard. "I would've said something sooner, but I didn't know," Carrie said. "I didn't realize until today."

Carrie noticed how the detective kept shooting looks at Allie. He seemed more concerned about Allie's suspected poisoning than her admission that Zoe had killed Johnny. He seemed to care about her. Carrie knew she'd never have anyone care about her after all of this. The realization made her feel even lonelier.

All she'd had was Zoe and her father.

Now she had neither of them.

The Night Before the Murders

It was the first time in weeks that Zoe seemed somewhat like her old self. Not quite, but close enough to make Carrie relax a little.

As always, they were hanging out in Zoe's bedroom. Zoe sat painting her fingernails with pink glittery polish and watched *Modern Family* on the iPad. Carrie was on the other side of the bed, reading a book.

"Shit!" Zoe suddenly said, scrambling off the bed. "She's going to kill me."

"Huh? What happened?"

Carrie looked over and saw that Zoe had spilled some polish on the comforter.

"Crap. Want me to get some nail polish remover?"

"No, that's okay. I'll get it."

Zoe hurried out of the room. About twenty minutes later, the door flew open. Zoe was wide-eyed. She hurried to the bed, breathing hard.

"What happened?"

"Mother's planning . . . she's planning . . ." she started, then stopped to take a breath. "She wants to run away with Gary and take us with them! She wants to take us away from *Dad*," she shrieked. "She's serious, Carrie! They're making plans right now!" Zoe looked hysterical.

Carrie clamped her hand to her sister's mouth. "Shh. They'll hear you." She took her hand from her sister's mouth. "Calm down. You're not making any sense."

"They're going to take off and bring us with them!"

"What? Who said that?"

"Mother! And Gary!"

Carrie stared at her sister, her stomach suddenly aching.

She watched Zoe pace. The news was unsettling. But even more distressing at the moment was how upset Zoe was. Carrie couldn't stand for her sister to feel bad. Carrie felt a weird tightness in her chest. She'd heard that was a sign of a heart attack. She'd felt it before, but this was the worst yet. Could twelve-year-olds get heart attacks? She would have to Google it, she thought, her pulse racing. "Calm down," Carrie said.

But Zoe was too amped to calm down. Tears streaking her face, she stopped pacing. "And she's going to give Gary all of Dad's money so they can keep it for themselves."

"What? Are you sure about all of this, Zoe?"

Zoe stared at her. "Do you think I'd make something like this up?"

"No, I mean—"

"Then why would you even ask such a thing?"

"Sorry," Carrie said.

Zoe paced for a very long time, refusing to talk. She just kept muttering to herself, and shaking her head.

Carrie was definitely going to throw up.

Zoe finally turned. "Dad would take us if Mother wasn't around? She's lying when she says he won't take us, right?"

"I don't know."

"We need to do something," Zoe said.

"Like what?"

Zoe seemed to study her. After several seconds, she leaned over to whisper something in her ear . . . something that would change everything for both of them forever.

As soon as the words were out, Carrie raced for the bathroom and vomited.

CHAPTER 38

HER HEART HAMMERING in her chest, Allie jumped out of the Crown Victoria before it could come to a full stop and ran through the cold rain to the front door. She punched the doorbell several times, then frantically fumbled with her keys. Piglet was inside the house, barking like crazy.

Bitty opened the door, a wad of Kleenex in her hand. She was wearing her robe, and her hair was disheveled as though she'd just woken. "Allie? What's wrong?" she asked, her gaze moving quickly from her to Carrie.

"What in God's name? Carrie? She was with you? How—?"

"Where's Sammy?" Allie asked, out of breath, pushing into the foyer.

Bitty's eyebrows inched together. "Zoe told me he was with you."

Ignoring Bitty's words, Allie dashed into the living room, hoping to see Sammy on the couch or the floor, playing. Goose bumps broke out along her arms when she saw only Zoe. The girl was reading a book, her socked feet propped up on the coffee table.

"Where's Sammy, Zoe?"

Zoe's mouth opened, then closed. Then she caught sight of the red and blue emergency lights that were splashed on the far wall of the room. She stood up, her eyes nervously skating around the room.

They landed on Carrie and froze.

"Where's Sammy, Zoe?" Allie asked again, louder, her whole body trembling with both fear and fury.

Zoe hugged her body with her arms. "What do you mean?" she said, her voice quivering. "I thought he was with you."

"No you didn't! You said you would help watch him. Where is he? Tell me right now, Zoe! Right now!"

"But he left with you! I mean . . . didn't he? I'm not sure—"

Allie's blood turned cold. Zoe had done something bad to Sammy.

"Sammy!" Allie screamed, running to her bedroom only to find it empty. "Sammy!" she shouted again. She started to head to his bedroom, but Detective Lambert was just stepping out of it. "He's not in there," he said.

"Can someone tell me what's going on?" she heard Bitty say somewhere behind her. The woman's voice was high-pitched. It was never high-pitched. Hearing the worry in her voice only made Allie more fearful.

"Carrie thinks Zoe might've done something to him," the detective answered.

"What? Oh my God, no."

"We've been trying to call," he said.

"The landline's dead, and I can't find my cell phone."

"Sammy! Sammy!" Allie screamed again, looking around. But her little boy didn't come. Piglet was going berserk, barking her head off.

"She's been barking like that for the last few minutes," Bitty said to the detective. "I found her locked in Allie's room right before you got here."

The foyer was filling with people. The caseworker and forensic therapist had both arrived, along with three uniformed cops and Sergeant Davis. "Search the house," the detective said, giving them orders. "You," he said pointing to an officer. "Tear the place apart if you have to." He turned to the other two officers. "Check the perimeter, and the woods."

Allie ran back to Zoe, who was now cowering against the wall behind the couch. She grabbed the girl's arms. "Where is he, dammit!" she screamed. "Where *is* he? So help me God, I will kill you if you don't tell me, Zoe!"

Zoe's eyes held hers as she tried to wrestle her arms free, but Allie clung on. "Tell me!" she shouted. She shook the girl, and her head whipped back.

Strong arms pried her fingers from Zoe's shoulders, quickly pulling her away. "No. Allie. I'm sorry, you can't—" Detective Lambert said.

She bucked and twisted against the detective's hold, but he held on tight. "Tell me, goddammit!" Allie screamed.

Zoe shrunk away. She rubbed her upper arms and stared at Allie, her eyes going flat. Something frightening passed through them.

"You tell us right now where he is, young lady!" Bitty said, now at Allie's side. "This isn't a game, Zoe! This is a little boy!"

"I know exactly what he is! He's a spoiled little brat!" Zoe spat, her eyes never leaving Allie's. "This is all *his* fault!" she screamed. "He was jealous of me! Don't you see! All he wanted to do is screw everything up for me! He was so selfish! It's not fair!"

"I trusted you!" Allie shouted.

"That wasn't enough! I wanted you to *love* me!" Zoe screamed, her eyes shimmering with tears. "Why couldn't you just love me?"

Allie's skin crawled with horror.

She had never wanted to hurt anyone so bad.

"Does the dog always bark like that?" Detective Lambert asked.

Allie hadn't even realized Piglet was still barking. She turned her head in the dog's direction. "Only if there's something out there . . .

The two traded a look. "Open the door! The dog knows where he is," Detective Lambert told Sergeant Davis, who was standing closest to the door.

The sergeant flipped the lock on the sliding glass door, and Piglet, barking maniacally, leaped out into the darkness.

Allie pushed out of the detective's grasp and sprinted into the cold, wet night after Piglet, shouting her son's name.

CHAPTER 39

FEAR KNIFED HER heart as Allie darted into the wet wintry night after Piglet. With every step, icy mud seeped into her shoes.

"Sammy! Piglet!" she yelled, rushing deeper into the woods. A weak moonbeam trickled through the canopy of trees but barely illuminated her path. She could see little more in the darkness than the shadows of the trees.

It tore her in two to think of Sammy out here, alone. She knew if he was out here, he was afraid. "Sammy!" she cried, her arms extended in front of her face as she ran, pushing aside low-slung branches. She missed one, and an ice-encrusted branch whipped at her face and sliced into her forehead. She cast it aside and kept running.

Were Piglet's barks growing fainter?

She stopped and listened, her heart racing so fast she thought it would burst out of her chest.

"Sammy!" she yelled, turning and running the other way. Her lungs were so tight, she could barely breathe. After a few yards, she stumbled on something and fell hard, sprawling flat on her stomach, cold mud splashing her face.

A sudden storm of footfalls pounded the forest's floor. Still on her stomach, she turned and saw the men spreading out into the woods. A cacophony of voices were shouting Sammy's name, their cries echoing off the trees.

Piglet was howling now. Deep, long, mournful howls that made Allie tremble even harder.

Flashlight beams bounced off the trees in every direction. Three different beams were headed toward her.

Please, God, let him be okay. Please. I'll do anything. Oh God, please.

Her thoughts started firing slowly again as the last bits of adrenaline drained from her body. The wind gusted through the branches, chilling her to the bone as she staggered to her feet.

Please, I'll do anything. Just please, keep my son safe. Please . . . let him be okay.

She turned in a full circle, watching the flashlight beams shine off trees in the distance.

She heard a deep voice. "Over here! The boy's over here!" Her eyes jerked in the direction of the man's voice. She could make out a small circle of light through the trees.

"Sammy!" she screamed.

Her lungs on fire, she limped toward the light, feeling as though she were moving through quicksand.

Another light shone from behind her, glancing off a tree. She peered over her shoulder, shielding her eyes from the beam. It snapped off and she felt a strong hand on her upper back. "Here. Let me help you." It was Detective Lambert. He draped her arm over his shoulder and helped her walk.

Despair washed through her as they neared her son. Was he okay?

She moved to him as quickly as she could. As she drew closer, she saw Sammy on the ground, curled up on his side in his Spider-Man pajamas, his thumb in his mouth. Piglet lay on the ground whining, pressed against Sammy's back. Two officers knelt beside the two. One was pressing fingers against Sammy's neck.

"Over here!" the other man kept shouting.

Tears exploding from her eyes, Allie fell to her knees and touched his shoulder, instantly smelling the sharp odor of vomit. "Oh, Sammy!"

His eyes remained closed.

"Sammy?" A shiver passed through her. "Sammy, Mommy's here." In the distance she heard radios going off.

"Ma'am, please. Make sure not to move him. EMS is making its way in and will be here in a few seconds," the officer said.

It took all she had to not cradle Sammy in her arms. She lay on the forest floor, pressed up against him, trying to keep him warm. Vomit coated his lips and the side of his face and his neck. His pajama shirt. In his hand, he clutched something sticky.

"Oh, Sammy," she whispered. "I love you so much. Please . . . please be okay."

His little eyes fluttered open. His lips turned up a little at the corners. "Mommy," he said, sounding relieved to see her. "Mommy, I cold." Then his eyes closed again.

Relief washed through her. "It's okay, baby," she said, smiling through her tears. "They're going to warm you up in just a minute, okay? You're about to be so much more comfortable."

"EMS. Clear the area," a man announced. Allie sat up, but continued holding her son's hand. Two men knelt down on either side of her son and began taking his vitals. She sat, rubbing the back of his hand with her thumb, and continuing to reassure him.

Until everything faded to black.

CHAPTER 40

BACK IN THE living room, Carrie could feel the hate in her sister's stare.

"Where were you?" Zoe asked. Even though she looked angry, she sounded terrified.

Zoe truly looked shocked Carrie would turn on her. Didn't she realize that when she continued to hurt people—Carrie included—she hadn't given her a choice?

Most everyone was in the yard and woods now. The only people left in the house were Carrie, Zoe, Miss Judy, Renee, and Sergeant Davis.

Zoe kept blinking hard, as though hoping when she opened her eyes, she would see something else. That it would all turn out to just be a bad dream.

"What did you do, Carrie?" she asked again, louder this time.

Carrie didn't answer her.

She remembered all her nasty words over the last few weeks. Zoe snapping at her. Threatening her. Warning her.

Do something brave for once . . . Stop being such a freak, Carrie! They're going to think something's up . . . Oh my God . . . Act normal for once, okay? Get over it, Carrie. Just get over it . . . Don't you want to see me happy?

She had put Zoe on a pedestal all her life, and Zoe had just thrown her away, making her feel small, worthless . . . completely disposable. It seemed almost everyone was disposable to Zoe.

From the beginning, Carrie had wanted to be honest about what had happened, but Zoe had begged and warned her to keep it a secret. She'd tried, but the secret had torn her mind into shreds.

Zoe was shaking with rage now, probably knowing without a doubt that Carrie had come clean. "Carrie? What did you tell them?"

"We need to separate them," she heard one of the women in the room say.

Carrie's knees felt weak, but she held her ground. "It's not just about you anymore, Zoe."

Lightning flashed behind Zoe's eyes. *"Anymore?"* she yelled. "Don't you get it? It was *never* about me."

Zoe's words only confirmed what Carrie had been thinking. Zoe was willing to do whatever it took to be loved, including getting rid of anyone who threatened to get in the way, or let her down. Their mother, Gary, Johnny, Sammy—and quite possibly even Joey, although Carrie probably would never know for sure.

Over the years she'd replayed that afternoon dozens of times: Zoe watching Joey as he ran toward the road and not even moving. Carrie forced the memory away and stared back at her sister. "You said to be brave for once, didn't you?" she said. "So I'm doing something brave."

Zoe narrowed her eyes. "You little bitch."

A bitter taste filled Carrie's mouth, as though she were tasting Zoe's rage.

Carrie's eyes flitted to Sergeant Davis, then back to Zoe. "Gary Willis didn't kill my parents," she said.

Zoe's face reddened and contorted with such fury, Carrie barely recognized her. She rushed toward Carrie, her arms extended straight out in front of her, screaming like a lunatic. But before she reached Carrie, Sergeant Davis caught her in his arms.

"Don't you dare!" Zoe screamed. "Don't you fucking *dare!*" She thrashed around in the policeman's arms. "Don't say a word. Not a fucking word, Carrie!" she screamed. "Oh my God! Are you that stupid?" she yelled. "Really? Are you?"

Salty tears rolled down Carrie's face. She wiped them away, then shook her head. "No, I'm not stupid. Not anymore."

———

Carrie listened as the ambulances outside left with Sammy and Allie, the sirens screaming into the winter night. A police officer and senior caseworker had led Zoe out the front door several minutes earlier. The expression on her face was imprinted in Carrie's mind. She'd looked completely mortified.

The air was charged as Carrie sat at the dining room table across from Detective Lambert, Sergeant Davis, Miss Judy, and Renee. Detective Lambert's dark hair was soaked with rain and slicked back. His clothes were wet, and sticking to him. Carrie could hear commotion outside the house—Zoe screaming at someone.

Carrie wanted Detective Lambert to know that Zoe had lied about Gary. There'd never been an argument the night her parents were killed. In fact, Gary and their mother never argued. Zoe had also lied about waking up to find Gary in her bedroom. Yes, Gary was a big screw up. But he had never done anything bad to them.

Carrie was ashamed that she'd let him take the fall. She knew she was partially responsible for his suicide, because if she'd only spoken up earlier, it never would have happened. It was just one of many things she would never forgive herself for.

She remembered Gary that morning in the backyard, waving the gun. That was Gary under great distress, not the Gary she remembered. He'd been afraid, confused—and had known exactly how guilty he seemed.

Seeing Gary that morning had been like seeing a ghost. Zoe had figured they'd just arrest him and that would be the end of it. But Gary had hidden from the cops, knowing how bad everything appeared. How easily he could go to prison for something he hadn't even done.

He'd been at the house that night. There'd been witnesses to confirm it. His fingerprints were all over the house, his DNA, too. He'd also just been given a lot of money. Carrie was pretty sure her mother and Gary had been planning to run away together, but she now wondered if they'd really planned on taking her and Zoe—or if it had simply just been another of her sister's many lies. One of her many acts of revenge. Carrie wondered if she would ever know.

The room was silent. Detective Lambert's eyes were fixed on hers. "Carrie, if Gary didn't kill your parents, who did?"

She glanced at Sergeant Davis. The big man looked up from the notebook he'd been scribbling in and nodded . . . as if to tell her it was okay to go on. But again, she was having a difficult time getting the words out.

Everyone sat silently. Waiting, expectant.

"Did Zoe do it, Carrie?" Detective Lambert offered.

Carrie gazed at him through tear-filled eyes. "No. Zoe didn't do it. It was me. I killed them."

The Night Before the Murders

What Zoe whispered to Carrie had sucked the air out of her lungs. "That's not funny, Zoe," she said, a sense of disquiet quickly forming in her middle.

Zoe's eyes were flat. "I'm not joking."

Carrie couldn't believe what she was hearing. Was Zoe okay? She couldn't be thinking straight.

"Don't you see? It's the only way to stay with Dad," Zoe said.

She was serious.

Dead serious.

Carrie took deep breaths, trying to slow her thundering heart. "But you can't just go and kill people just because . . ."

"You don't understand." Zoe's cheeks were soaked with tears. Her eyes were wild. "If I have to live with her any longer, it's going to kill *me*. Either that or I'm going to kill myself. I'm not kidding, Carrie. I can't take this anymore. Living like this . . . I'm dying." More tears rolled down her cheeks, and her face crumpled. "I can't do this anymore. I can't!"

Carrie felt sick. "But I'm sure there are a million other ways. *Better* ways. We'll figure something out."

Zoe shook her head. "No." She marched to the closet and rooted around. Finally, she pulled out a plastic Wal-Mart shopping bag. She brought it to the bed and held it open. In the bottom lay one of her father's handguns.

Their father kept his guns in a box on the top shelf of the master bedroom closet. The girls had known about the guns for years.

Carrie's jaw dropped.

"I took it months ago. He hasn't even noticed."

"What? Why?"

Her sister stared at her. "Just in case."

"Of what?"

"Of something like this."

"Oh my God, Zoe! Have you lost your mind?"

Zoe's eyes bore into hers. "No. But I'm about to."

Carrie shook her head.

"And you are the one who has to do it," Zoe said. "They'd never in a million years think it was you. I have it all planned out. You can do it while they're in the shower. Right through the shower curtain. It would be so easy. So fast. You won't even have to see them."

Carrie shook her head vigorously. "No."

Zoe narrowed her eyes. "Come on. For once in your life do something brave. Mother's not a good person. Neither is Gary. You know he's killing people, dealing that meth shit, right? Everyone would be better off if they weren't around. Especially us." Zoe placed her hands on Carrie's shoulders. "Think about it, Carrie. We'd get to live with Dad. How great would that be?" Zoe smiled. "Life would be totally different for us."

Carrie shook her head again.

Zoe's smile skidded off her face. "We don't deserve to live like this, Carrie. We haven't done anything wrong!"

Silence fell between them.

Zoe watched her for a long moment. "I swear, Carrie . . . I don't know what I'll do if you don't."

"What do you mean?"

"With this," she said, clutching the gun and pressing the barrel against her cheek, "to myself."

Carrie felt the breath leave her lungs for the second time that evening . . . because she believed her.

———

After Zoe had fallen asleep, Carrie lay on her back in bed and cried so hard and for so long, the tears streamed into her ears.

She'd never been able to say no to Zoe. She'd never had to . . . before now. Zoe had to be insane to think that killing their mother and Gary was a good idea. That it was the solution to their problems. Right?

But she discovered the more she thought about it, the less shocking it sounded . . . and she started finding ways to justify it. After all, what other options did they have?

Living with Mother and Gary . . . and not being able to see their father . . . would be unbearable . . . and it would absolutely kill Zoe.

If Zoe didn't kill herself first.

And it was likely she would.

And Zoe . . . well, she was the one who really counted, right? Besides, what would Carrie do if Zoe was gone?

She trembled in bed, the logic starting to make sense.

———

When Zoe pulled out the gun the next afternoon and pressed it to her temple so she could see her reflection in the mirror, Carrie heard herself say she'd do it.

Zoe spun around to face her, relief in her eyes. She removed the gun from the side of her face and dropped it back into the bag, then hugged Carrie hard. They hugged for a long time, their hearts pounding against one another's.

Carrie was going to please her sister, do something brave—save her sister's life. After all, things couldn't get worse.

She just hoped she could really go through with it.

"You're going to have to do it tonight," Zoe said.

Carrie's stomach clenched. "What? Tonight?"

"Yes, tonight. The longer we wait, the harder it'll be."

Carrie swallowed nervously.

Zoe studied her. "What?"

"Nothing."

"Tell me, Carrie."

"I . . . I just don't know if I can."

Her sister frowned. "But you just said you would."

"I . . . I know."

"So do it," Zoe snapped.

"We're talking about killing people!"

"Just don't think about it."

"How can I not think about it?"

Zoe's hands were on her shoulders again. "Remember when I jumped off the high dive the summer we were nine? I was only able to do it because I didn't let myself think about it. I didn't give myself time to get scared. That's what you'll need to do, okay?" Zoe stared at her. "Carrie, don't you *dare* chicken out on me." Her eyes turned cold. "I swear . . . I'll hate you if you do. I'll hate you, and I'll fucking *kill* myself."

Two hours later, Zoe walked into the room with two red plastic cups full of rum and Sprite. She told Carrie to follow her into the closet, and they sat in the dark with a flashlight and drank together.

Carrie took a sip to calm her inflamed mind. Her brain felt like it was actually bleeding. Once she was a little calmer, she'd again tell Zoe that she just couldn't do it. She never should've said she would.

What had she been thinking?

As she took her first sip of the strong drink—her second drink ever in her twelve years—she heard their mother laughing in the master bedroom. Then she heard the bang of her headboard against a wall. Carrie glanced nervously at Zoe, knowing that this time she wouldn't scream for them to stop. She had worse things in mind for them.

Zoe fumbled for her earbuds and pressed them into her ears, then sat rocking and nursing her drink.

After Carrie'd swallowed about a third of the drink, her eyes went out of focus a little and she got sleepy. When she looked up at Zoe again, she noticed her eyes were closed and she was slumped over to her left, the side of her head pressed against the wall, her small chest gently rising and falling.

She had fallen asleep.

Relieved, Carrie pulled some shirts from their hangers, balled them up, and lay her head on them. Letting her own eyes close, she took a deep breath and hoped Zoe wouldn't wake until the morning.

But what only seemed to be a few minutes later, Zoe was shaking her. "Crap. We fell asleep!" she said. "Hurry. It's time."

Carrie heard the pipes in the walls clank. Their mother and Gary were in the shower.

"It's a good plan, Carrie," her sister said, swinging the closet door open and pulling Carrie to her feet. "No one will ever know it was us."

———

Two minutes later, Carrie found herself walking, unsteadily, from her bedroom into the hallway, her sister's hand on her back, guiding her forward. In Carrie's right hand was the loaded gun.

Her brain was screaming at her to stop . . . to turn around and go back to her bedroom . . . but she knew she couldn't back out. She was going to make her sister happy. That was what she did. Zoe would never forgive her if she didn't do it. Besides, she was saving Zoe's life, which would save them both—and their lives would be so much better afterward.

Everything would finally be okay.

Her blood was electric as Zoe pushed open her parents' bedroom door and nudged her forward. Carrie walked into the room, the gun bobbing with every shake of her hand, her finger already on the trigger. She could smell the clean, spicy scent of Irish Spring soap in the room and could hear shower spray coming from the bathroom.

Her breath left her with a jolt when she saw their mother walk toward them, toweling off her long, blonde hair. She was supposed to be in the shower!

The woman frowned, seeing the gun. "What the hell? Carrie, give that to me this minute!"

The woman held out her hand expecting Carrie to surrender it.

Carrie's heart pounded in her ears. She was shaking. The gun was shaking.

"Do it, Carrie!" Zoe hissed. "Now! Stop thinking!"

Their mother's eyes went from hers to Zoe's, then, to hers again . . . and they filled with fear.

She took a step backward. "Carrie—"

"Now!" Zoe screamed.

Carrie's skin flashed hot then cold. She did as Zoe instructed. She squeezed her eyes closed and fired off two rounds. When she opened her eyes again, her mother was on the floor. She was holding her belly, staring up at them. She made a gurgling sound, then blood trickled out of her mouth and her eyes went still.

Carrie trembled. It had happened so quickly.

She dragged her eyes away and forced air into her lungs. She was going to vomit.

An iciness ran slowly from Carrie's head to her feet as Zoe shoved her closer to the bathroom. "Hurry, while he's still in the shower."

In the middle of the steamy bathroom, Zoe turned Carrie so she was facing the shower.

Carrie listened to the water roar down from the pipes.

"Do it!" Zoe hissed, leaving drops of spit on the side of Carrie's face.

Carrie's hands shook so much she wondered if she might drop the gun.

The water suddenly stopped.

"Do it, dammit!" Zoe demanded.

From the other side of the shower curtain: "Julie?"

Carrie looked away as the curtain screamed open. Her brain was trying to tell her something, but at the same time, Zoe was shouting for her to pull the trigger. Unable to think clearly, she looked away and squeezed the trigger twice more, shooting off two more rounds. Just as the gun discharged the second time, she heard Zoe scream, "NO!"

The command baffled her. Plus, she'd already done it.

The man fell toward them, in a tangle of blue plastic shower curtain.

"Oh my God! Oh my God!" Zoe screamed.

Carrie concentrated on the water bouncing off the tiled floor of the shower and onto the man's hairy arm. She watched the blood quickly mix with water and swirl past a clump of her mother's wet hair . . . and down the stainless steel grate.

Zoe kept screaming.

Carrie wished she would stop.

She knew that something more terrible than even what they'd set out to do had happened. Something else that they could never take back. But she didn't want to know what that was.

After a while, she reluctantly let her eyes crawl to the man's face, and she screamed, too.

Her father had come home early . . . and now he was tangled in the shower curtain, his lips parted, as though he'd been in the middle of trying to say something before he fell. His beautiful brown eyes were half open, but unfocused.

He was already gone.

Her father, who she loved so much. One of the only people who could make her smile. One of the few who had ever loved her. Feeling as though she'd gutted herself, Carrie let her arm fall limply to her side, and the gun slammed into the top of her foot, its hot barrel scorching her skin. She fell to her butt and backed into a bathroom cabinet and cried, trying not to listen to her sister bellow like a wounded animal a few feet away from her.

After that, Carrie lost all sense of time. At some point, she felt Zoe drag her back to her bedroom closet, where Carrie didn't move for days—until paramedics carried her out.

CHAPTER 41

ALLIE SAT IN Sammy's hospital room, feeling nothing but gratitude. She held her son's small hand as he slept, thankful that he was still with her. They'd given him Flumazenil in the emergency room, an antidote for the Xanax poisoning, and an IV drip . . . and assured her that he would be just fine.

He didn't seem to remember most of what happened and didn't appear at all frightened. He just kept telling her that Zoe had given him medicine, then let him have only one gummy worm when she said she'd give him more.

Allie had regained consciousness as they were strapping her to a gurney in the woods. After an initial examination in the emergency room, she had signed a waiver to discontinue treatment so she could be with her son.

Sergeant Davis had called to confirm that her antidepressant had been switched. The doctor on duty had refilled her prescription for her antidepressant and given Allie twice her usual dose. Since it had been several hours since she'd taken the Xanax-filled capsules, she was feeling more clearheaded, less lethargic. The spasms in her brain were also becoming duller and more infrequent.

She was pleasantly surprised to find that her mind hadn't broken after all, even with the stress and chaos of the last several weeks. The depression and lethargy had just been the result of Zoe switching drugs on her.

Not a sign of impending mental illness.

Bitty walked into the room. "Detective Lambert just called. He's on his way."

"Where are the girls?" Allie asked.

"They're being held at the juvenile detention center in Tyler."

"Carrie, too?"

Bitty nodded. "I'm so sorry, Allie. I didn't know how disturbed Zoe was," she said, her eyes red and swollen. "Or I never would've let her near Sammy. I feel awful."

Allie didn't blame Bitty at all. In fact, right now she didn't blame anyone. She felt no anger or resentment . . . no negative emotion of any kind. She was just grateful that her son was going to be okay.

That her mind was still whole.

That they'd gotten through the nightmare in one piece. "Don't," Allie said. "It wasn't your fault. Neither of us knew. The important thing is that Sammy's okay. Everything's okay now. Everything's okay."

And she smiled, because for the first time in weeks she actually felt like it would be.

EPILOGUE

Three Weeks Later . . .

THE TRUTH *HAD* set Carrie free . . . in some ways.

The horror of what she'd done still paralyzed her from time to time, and she knew she'd never completely forgive herself, but the guilt, coupled with trying to keep it a secret from everyone, had made it so much worse.

She was so thankful that Zoe had run out of bullets after killing Johnny—and had been forced to resort to the Xanax . . . or things would've turned out *much* differently for Sammy. Allie had explained that Zoe had panicked when Sammy found their mother's cell phone in their closet. She feared that if it were discovered that she had it, they'd know that she'd been the one making the calls after Gary's calls had ceased. Zoe had made the most recent calls herself so that she could pretend to be frightened, reasoning that if she had good reason to be fearful, Allie would allow her to sleep in her bedroom again.

Carrie knew Zoe would hate her forever for telling the truth—and blame her for just about everything that had happened. But that was okay. Zoe wasn't the sister Carrie thought she'd been, and Carrie no longer felt the overpowering need to please her.

She'd been shocked when Allie and Bitty first visited. She was stunned that they still wanted anything to do with her. But they said they'd always be there for her, and would be there to help her with whatever she needed when she got out. They'd even brought Sammy once, and his face had provided her some sunshine. In Sammy's face, she still saw her brother, Joey, who she missed so much.

She was still overcome with grief over what she'd done. And she still missed her father so much. She knew she'd never heal from it all, but she let a tiny part of herself welcome the possibility of feeling better.

She liked her new therapist, and she'd even made friends with her roommate, another twelve-year-old girl. And for the first time she was starting to get to know herself for who she was . . . not for what she was to her sister.

She didn't know yet what the full extent of her punishment would be and when exactly she'd be moved. She was still being held at the detention center and had already had three detention hearings. Tomorrow she'd have a fourth.

She was told that she would probably be moved to the Texas Youth Commission soon, where she would stay until she was eighteen. After that, her sentence would be transferred to the Texas Department of Criminal Justice, where she'd serve out the rest of the time the judge would render. It was likely she'd get forty years, but would be eligible for parole after twenty.

She was okay with whatever sentence they decided to give her. She knew what she'd done had been unforgivable, and that she needed to pay.

For the first time in her life, she didn't even know where Zoe was . . . but that was okay, too. She was ready to just concentrate on herself.

The little flame in her that had almost been completely extinguished since she murdered her parents seemed to spark a teeny bit brighter now.

It gave her a little hope.

And a little courage.

———

Allie sat at the dinner table, watching Sammy as he happily engaged Detective Lambert—who now insisted they call him Adam—and Bitty, excitedly telling them about a new Avengers game he'd seen a trailer for.

Knowing he had no family in town, Bitty had been inviting Adam over for dinner regularly since that dreadful night . . . the night that Allie almost lost everything. Thankfully, though, neither Allie nor Sammy had suffered any long-term effects from the drugging. Just some minor bumps and bruises from the ordeal.

The girls' bedroom was now empty; so was Carrie's favorite spot on the couch. It almost seemed as though they'd never even been there.

Because of everything that had happened since the twins' arrival, Allie had learned that her mind was much stronger than she'd thought. Despite her fears, Allie had let the girls in, and now her world was bigger, broader, richer. She had Carrie and Adam in her life, and she was considering a new career, working with troubled youth. What Carrie and Zoe had gone through had shown her that she hadn't been the only troubled child to use immature logic to make horrible decisions.

And after visiting the detention center, she'd seen there were many.

Allie's eyes still stung a little every time she thought about the sentence the girls would get. She still felt an undeniable pull to Carrie and cared for her. It pained her to know she'd be locked up for a good portion of her life. No matter the term rendered, Allie had committed to visiting Carrie on a regular basis, and would do whatever she could to help her, going forward.

Although it had been difficult, she had also forgiven Zoe. As Bitty always said, not forgiving was like drinking poison and expecting the other person to die. She forgave, but she would never forget. The one time she visited Zoe to tell her that she forgave her, Zoe had refused to look her in the eye. She looked much different than the tough little girl that Allie had seen when Zoe and her sister first arrived at the house. She was much thinner. More timid and much less sure of herself. Allie hated to see her that way.

She wondered how soon Zoe would get out. Where she would end up. Who she would try to attach herself to next. During the visit, Zoe didn't even attempt to apologize for what she'd done. Instead, she stood up after only a couple of minutes and, with a staff member's permission, left the room. Bitty had visited her twice since, and received the same treatment.

Telling Sammy about Johnny had been complete hell. Johnny's funeral had been even worse. And worse than both were the days that Sammy forgot that death was permanent and asked when his daddy was going to visit again. But in the last two weeks, he hadn't asked very often.

Bitty had heard that Laura Willis ended up getting the seven hundred thousand dollars that Julie Parish had given Gary. Since there was no reason to believe that Julie hadn't signed the money over to Gary of her own free will, and it hadn't been contested, Julie was able to collect it from Gary's account.

Bitty retreated to the kitchen to brew a pot of decaf coffee to serve with her famous healthy version of Bananas Foster. But before she did so, she winked at Allie, her eyes twinkling.

Bitty adored Adam, and she knew that there was something happening between them, albeit very slowly. Something that might not have developed had Bitty not taken it upon herself to get the two in the same room together as many times as she had.

Sammy took the break as an opportunity to scurry off to get a mini-figure from his toy box to show Adam. When they were alone, Adam reached over and laced his fingers through Allie's, and something deep inside of her stirred. It was the most intimate of their touching so far. Up until this point, there'd only been a touch on the shoulder, the back, the top of her hand . . . or a quick hug.

Adam had been instrumental in saving Sammy's life . . . which had saved her own. He also spent several hours with them during Sammy's short hospital stay, constantly making sure they had everything they needed. What's more, Allie had come to realize that when he was under their roof she felt safer.

"How are you holding up?" he asked, his blue eyes piercing hers.

"Pretty well," she said, and it was the truth. Every day was a little easier, and a little better, than the one before.

Hearing Bitty's footsteps approach, he gave her hand a quick squeeze, then let it go. A moment later, Bitty came shuffling in with the coffee. Her eyes met Allie's, and she winked again.

After dessert and coffee, Bitty offered to give Sammy his bath, then read to him. Allie and Adam retreated to the deck, into the chilly night air. After closing the door, he took her hands in his and backed her up against the house. Then he leaned in and kissed her. Gently at first. Then hard.

Her stomach did somersaults.

Weak in the knees, she kissed him back—but a troubling thought kept nudging her. He didn't know about her past yet—and that concerned her . . . a lot.

He stopped kissing her, then tilted her chin up so he could see her eyes. "How about we take Sammy to the movies tomorrow?" he asked, his breath tickling her ear.

Allie hesitated, knowing that she couldn't take things with Adam any further without him knowing the truth about her. About her mother, her brother—and the things they'd done.

She didn't want to live forever afraid he'd find out where she came from. What her family had done. She was tired of hiding.

She took a deep breath and stared into his eyes. "There are things you don't know about me."

"And there're plenty of things you don't know about me."

"That's not what I mean," she said. "There are things—"

"Are you talking about your family? If so, I know."

Her breath caught in her throat. *He knew? How—*

"I'm a cop, Allie. I did a background check."

She stared at him, stunned.

"I'm just joking." His smile was gentle. "Bitty told me. She knew I was interested in you, and she didn't want to see you hurt, so she wanted me to know before I pursued anything. To see if it would change the way I feel about you."

Her eyes began to sting. "So you know about my mother?"

"Yes."

"My brother?"

"That's affirmative."

"And . . . you're still interested?" she asked, her vision clouding.

"More than you know," he said, embracing her, pressing his strong chest against hers. His warm breath was in her ear. "You can't help what they did. You're not them."

Her pulse quickened. He'd seen her pretty much at her worst, more than once. He knew about her family. And he *still* wanted her? Not only was he gorgeous, he was kind, considerate, solid, and honored his word. And on top of it all, Sammy and Bitty both loved him, and she felt safer when he was around.

How had this even happened to her? How in the world had she gone from living on the streets as an orphan to having such a beautiful life with a loving family, the most amazing son and mother, and the interest of a man like Adam?

He pulled away to look at her. "You're smart, kind, strong, a great mother . . . not to mention stunning . . . inside and out." With his finger, he began to trace the scar on her forehead, one she'd suffered from a tree branch during her frantic search for Sammy.

She was amazed when she didn't feel compelled to shrink away from his touch. After all, the scar was one of her many imperfections. "I would consider myself very lucky to be with you, Allie."

She wiped at her eyes with the heel of her hand. They held each other a few more moments, Allie savoring his warmth and strong embrace, until they heard Sammy's high-pitched chatter in the living room. Adam pressed his lips against hers one more time, then released her. Placing his hand lightly on her lower back, he guided her back inside the house.

Later, as she watched his taillights disappear around the corner, she found herself already anticipating when he'd be back.

Once in bed, she lay beside her sleeping son and reflected on the last several weeks. She remembered Bitty's wise words: Fear makes the wolf bigger than he is.

Well, the wolf wasn't very big today. In fact, at the moment, she couldn't even sense his presence.

In the darkness, she smiled, turned over, and closed her eyes.

ACKNOWLEDGMENTS

I am grateful to many people who helped bring this book to life. First of all, a huge thanks to David Wilson, Ashley Previte, Chelle Olsen, Charlotte Herscher, and Maxine Groves for their insight and keen eyes. I am also grateful to all of the experts who helped answer technical questions: Kari Schultz; Travis White; Detective Carlos Flores; Police Chief Richard Penn; retired homicide detective Brad Strawn; Roger Canaff; Gena S. Dry, RN; Desiree X; Shannon Hysell; and Donna Crisler.

Thanks to my husband, Brian, for being a first reader, giving me constructive notes, and most of all for helping with the kids all summer so I could write. I think I left the house less than ten times the whole summer. Seriously! It was a pretty intense time.

Thanks to Reida O'Brien and Terry O'Brien for their unflagging support and encouragement in everything I do—and for always being there for me; Sage Gallegos for being an amazing and patient friend, encourager, and wonderful auntie; Mark Klein for being such a wonderful pen pal for the last fifteen years. Without your continued belief in me, Mark, I wonder if I'd even have completed my first book.

Thank you to all the wonderful people at Thomas & Mercer, especially JoVon Sotak, Anh Schluep, Jacque Ben-Zekry, and Alan Turkus. Thank you for believing in my books and for getting them in front of so many thousands of readers here and abroad. I couldn't have imagined a better, more fulfilling experience with a publisher.

And last, but certainly not least, a big thanks to my amazing twin sons, Christopher and Ryan. Thank you for making Mommy's life so much more beautiful . . . in so many incredible ways.

ABOUT THE AUTHOR

Photo © 2014 Alan Weissman

Since graduating from Old Dominion University with a bachelor's degree in health sciences and a minor in management, Jennifer Jaynes has made her living as a content manager, webmaster, news publisher, editor, and copywriter. Her first novel, *Never Smile at Strangers*, quickly found an audience and in 2014 became a *USA Today* bestseller.

When she's not writing or spending time with her husband and twin sons, Jennifer loves reading, cooking, studying nutrition, doing CrossFit training, and playing poker. She and her family live in the Dallas area.